Flowers for Her Grave
Jean Sheldon

BAST PRESS

FLOWERS FOR HER GRAVE
Jean Sheldon

Flowers for Her Grave is a work of fiction. Characters, places and events exist only in the author's imagination or are improvised for the story. Resemblances to real occurrences, locations or people, living or dead, are unintended.

ISBN 13: 978-0-9723541-9-6
Library of Congress Control Number: 2011927555

BAST PRESS
an imprint of

WELLWORTH PUBLISHING
www.wellworthpublishing.com
Oregon USA

To Mom and Dad

*Flowers leave fragrance in the
hand that bestows them*
Chinese Proverb

PROLOGUE

The journal cover felt smooth, pleasing to Louise Vandenberg's wrinkled fingers as she placed it on the shelf. It was the last of dozens filled during her undertaking, and though the answers saddened her, they brought a small amount of peace—a peace two decades in coming. For years after that horrifying night, immobilized by shock and despair, she barely moved. Seconds, minutes, hours, laden with grief, gathered one atop another, but even their suffocating weight was not enough to answer her prayers and end the ordeal. Those days without light did little to dull the image of her husband's bloodied body, or dim the memory of her missing daughter's smile. Her dear friend, Anna, helped her endure from one hour to the next, offering kind and comforting words or simply quiet companionship. In time, Louise understood that until she knew what happened to Jack and Kimberly, nothing would console her.

After years of numbed anguish, she bought the first journal and began her search. She questioned everyone in Raccoon Grove, filling pages and then books with rumors and fading memories. Many she interviewed considered her search futile, a journey destined to add to her pain. They helped out of pity, but they helped. In the end, despite their shaky support and strenuous efforts by the ex-sheriff to thwart her investigation, the answers emerged. When the truth became clear, Anna and she agreed that even though it would bring more pain, her findings belonged in the hands of the authorities. Only days after that conversation, Anna acquiesced to her frail heart and died peacefully in her sleep. Louise believed her supportive friend had struck a deal with the almighty to postpone departure until they knew the truth. An angel on earth would have no difficulty with such negotiations.

Anna's funeral drew a large crowd, including the man responsible. Louise made the decision to face him before surrendering the diaries. When the service ended, she took him aside and revealed her discoveries. He denied everything, of course, but she saw his discomfort and heard the panic as he fumbled for answers.

As she replaced the final diary and sat on her bed, Louise wondered if the confrontation been a mistake. What else could she have done? In a few weeks, it would be the twentieth anniversary of that day. By then, the police would know the truth. A noise interrupted her thoughts and she turned toward the door as someone entered.

"Hello, Louise."

"Hello."

"You knew I'd come."

"Yes. I suppose I knew you had to."

CHAPTER 1

Spectators in Raccoon Grove High School's auditorium made good use of the programs found on their seats. After admiring familiar faces of daughters, sisters, friends, and neighbors, visitors used the booklets to fan muggy, unmoving air. They packed the sweltering hall to watch young women from the 1965 senior class compete in a beauty contest.

A number of the youthful participants signed up knowing it was their once-in-a-lifetime chance to enter such a competition. Others, preened and prompted by Hollywood-dazed parents, agreed to the embarrassing display as a final concession to waning parental control.

One contestant, Kathleen Chandler, stood out from the rest. Viewers could not know as they watched the young beauty cross the stage with practiced, deceivingly confident strides, she longed for nothing more than to fade into the darkness beyond the footlights. Nor did they guess that beneath a healthy radiant glow her stomach churned. Determination, which she could only attribute to confusion, helped quiet her uneasy stomach and propel her forward in the line of smiling women.

Stunned at winning the high school pageant, but convinced it was a fluke, she entered another competition. Defeat would force her to abandon the pointless exercise and she could return to a normal life, whatever that was. To her shock, she won the next contest, and then the next. In the years that followed, Kathleen regularly found herself on a stage, head tilted to receive the crown and arms open to embrace a bouquet. A ready smile cut through the veil that seemed to separate her from the rest of humanity. She was grateful for the shroud. No one ever looked deeper. Nothing told her what she searched for, or why she believed it existed on a stage or runway. Eventually she stopped questioning her motives. When she tried to imagine herself working a job, or attending a university, the answer was clear.

For six years, she applied suffocating makeup and poured her body into garments that pushed and pulled in unimaginable ways. At the age of twenty-four, an agent suggested she enter the Miss Illinois contest, assuring her she would win and go on to compete for Miss America. At the same time, Kate received another proposal. Dirk Harrison wanted her to become his wife. Most pageants barred married contestants and Dirk's offer gave her an opportunity to end the pointless journey. She heard, and effectively ignored an inner voice that predicted continued uncertainty and despair.

Satin opera gloves gave way to heavy-duty latex, and flowing gowns to aprons. The veil followed her from stages and runways to the bedroom where Dirk, like pageant audiences, failed to notice her lack of interest. He expected only two things from his wife, to maintain his house and her beauty.

To some, housekeeping was drudgery. To Kathleen, it was a way to keep busy. She could focus on the waxy shine of her furniture and ignore the dull ache in her heart. Her looks required little effort and while they remained youthful and fresh, pleased Dirk. He savored opportunities to plump his feathers when friends and co-workers complimented him on the gorgeous figure attached to his arm.

To play the role, she simply recalled the runways, never considering the effect those performances had on her spirit. Nor did it occur to her that life offered anything more. She assumed all of humanity lived with a gaping hole inside, and when change occurred, it moved you laterally from one empty reality to another. She had traded what she perceived as the normal unhappy life of a teenager for the tedium of diets and exercise to strut down joyless runways. She exchanged that to raise two children and make a home for her husband. Twenty years later, she rarely heard from her son and daughter who attended college in nearby Chicago and found excuses every weekend to avoid coming home. Her husband, still infatuated by young beauty queens, checked out the runways again when Kate took a rare stand and refused to color her hair or surgically enhance anything. Dirk considered the action a breach of their marriage contract.

When he moved in with his next contestant, Kate was forty-four and terrified to be without a role to play. Just as the emptiness threatened to consume her, she recalled a long forgotten pleasure—a love of flowers. She had worked in her mom's garden when she lived at home and knew the delight of a single new blossom, a pleasure nearly lost in shadow.

At first, she planted only a small number of flowers in the backyard of their three-acre lot. The more time she spent with them, the further her spirits lifted and the garden grew. Soon, aroma and color filled the empty spaces in her yard and her soul. At sixty-four, forty-six years after strolling down her first runway, Kate understood that what she wanted did not come from a Pauline Trigere evening gown, or Helena Rubenstein lip gloss. It came from rich black soil that nudged forth a fragrant rainbow and revealed a beauty in her heart that she'd nearly forgotten existed.

"Kate, are you home?" Tracy Kendall's familiar voice carried through the kitchen to the garden.

"Out back. Grab something to drink on your way."

"The gardens look great. I like the spring blossoms best." The local journalist and Kate's best friend pointed her water bottle toward the flowers before raising it to her lips.

"You say that about the summer and fall flowers, and I believe I've heard you swear your undying devotion to the greenhouse collection. What brings you out this way, a breaking news story or a hot bit of gossip?"

"Neither. I had to get out of the house and couldn't think of a prettier place to park it. Any new customers?" The women lowered themselves into two cedar Adirondack chairs overlooking the yard.

"Funeral parlors are still my best clients. I try not to dwell on the fact that my business depends on people dying. What about you, anything exciting at the paper?"

"Since dying is news, my business depends on it, too, but a weekly newspaper in a town of five thousand isn't exactly a hotbed of excitement and intrigue."

"I know. That's why I read it."

"I did get two interesting letters in response to last week's column. They don't seem related, I mean as far as who sent them, but both involve a Vandenberg. One was about Jack, and the other, Kimberly."

Kate kept her ears tuned to Tracy, but her eyes scanned the gardens while she listened. When a wilted marigold came into her line of vision, she rose and deadheaded the blossom, laying it on the flat wooden arm when she returned to her chair. "What did they say?"

"Did you read last week's column? It was the twentieth anniversary of Kimberly Vandenberg's disappearance."

"Yes, and I remember quite well what happened in Raccoon Grove twenty years ago. I had more than a passing interest."

"Right. Well, I didn't mention your involvement. The article simply told how Louise found Jack dead and Kimberly gone."

"Thank you for keeping my name out of it. Who sent the letters?"

"I have no idea. They were both anonymous. One said he or she knew who killed Jack Vandenberg."

"Everyone in town had an opinion about who killed Jack. The sheriff thought I did it. Where is that water bottle?" Kate had been waving her hand erratically under the chair to locate her drink with no success. She leaned down for a better view and frowned as she recovered the empty bottle.

"If I remember correctly, it wasn't only the sheriff." Tracy intended the comment as a joke, but at Kate's frown, amended her response. "I knew you weren't involved."

"Thank you. What did the second letter say?"

"That Kimberly Vandenberg is alive and living in Chicago. There was a phone number, but when I called, it wasn't in service. I found that rather strange. Unless it's a tacky practical joke, what's the point of sending a number to contact if it isn't connected?"

Any words that followed 'living in Chicago' dissolved before they reached Kate's ears. She sat forward, eyes wide, and uttered a few brief and disconnected sentences. "What? How? Kimberly is alive? Why didn't she come home? Her mom only passed away a few weeks ago. Peter told me they haven't even settled the estate. Isn't he Louise's attorney?"

"We don't know if the letter is true, but you're right, until the estate is settled, even though she's dead, Peter is Louise's attorney. He ran an ad in major papers hoping to contact relatives, but he doesn't think there's any family left. The person that sent the letter didn't say they were Kimberly, they said someone they knew might be her. She was only five when she disappeared. If someone kidnapped her, she could have been brainwashed, or kept locked in a basement. Maybe she forgot everything about her childhood."

"Keep a happy thought. I need water. What about you?" When Tracy lifted the half-full bottle and shook her head, Kate went to the kitchen where she held the refrigerator door open to stare blankly at its contents. Her mind was too full of images from long ago to focus on the shelves or the size of her carbon footprint.

Twenty years earlier, when Dirk told her he wanted out of the marriage, she took the advice of a few other women in town and hired Jack Vandenberg as her divorce attorney. She liked him immediately. At first, they met in his office where he advised her on what to discuss with Dirk and what papers to file. Later, they went to quiet, out-of-town restaurants. Their meetings were not clandestine, but they were, for Kate, a pleasant diversion from the house and Raccoon Grove. Conversation was easy with Jack, and their time together gave her more of a sense of being alive than she'd felt for a long while. It was no more than a friendship, but that friendship came at a time when she needed it desperately. It ended abruptly.

1991

The *Raccoon Grove Gazette*, a twenty-four page weekly that covered predominantly local news and events, came to town in 1984. It offered little competition to the bulkier papers from nearby cities, especially since two major dailies represented the largest city in the Midwest. You could purchase either Chicago paper, or Kankakee's daily at a number of outlets around town. If, however, you wanted to catch up on local gossip, or sales at nearby stores, you bought the Gazette. Every Friday, subscribers found the paper on or near their front porch. For those who didn't subscribe, a few coins bought the latest edition at shops and boxes throughout the community.

Tracy Kendall wrote two columns. 'Tracy's Tidbits', the gossip column that bore her name, provided an important service to the community. Small towns thrive on gossip and the loved and hated columnist dished out dirt with the best of them. Over the years, several larger papers offered her syndication, but she declined. She liked the control that went with being owner of her column and the Gazette. A title she shared with her husband and publisher, Dave Kendall.

Her news column ran under the pen name, Maureen Fitzpatrick. Maureen was her mother's name and Fitzpatrick her maiden name. Although everyone in town knew she wrote the column, Tracy enjoyed what she considered her secret identity. In her eyes, she was a journalist first, and a gossip columnist out of necessity, although you'd have a hard time convincing her fans. Tracy's followers considered her as brassy and brutal as any gossip queen. She lived up to that praise, but she also made it a rule to confirm any item before it made the paper. If she received a tip that someone appeared in company other than his or her spouse, Tracy liked to hear both sides of the story. Those ethics led her to request an interview with Kathleen Harrison, retired beauty queen.

A number of reports had reached her desk alleging that Dirk Harrison, Kathleen's husband, was involved with a young woman from a neighboring town who actively competed in beauty pageants as Kathleen herself had twenty years earlier. Tracy planned to telephone Mr. Harrison for a firsthand account of his escapades. That plan changed when other sources reported seeing Harrison's wife dining with her new divorce attorney. Tracy decided a face-to-face interview with Kathleen would be best, but before she had the chance, Jack Vandenberg, turned up dead.

CHAPTER 2

I n the closing decade of the twentieth century, newspaper headlines announced the release of Nelson Mandela, the dissolution of the Soviet Union, the Gulf War, and the launch into orbit of the Hubble Space Telescope to name a few. In Raccoon Grove, the death of Jack Vandenberg and the disappearance of his daughter overshadowed even those newsworthy events. People died in small towns just as they did everywhere, but local deaths seldom drew a column in the Chicago Metro pages and even more rarely mentioned murder.

Tracy waited for what she considered a reasonable amount of time after Jack's funeral to request an interview with Kathleen Harrison. Three days seemed adequate and the most her curiosity could abide. Armed with questions about the couples divorce and Mrs. Harrison's relationship with her attorney, she pressed the retired beauty queen's doorbell, ready for a juicy bit of gossip.

"Hello, Mrs. Harrison, I'm Tracy Kendall. You might be familiar with my column in the Gazette." Kathleen's long silence almost prompted Tracy to repeat her introduction, until she noticed her damp red eyes. The woman had been crying, and needed a minute to regain her composure.

When her visitor's words registered, Mrs. Harrison slipped a wad of soggy tissue into the back pocket of her jeans and used the freed hand to smooth a loosely gathered ponytail and wrap escaped strands behind her ears. She backed away from the door and waved her in. "Please call me Kate. I'll be Kathleen Chandler again soon and I prefer Kate. I'm familiar with your column, Mrs. Kendall. I suppose my divorce makes me a person of interest."

Tracy made a subtle scan of the house as she entered and saw that someone took pride in the furnishings and upkeep. She hadn't heard that they'd hired domestic help, so it would have been Mrs. Harrison's handiwork. Although she'd seen her around town over the paper's eight year tenure, there had never been occasion to strike up a conversation. Her pageant career ended before the Gazette came to Raccoon Grove and Kathleen was distant, unapproachable. One thing was clear as she studied her, even though most gossip came to the paper slightly embellished, no one had exaggerated the woman's remarkable beauty. If she hadn't known from her research that the Kate had recently turned forty-two, Tracy would have guessed her in her early thirties. "Call me Tracy. I'd imagine you've been a person of interest for a large part of your life. I gather from the remark, rumors about your divorce are true."

Kate led them to chairs in the parlor. "Yes. They're true. I was just thinking that I need to find a new attorney, because Jack…" She retrieved the wadded tissue. "Because of what happened to Jack Vandenberg."

"You've lived here your entire life, Kate, and know the well-oiled efficiency of our rumor mill, so I'll come right to the point. I've heard from a few different sources that you and Jack had more than an attorney-client relationship."

Tracy expected a defensive response, and Kate might have been about to supply one, but as her head shot up, the annoyed expression faded and she regained control. "Sometimes I do forget how small Raccoon Grove is. Yes, I knew there was gossip about Jack and myself, but beyond our professional relationship, we were friends, nothing more." She wiped large brown eyes that neither required nor wore makeup.

The attorney's friendship with Kate wasn't a surprise. Jack understood the potentially painful effects of gossip in a small town and planned dinner meetings away from Raccoon Grove to give his usually female clientele a break from whispers and sidelong glances. What did surprise her, were rumors that Mrs. Harrison was a suspect in Jack's murder. "Why did Sheriff Crayton question you?"

"He said I was one of the last people to see Jack alive and that made me a suspect."

"Did he accuse you of murdering him?"

Kate's previous uneasiness became anger. "He suggested I had something to do with Jack's death. That I was the kind of woman who caused men to behave badly and I shouldn't think I could get away with murder just because I was pretty."

"Oh." Familiar with the sheriff's irritating misogynistic attitude, Tracy refrained from groaning, but just barely. "What did you say to that?"

"Not what I wanted, which was to get the hell out of my house. His accusation surprised me. I told him what I told you, that Jack and I went to dinner, but he was my attorney and nothing more. I'm aware that he befriended many of his clients. I was lonely and enjoyed his company. I told Sheriff Crayton that after Jack dropped me off at home, I spent the remainder of the evening reading. He said that meant I didn't have an alibi. To be honest, that's when I began to think he'd been drinking. He became hostile and didn't make sense. He said that I'd charmed Jack into helping with my divorce and I planned to dump him when it was final. What is that supposed to mean? I paid Jack to help with my divorce and once it became final, he wouldn't be my lawyer. That's not charming or dumping, and how would that make me guilty of murdering Jack or doing something to Kimberly?"

"You're right. It doesn't make sense. I'm afraid our sheriff has a few problems of his own that he needs to deal with. Well, that we all need to deal with. Your divorce, Jack's death, and the sheriff hassling you have been a handful. I'm sure it's been a dreadful time."

"Thank you. I hope you don't think there's anything about me worth printing. I doubt that your readers are interested in the problems of a retired beauty contestant."

Another glance at the surroundings showed Tracy what she failed to see the first time, a loneliness so intense she nearly shivered. "If you don't mind, I'd like to call on you again. I've heard some gossip about your flower garden and would love to come back and take a look." She showed herself out and used the short drive back to the newspaper to decide that there would be no gossip column involving Kate. She was considering, however, a news story on the failings of their local sheriff.

∗✦

The three-story frame building, home to Raccoon Grove's weekly paper, once housed a feed store—the heart and business center of an agricultural county. By the 1990s, only a handful of family-owned farms remained on the fringes of the nation's third largest city. The ones not swallowed by corporate farms, became casualties of the super producers.

The structure sat on the main drag, prominent because of its size and nestled between the Farmers Credit Union and the phone company. Across the street were Mike's Diner and a two-room county library. Local businesses had succumbed to the mammoth department stores that infiltrated nearby Chicago suburbs. They, like the family farms, could not compete.

The uniqueness and history of the building helped to persuade the Kendalls to move from Chicago and start their own weekly. Tempted by other towns, Tracy claimed that from the moment she entered the empty feed store, she could hear the sheet-fed printing presses in the basement, where they still cranked out newspapers every Thursday night.

On the third floor, most of the walls from the feed store's offices came down to make space for prepress production and assembly. The arrival of computers and sophisticated layout software eventually doomed the space to storage. From the beginning, the second floor was command central, housing the offices of Gazette owners Tracy and Dave Kendall and a few smaller offices for their largely freelance staff.

Tracy returned from her interview and slid into the chair in front of Dave's desk. "How did the interview go? Is there a story?"

"Somewhere, I suppose, Dave, but I won't write it. I haven't seen a woman look quite that abandoned in a long time. You know my nurturing instincts are not my greatest asset." She frowned at his quick nod, but continued. "I felt so bad I almost offered her a shoulder to cry on. She doesn't look fragile, but she's carrying a heavy load."

"They're divorcing?"

"Yes, but there's more going on. I see it as a combination of things. She gave up her career to marry, raise kids, and keep house. Suddenly, the house is empty and she's alone. She's too old to return to pageants, and didn't take the opportunity, if there'd been one, to learn another trade. I found it interesting that she wasn't as upset about her divorce as she was about Jack's death."

"By the time some couples decide to divorce they don't like each other very much. She might be at that point and just wants it finished. You said her kids live in Chicago?"

She nodded. "Jack earned his reputation as a competent and compassionate attorney. Some people thought he took the latter to the extreme."

"Jack befriended the women whose divorces he handled. No one ever said it went beyond that, except for a few of the disgruntled ex-husbands. Those boys accused him of everything from immoral behavior to double billing. He was a good attorney and good company to a number of people. Kate needed his friendship. She's still a beautiful woman. Not by the youth-oriented standards of today, but I'd think if you're that attractive, you don't spend much time alone." Tracy reconsidered her words. "You know, I'm not sure that's true. After meeting Ms Chandler, I have a sense she isn't comfortable in social settings. That's odd for a beauty queen. I wonder if I should investigate her personal survival story."

"What did Ben want with her? She doesn't fit my image of a murdering sort of woman. Not that I'd know how a murdering sort of woman looks." He lifted a picture of Tracy from his desk. "I do know how one doesn't look. This is definitely not the murdering sort."

"Good answer." Her frown disappeared in a chuckle as she removed the picture from his fingers and returned it to the desk. "Mrs. Harrison said our sheriff paid her a visit and practically accused her of murdering Jack, or at least of jerking him around. That man hasn't been right since his divorce last year. He's become downright hateful, especially toward women. Kate's floundering, Dave, and I can see why."

Tracy liked Kathleen Harrison, soon to be Chandler, and wanted to become better acquainted. Neither woman could have guessed that twenty years later their friendship would remain one of the strongest bonds in their lives.

CHAPTER 3

E ven as a child, Kate rose at first light, a habit unchanged by over twenty-three thousand rising and setting suns. By midmorning, arrangements due that day waited in the van for delivery while she went to shower and change. Over the years, she'd learned numerous lessons about running the business. One of the first came from now deceased Nathaniel Thompson of Thompson and Sons Funeral Home.

When life on the pageant circuit ended and fashion trends no longer dictated what she wore, Kate chose clothes that offered comfort over style. Except for her husband's events, she wore lose garments made of natural fibers and rarely anything but jeans and tee shirts to work in the yard. After the divorce, without dinners and parties to attend, she lived in cotton, often not bothering to change when she delivered her arrangements. That practice ended the day Mr. Thompson saw her entering the funeral home in her dirt and grass soiled jeans. He blanched and ushered her out of the building. "We have families here mourning the loss of their loved ones." The reprimand was brusque, but whispered in a voice experienced with soft reproach. "They do not expect to see vagabonds come through the door, even if they are carrying flowers." He checked the arrangements and found their appearance more to his liking. "They're beautiful, Ms Chandler, but I'll have my sons bring them in. Please wait here."

That encounter taught her to take the time to dress before making deliveries. Mr. Thompson, pleased by her efforts, forgave her. "Hello, Ms Chandler, the arrangements are lovely, as are you. Come to my office and I'll show you what I need." It was a trade-off. The extra half hour it took to change from gardening clothes into more acceptable attire made life easier and her customers happy.

Jack Vandenberg suggested the arrangement business after he noticed a floral piece when he came to pick her up one night. "That's a beautiful arrangement, Kathleen. Where did it come from? There isn't a florist around here who produces such quality work."

She rarely blushed, but her face grew warm. "They're from my garden. Thank you."

"You grew the flowers and made the arrangement? It's breathtaking. You should sell these." She hadn't taken his compliment seriously, assuming he said it to be kind. He was always kind.

A few months after his death, while working in the garden and wondering what to do with the rest of her life, she recalled his words. She didn't doubt her ability to grow flowers or create arrangements, but she lacked entrepreneurial skills and wondered if she could maintain a successful business. Tracy Kendall, who had become her closest pal and advisor, thought she should try.

Kate was by nature organized, and a brief search of the basement turned up a plastic bin with photos of different arrangements. She put together a selection for potential customers and in a short time, developed a list of clients, supplying displays for three funeral homes in the area and working with various consultants and flower shops on an as needed basis for everything from weddings to luncheons.

Necessity and good business sense convinced her to add a large greenhouse to grow year round. Word of mouth, along with the unquestionable quality of her designs, supplied her with enough work to pay off the loan in a short time.

The business provided more than income. It gave her a sense of self she hadn't previously known. Twenty years after planting her first garden, she could retire if she chose, but she suspected she'd design arrangements and grow flowers, as her mother had, right until the end.

Kate finished the deliveries and returned home contemplating a nap. The phone rang. "Kate." It was Tracy's 'have I got news for you' voice. "Peter called. Someone's meeting with him who claims to be Jack's nephew and heir to the Vandenberg estate."

"Wow. He must have seen Peter's notice in the paper. Did he say where he's from?"

"Chicago, but he moved there recently from California. I didn't think Jack had any relatives left."

"First the letter about Kimberly and now a nephew. This is getting more interesting by the minute."

"It is. Maybe it's time to do a little investigating."

Kate didn't reply.

"Look, Mr. Zabicki. What's the problem? Louise Vandenberg is dead and I'm the only living relative. That means I inherit the property."

"I'm afraid, Mr. Vandenberg, that we have two problems. First, you have offered no proof of your family's relationship to Jack or Louise Vandenberg. Your identification shows that you are a Vandenberg, but your family is not mentioned in my records of the estate." Peter Zabicki shuffled through a pile of papers until he found the one he wanted. He read for a few seconds and without lifting his eyes, spoke to the man seated on the other side of his desk. "You claim your father, Frank, was Jack Vandenberg's cousin and as his son, you are the heir."

"That's what I said. I'm his son. I'm the heir." Joseph slouched in the chair, bored and impatient.

"If Frank were Jack's cousin, then, as Frank's son, you would be his heir, but I find no evidence that Jack had a cousin Frank. You stated that shortly after your father died his house burned, destroying records that prove his relationship, and yours, to the family. Is that also correct, Mr. Vandenberg?"

"It sounds a little out there, but it's true. What's your point?"

"Have you ever met the Raccoon Grove Vandenbergs, or been to their home?"

"Once. When I was a kid. We came here on a vacation. Kimberly and I hung out together. We hit it off pretty good and wrote to each other for a few months, but it didn't last. Kid stuff, you know. I still don't see your point."

"You'll need to procure documents that prove you belong to this family. Perhaps you could work with a genealogist. Having the same last name as someone, doesn't necessarily make you a relative. The second issue to be resolved is Louise Vandenberg's will. She didn't change the one that left everything to Kimberly, at least not the one she has filed with me, although before she died, she told me she'd written a new one and would bring it in. It is my sworn duty to try to locate that will before we settle the estate. If I can't find it, the existing will, naming Kimberly as heir, will stand. If you prove that you are Kimberly's cousin, you may be the legal claimant. Your attorney can contact me about having her declared dead and claiming any possible inheritance."

"You're an attorney, can't you do it?"

"I'm Louise Vandenberg's attorney. You'll need to hire your own."

"How do I do that?"

"Don't worry about that yet. For right now, focus on proving your relationship to Jack Vandenberg or his family. In the meantime, I'll do what I can to locate the new will. If I find it, you'll have to abide by the terms even if Mrs. Vandenberg decided to give her money to charity. Since the amount of money and property involved here is large, it'll take anywhere from six to eight months to settle."

"I don't have six to eight months to settle." Joe shot forward in his chair and then eased back, failing an attempt to look relaxed. "I mean, my finances aren't in great shape. I maxed out my credit cards, my mortgage is six months overdue, and they've repossessed my car. I need the money now."

"If you find documents to prove your connection to the Vandenberg family, your attorney can start on the settlement proceeding. Perhaps someone will give you a loan based on your pending inheritance."

Joe slumped further in the wing chair. Credit card bills weren't the reason he needed to collect in a hurry. He'd gambled with the wrong people in Chicago and they wanted their money. He'd found the ad the attorney ran after Louise Vandenberg's death and figured with the right phony documents it would be easy to fool a small town lawyer. It might not be as easy as he thought, but he didn't intend to lose that money, even if it meant coming up with another plan. As soon as he left Zabicki's office, Joe made a call. "Yeah, it's me."

"What did the attorney say?"

"He wants me to bring in proof that I'm related to the Vandenberg family."

"What about all the documents you had made?"

"He believes I'm Joe Vandenberg, but I need to prove I'm related. He says he can't take my word or give it to me because my last name is the same."

"Did he give you an idea of what he'd accept as proof?"

"No. He told me I should go to a gynecologist or something to do research."

"Do you think he might have said genealogist?"

"That could have been it. I'll go back to the house and look around inside. There has to be something I can use to prove I'm related. I had another idea. I told the attorney I wrote letters to Kimberly when I was a kid. If I made fakes and planted them in the house, they would back up my story that I'm family."

"That's not a bad idea, Joe."

Tracy finished the call with Kate and eyed her desk. She wanted to reexamine the responses to last week's column, but that required finding the letters and her reading glasses. Her annoyance at deteriorating body parts only increased a natural tendency toward impatience. Luckily, as she raised her arm to sweep the desk clean and locate the missing objects in the rubble, light reflected on the lenses. Beneath them lay the letters.

She set the contents aside for a moment to focus on the envelopes. The individual who claimed to know Jack's killer posted the letter in the nearby town of Beecher. The envelope from the person who alleged Kimberly Vandenberg was alive bore a Chicago postmark. "That doesn't tell me anything." She flicked them to her desk with annoyance and leaned back removing the glasses. Even they couldn't see through the fog surrounding events from twenty years earlier.

Jack's murder and his daughter's disappearance tested their town. For every person who liked the attorney, another professed an equal amount of hatred, but no one wanted to believe a murderer lived in their midst. Most came to accept that a stranger killed Jack and stole Kimberly for evil purposes. Purposes the good people of Raccoon Grove could not imagine. Even the most stalwart gossips found the crime too heinous to reflect on over coffee. After a few weeks, it rarely came up in conversation. Only Louise Vandenberg continued the search for what lay beneath the darkness. If she discovered the truth, she chose not to share that knowledge with Tracy.

"Why would someone send these letters now? What's the point?"

"Maybe he or she knew what happened twenty years ago but didn't come forward. When the story appeared, guilt forced the confession." Tracy turned to the voice and found Dave in the doorway eavesdropping on her one-sided conversations. He entered and planted a kiss on the top of her head before settling in the chair in front of her desk.

"But it's not a confession. The writer didn't say who killed Jack, or who to contact for more information. How would that alleviate guilt?" Dave's shoulders moved so slightly that Tracy wasn't sure if it was a shrug or an attempt to adjust in the uncomfortable chair.

When he leaned back and wove his fingers behind a mass of gray hair, he confirmed the shrug. "I don't know, but it's hard to imagine that someone in Raccoon Grove could have known what happened and never said anything. That's a long time to keep a secret in this town."

"That's true." She slipped into her shoes and walked the few feet from her desk to the coffee pot. When Dave nodded at the raised decanter, she filled two cups and brought them back to the desk. "But there are still a few secrets in the Grove."

"Like what?"

"Like the fact that Natalie Gilford out on Hilltop Road used to be a Playboy bunny."

"Ha." Dave snorted. "Tracy, everyone knows about Natalie. Her past is no more a secret than the natural color of your hair."

She looked stunned. "You think people know my hair is really grey?"

Her absolute surprise prompted Dave to soften his reply. "You're over sixty, my sweet. It's acceptable to be gray. Why don't you let it grow out?"

"I've been considering that possibility. I wish I hadn't colored it in the first place, but when the little intruders appeared, I panicked and ran screaming to the salon. I don't suppose I'd have ever been ready for its arrival. Kate looks fantastic gray, but she would no doubt look good bald. I'm being crazy about this, aren't I? No, don't answer. Okay, dear husband, at a yet to be determined date, the no longer natural hair color will go the way of reading without glasses. What do you think about the letter? Does someone in town really know who killed Jack?"

Over the years, Dave learned not only how to follow, but to keep up with Tracy's sudden shifts from subject to subject. "If it's a clue to Jack Vandenberg's murder, you'll unravel it. You have one or two solved crimes under your belt."

"Not according to Ben Crayton. He wouldn't admit I did anything to help crack those other cases. His only comment was that I'd have been in big trouble if I messed up his evidence. He never had evidence for me to mess up that I knew." As the topic shifted from her hair color to her detecting skills, Tracy's excitement returned. "A murder investigation is thrilling in a creepy way. What are your thoughts on the letters?"

"The one that claims to know who killed Jack isn't as strange to me as the one that says Kimberly Vandenberg is living in Chicago. What motive would a person have to write that letter and include a phone number that doesn't work? I think it might be a prank."

"If the person were really Kimberly, then she was kidnapped, and who but her kidnapper would know her whereabouts? Would they risk revealing themselves after all these years? Everyone knows there's no statute of limitations on murder or parking tickets."

"That's another good reason that it might be a prank. What do you plan to do with them?"

"I've already done something. Since we don't print letters of the anonymous variety, I've been telling everyone I run into what they said. Sometimes the gossip channel spreads news more efficiently than the Gazette."

"While you're spreading the news, you might want to mention that the contact number didn't work. If it isn't a hoax, maybe it's a typo and the writer will hear the gossip and send the correct number." Tracy looked doubtful. "Okay, legitimate or not, those letters have given me a headache. Why don't we stop at the Boar's Head Inn and see if a little scotch can ease my pain."

"If the scotch doesn't do the trick, we can head home and see what kind of magic I can work." The sixty-four-year-old reporter circled her desk and kissed the publisher's equally mature cheek. She couldn't help but smile remembering the first time she'd kissed it three and a half decades earlier. After dating for only a few weeks, the young reporters decided to share a byline. Ten years later, they left the Windy City to run a small weekly paper in a town that, at their arrival, sat in the middle of farmland. Chicago suburbs now approached its borders, but Raccoon Grove, modern in every way, had no desire to be a part of the greater metropolitan area.

"About your offer, I'd be willing to skip the scotch and try a little of your magic."

CHAPTER 4

L ook, Sheriff Crayton, let me call someone to give you a ride home. I can't serve you any more." The young bartender shifted nervously, having taken a step further from his customer's reach before denying him service. He'd seen Ben throw a punch at a bartender who had cut him off and did not want to be on the receiving end of his broad fist.

"Don't call me sheriff. You know damn well I ain't been sheriff in this town for years. Give me another shot or I'll throw this thing through the window." If Ben had been sober enough to hurl the shot glass as hard as he slammed it on the bar, they would have been sweeping up glass at the post office across the street.

"I can't serve you, Ben. Let me call someone to drive you home."

"The hell you can't." The retired sheriff bellowed as he tried to climb from his stool. An unsteady floor and shaky legs kept him seated, but his size and the volume of his shouts were intimidating enough. He reached for the blurred figure, but before he could finish his intended, no doubt, unintelligible response, the front door opened.

"Hey, boys, what's the commotion? We could hear your discussion outside." An inch shy of six feet, Tracy was no shrimp. When Dave's six foot five inch frame moved to her side, they made a formidable presence.

Dave not only enjoyed a lengthier inseam, he also outweighed Tracy by forty pounds, but unlike his reactionary wife, he rarely found reason to raise his voice. He directed a calm inquiry at the two figures facing off across the bar. "Do we have a problem?"

"I told him I couldn't serve him anymore, Mr. Kendall, and he doesn't want to leave." The bartender's eyes strayed from Ben for only a second and he missed Tracy's almost imperceptible nod. Dave didn't.

"Come on, Ben. Tracy has kindly volunteered to take you home. You'd be a danger to the rest of the neighborhood if you walked and I have no intention of carrying you." He fastened a hand on Ben's shoulder, increasing his grip when the intoxicated patron tried to remove it. "You're as big as me, Ben, and stronger, but you're also blind drunk. If you want to walk out, we can do that, or I can knock you unconscious and we'll call a squad car to take you home. Make up your mind." Dave rejoined Tracy at the door and met Ben's glare.

"All right. All right." He untangled himself from the stool and slid the money from the bar into a pocket. "I ain't leaving you a tip," he growled.

"You never do, Ben." The bartender gave Dave and Tracy a relieved nod.

With Ben's unsteady assistance, Dave loaded him into the back seat of Tracy's mid-size Toyota. The problem came when they arrived at his house and found him unconscious, a mass of dead weight. Tracy opened the back door and chuckled at the inebriated ex-sheriff. "This should be fun."

His catatonic state didn't amuse Dave. "Brother. Trace, you climb in behind him and push on his shoulders. I'll pull him this way." Tracy leaned in and braced herself to shove Ben's bulky shoulders. As she pushed, Dave pulled him to the end of the seat and straddled the unconscious body. He leaned him forward, wrapped his arms around his barrel chest, and pulled upward. Unfortunately, he yanked a little too hard. When Ben fell forward, Dave couldn't support him and they toppled to the ground. "Shit."

Tracy hurried to see what incited her husband's infrequent colorful response and found a two-person pileup in one of the large mud puddles dotting Ben's unpaved drive. Dave was on the bottom. "Pull him off. This is one of my best suits." The sleeve of his recently acquired Hugo Boss suit waved helplessly under Ben's massive body. Tracy grabbed an arm and pulled as Dave pushed until they managed to roll him aside.

Dave rose and caught his breath while Tracy called the Sheriff's Department. "Could you send a deputy or two to carry Ben into his house? We made it as far as the end of his drive and hit a major snag. Great, we'll wait until you arrive." She closed her phone and joined Dave. "Would you have hit him?"

"What?"

"You said in the bar that you would knock him unconscious. Would you really have hit him?"

"I wouldn't have then, but if he comes to, I might."

"When the deputies take over, you and I can head home. I'll pour you a scotch while you take a shower, and then I promise to make your headache go away." She eyed his muddy clothing. "Would you mind taking off the suit before you get in my car?"

Sheriff Benjamin Crayton couldn't have known when his wife divorced him that it would lead to the end of his career. Years later, he wouldn't remember that his premature retirement took him to the local tavern where he spent a good portion of his time and money.

Ben groaned as he approached a dull consciousness. Sandpaper lined the insides of his eyelids and he rubbed with his fists to separate the top lid from bottom. It took another couple of minutes to focus. He wasn't surprised to find himself stretched out on his couch along with magazines, dirty clothes, and a few empty beer cans, but he wasn't sure how he got there or why his clothes were covered with mud.

He'd gone to the Boar's Head the previous night. He remembered driving over, but he had no clue what happened when he left. Someone must have brought him home, because if he couldn't remember leaving, he most likely couldn't drive. Who would have given him a ride? Everyone in town avoided him when they could, and the ones that didn't, saw him as a pathetic old drunk and bought him shots for their own amusement. "This is her fault. She shouldn't have divorced me." He repeated the same words he'd been shouting for twenty-one years.

His marriage hadn't exactly been wedded bliss, but they'd done all right. She had no cause to complain. He gave her a big house and enough money for food and clothes. What more did she want? They didn't have any kids and she never worked a day in her life. She still bitched. Ben didn't know she planned to divorce him until after she had gone to see Vandenberg, who filled her head with a bunch of crap about her rights. The only rights she needed were the ones her husband gave her.

He didn't feel bad about Vandenberg dying. A few people in Raccoon Grove figured he deserved it after what he did to families around town. Ben was one of those people. He did feel bad about the little girl, Kimberly. It wasn't her fault her old man was a jackass.

Even with the curtains drawn, the room was painfully bright. He groaned again, keeping a hand over his eyes as he struggled to sit up. He couldn't remember a hangover that bad since he'd gone to see Louise Vandenberg shortly before she died. She'd invited him for a drink and poured expensive scotch like it was water. His glass was never less than half full. He couldn't remember much about that night either. It worried him some that he might have talked about the murder, but none of that mattered anymore. Louise wouldn't be telling anyone anything. If she said something before she died, he'd have heard about it. Nobody knew how to keep their mouth shut in Raccoon Grove. Nobody but him.

Steady enough to stand, Ben lumbered to the front window and pulled back the curtains. He looked through the scattering dust at the empty driveway and sneezed, which did nothing to help his headache. "Damn, I hope the truck's at the bar." A banging he thought came from his head grew louder and more persistent. "Oh, jeez, what idiot is hammering on the door? Stop it. I got enough of that without any outside help." His left hand pulled the door open and his right flew to his face to block the sun. He peeked through his fingers at the visitor. "What the hell do you want, Kendall?"

Without waiting for an invitation, Dave pushed on the door and let himself in, brushing a pile of debris from a chair to sit. "Did your maid quit, Ben? I wanted to see how you were doing this morning. You didn't look your best last night."

"You brought me home?"

"Tracy and I drove you back here and moved you as far as the end of the driveway, where you proceeded to put us both in a large mud puddle." He pointed at the dried mud on Ben's jeans. "I should send you the bill for cleaning my suit. Ben, you're not going to make it much longer if you keep this up."

"What'd you do, Kendall, retire from publishing and go into preaching? I suggest you go back to your old job even if you ain't good at it. Something tells me you'd be a lousy preacher."

"I'm not preaching, Crayton. I'm telling you the facts. You've been drunk more often than you've been sober, and your body won't take much more. If you kill yourself, I'll have to waste a lot of valuable space running your obit."

"It's no business of yours or anybody else in this town if I kill myself." He stood and Dave followed.

"Fine with me. By the way, you might be interested to know that Tracy and Kate have decided to look into the Vandenberg case."

"Yeah, I heard, but I don't know why the hell they want to do that."

"If you remember, it was never solved. Some people want to know what happened."

"Then some people ought to have their heads examined. Thanks for the ride, Kendall. Now beat it."

"Don't let it be said that I can't take a hint, even one as subtle as yours." Dave let himself out.

Perfect weather and a lack of new orders allowed Kate time to check the drip lines that wove through her gardens. It took her a few hours to inspect the entire watering system, but she had a surplus of energy that morning and went section by section pulling invading weeds. Chemicals were a rare and last resort, so she removed the intruders by hand as soon as they dared make an appearance.

The physical work required to maintain her gardens involved little concentration. That gave her plenty of time for reflection. The younger Kathleen left little room in her life for thinking because her thoughts inevitably followed the paths of self-pity and despair. As the flower business became successful, her sky lightened and her fear lessened. She also learned to take advantage of two wonderful sets of ears, which were hers to bend—those of her mother and her friendly gossip columnist.

Tracy Kendall proved to be a good friend, and friendship was one of the many things that came to Kate later in life. Close relationships rarely formed at beauty pageants. People you met on the runways were adversaries and any appearance of closeness was as phony as their practiced on-camera smiles.

Kate's mother supported her choice to enter the high school beauty contest, but she didn't encourage it, or suggest she continue. In fact, though she never said, Kate knew her mom did not approve. She worried about her daughter's future and on more than one occasion suggested Kathleen take a few classes at the community college. Kate knew being pretty would not help her in college. It terrified her that the other students and teachers would see the empty, stupid person she saw in herself. Her excuse to her mom was that college had nothing to offer. In reality, she stayed clear of academia to avoid the embarrassment of failure. She would live on her looks for as long as possible.

Her mother once told her that without a light burning inside, beauty faded quickly. Kate didn't know what that meant until she noticed the darkness pushing on both sides of her skin. She did the pageants because she believed she had no choice. She looked the part of a beauty queen, but didn't feel it. Once she walked down her first runway, she saw no way out.

A memory that still made her smile was her reaction when they handed her flowers after a victory. She instinctively held them close to adjust the arrangement. Her true calling might have surfaced sooner had she paid attention to the only part of the competitions that brought her joy.

When she finished weeding, Kate went to the shed for a rake to fluff the mulch. Packed down it didn't allow rainwater through. As wonderful as the irrigation system was, it would never match the effectiveness of a summer rain. She remembered the shower that ended minutes before Jack came to pick her up the last time they met. The reemergence of the sun with Jack's arrival had seemed such a good sign.

"Hello." Tracy stood at the back of the house waving a picnic basket. "How about a lunch break?"

"Sure, where do you want to go?" Kate returned the rake to the shed and noticed Tracy's chic pantsuit. She removed her gloves, dusted loose soil from her jeans, and pushed escaped strands behind her ears. It was futile. "If you have something fancy in mind you'll have to wait until I shower and change."

"Even in your grubby old jeans, you look better then most of the women in Raccoon Grove. That, by the way, puts a lot of pressure on the rest of us." Tracy feigned a snarl, but it disappeared with one glance at the yard. "Why would we go anywhere when we can dine in this exquisite backyard? I brought sandwiches." She led the way to the gazebo and flipped open the woven basket to retrieve boxes of food and a bottle of wine. "Grab some glasses, Kate. This is an excellent pinot noir, the perfect accompaniment to a discussion on murder."

CHAPTER 5

W"here did you get these sandwiches, Tracy?" Kate waved the half-eaten item in question. "This is wonderful."

"There's a new place around the corner from the bank called Alice's Restaurant. It's done in a 1920s Paris motif. We should have lunch there. Not Paris, the restaurant." Tracy's eyes fixed on the glass of deep red liquid as though it were a crystal ball. Her growing smile suggested a bright future. "Maybe we should go to Paris. You can investigate the flowers, and I'll check out a winery or two."

"Okay, but for now, it will have to be the restaurant."

"Let's do it soon. Trendy places tend not to last long in this town. Kate, I don't want to talk about *le café de jour*. I've gathered us here with good food and wine to discuss Jack's murder." She emptied her glass and pulled several sheets of paper from her purse, placing them in the center of the table. "I think we should reopen the case."

"When you say we, I assume you mean the Gazette and the sheriff's department plan to collaborate on reopening the case." Kate didn't assume any such thing, but decided it wouldn't hurt to introduce the idea. She found Tracy's enthusiasm and willingness to participate in various adventures an admirable quality, but her eagerness to involve her friends in those adventures, though thoughtful, was much less endearing.

"Silly, silly, Kate, of course, I mean you and me. Surely you've wondered over the years why someone killed Jack and possibly kidnapped Kimberly."

"I've wondered for two decades, but never came up with an answer. Is it the arrival of the anonymous letters that has you thinking about reopening the case?"

"That's part of it, but it started when I wrote the anniversary piece. The letters just added fuel to my curiosity's fire. Dave thinks the letter about Kimberly with the nonworking phone number is a prank. I disagree with my cute, but uncurious, husband."

"Maybe Dave is right. If it was a real tip, wouldn't the number work?"

"He also said it could be a typo."

"That's a stretch. Why would a person go through the trouble of composing and sending something like that and not bother to check the number?"

"I'm sure you've noticed that accurate information isn't exactly a requirement in communication these days."

"There do seem to be a large number of errors slipping through. I read an article by a professor who thinks our excessive use of computers is contributing to an inability to concentrate. Maybe that's a clue. The person who wrote the letter may have one of those attention disorders."

"Since some research says over twenty five million Americans have it, that doesn't narrow down the field."

"Do you think it's possible that the letter is true? That Kimberly is alive."

"Anything is possible. I never believed the kidnapping theory. The only thing that made sense to me was that she saw whoever killed Jack and that person had to kill her so she didn't talk. If that's true and we discover who killed Jack, we'll know who killed Kimberly."

"Why would they have bothered to hide Kim and not Jack?"

"Maybe there wasn't time. Remember, when Louise showed up Kimberly was gone. Maybe this person planned to hide both bodies and make it look like Jack took Kimberly and left. When Louise showed up, his plan fell apart."

"Why in heavens name would anyone believe that Jack kidnapped Kimberly?"

"Because…well…I don't know. Okay, that's a little implausible. Let's just leave Kimberly's disappearance separate for now and think of reasons for wanting Jack dead." Tracy refilled the glasses before tapping a finger on the papers. "So, do we reopen the case?"

"One of Jack's clients' ex-husband could have blamed Jack for the divorce. I remember hearing rumblings back then. Some of the guys weren't pleased." She paused for a sip of wine. "This is good, but I'm sure I haven't seen it at Tommy's liquor store."

"I buy it online by the case. They have some remarkable deals which I'll be glad to show you, but finish your thought."

Kate knew that Tracy intended to reopen the case and only asked to be polite. That counted for something. "Maybe it wasn't a divorce. What if Jack had an unhappy client on another case? If someone he represented thought he handled his or her case poorly, they may have wanted revenge, except that I can't imagine Jack Vandenberg handling a case badly."

"Jack worked exclusively as a divorce attorney, and I agree. I doubt he handled any legal action badly. If someone killed him because of a case, it would have been because he did a good job for his client. I think we should start our investigation with the ex-husbands." Tracy unfolded the papers and turned them toward her reluctant partner. "This list shows every divorce Jack handled five years prior to his death. That's right after he opened his practice here and should include most of his clients."

"Maybe it was a client from before he came here and he found out where Jack lived."

"I doubt it. He spent ten years in the Air Force before he went to law school and had only recently passed the Illinois Bar when he married Louise and they moved into that house. Jack inherited it from his grandfather." She pulled the second sheet from underneath and put it on top. "This is a list of the ex-husbands from our little town whose wives used Jack as an attorney. You'll recognize many of them, I'm sure."

In no hurry to spoil a perfectly pleasant lunch discussing murder, Kate savored her wine and absently studied the list. Midway through the names, her eyes widened. "I'd forgotten about Dirk. Jack didn't finish the divorce, but he did ninety-nine percent of the work. No matter how much anger I had for him back then, I can't imagine Dirk killing anyone. He's the embodiment of the phrase 'a lover, not a fighter.'"

"Were you angry with Dirk? I don't remember you having a great deal of interest in his change of address at the time."

Kate's brief look of astonishment disappeared with a chuckle as she rested her elbow on the table and her chin in her hand. "No, I don't suppose I was that upset. The only thing that surprised me was how long he stayed in the marriage. I didn't like myself much back then. I do however, like this wine." She continued to sip as she reviewed the list of names. "A few of these people are dead."

"Yes, but if they were alive when Jack died, they could be a suspect. I checked records and two were dead at the time of Jack's death. I put red dots next to those. The yellow dots indicate people who died after the murder."

"Tracy, I'm not sure what good this information will do. We're not certain any of these people killed Jack, and if one did, how do you plan to get a confession after all this time?"

"Granted, it's meager, but don't you want to know what happened? Remember, Sheriff Crayton wanted to pin it on you."

"Yes, I want to know. You're determined to do this, aren't you? Okay. I guess the best place to start would be with the messier divorces. That should be easy enough for our local gossip columnist to discover."

"That a girl." Tracy raised her glass, an action Kate mirrored while remembering the end of her marriage. The divorce had not been messy, but it was a time she wouldn't forget.

As the divorce neared completion, Kate found herself thinking less of the end of her relationship with Dirk, than of the end of her meetings with Jack. "Please call me Kate, Jack. Everyone does."

"That's why I prefer Kathleen. Does it bother you?"

"No, and that surprises me. Besides you, my mother is the only person who calls me Kathleen without making it sound like a reprimand. I suppose your speaking skills are part of what makes you such a good attorney." He offered only an amused smile. "Do you read a lot, Jack?"

"I do. How about you?"

"I didn't read much until recently. That probably sounds strange to you, but when I was younger, books intimidated me. No, it was more than that. They scared the heck out of me. I never considered myself very bright. After my children moved out and Dirk wasn't around, I began reading the books they left behind. It wasn't long before I was hooked."

"I don't believe it."

"You don't believe I read?" She wondered if he saw her as an empty-headed beauty queen.

"No, that you don't consider yourself bright. You're an intelligent, articulate woman. Where did that idea come from, your parents?"

"No, not at all. I don't remember much about my dad, but mom always told me I was smart. I just never believed her. Most people told me I was pretty, not intelligent. I thought my life would be easier if I kept my mouth shut."

"Your beauty is indisputable, but your mother was right." She watched her dinner companion swirl his wine. Much more than a mastery of the language made Jack attractive. He seemed to have it all, thick brown hair, dark sensitive eyes, good health, a successful practice, a great personality, a large home, and a wife and daughter. He had never given her reason to think he wanted more than a professional relationship and friendship. Kate wasn't certain how she would have responded if he had, especially with the way her chest tightened as an end to their meetings approached. She could never have guessed how soon that would end would come, or how permanent it would be.

"I'm sorry to have to cut this short, Kathleen, but we have our quarterly card game tonight. I'm glad you could make dinner. Losing my shirt will be at least tolerable."

After Jack dropped her off at home, she returned to the book she'd been reading, a collection of short stories by J.D. Salinger. She delighted in how Salinger made her feel a part of the characters lives. Later, it occurred to her that she enjoyed them simply because they made her feel. Her dad's death had left her terrified of emotion. She grew up doubting she could survive pain that intense a second time.

Months after Jack's death when Kate finished the books her family left behind, she asked Tracy and her mom to recommend others. Then, she joined the library and became almost as addicted to reading as working with her flowers. One of the greatest gifts to come from her new passion was that it gave her a chance to share books with her mom for the last few years of her life. She spent her final days with Kate, often sitting in the yard by the flowers while Kate read aloud. Eventually her mom's patient love helped her see that if she didn't allow herself to feel the pain of loss she couldn't know the joy of a life shared with others. When her mom died, Kate felt the full impact of both.

❧

"I'm glad your gardens let you out to play from time to time." Dave came out of his office when he saw Kate at the top of the stairs. "Visit with me for a minute before you join Tracy. Once you two start detecting, I won't see you again." He kissed her cheek and escorted her to a soft leather chair in front of his desk, a chair with which she developed an instant rapport.

"How in the world do you persuade people to move out of this thing once they're in its grasp?"

"I don't always. You'd be surprised how many visitors I've poked with a pencil to send them on their way. I bought that one to replace one that sat there for over twenty-five years. It was as comfortable as its replacement. So, Tracy tells me you two plan to reopen the Vandenberg case."

"We'll see how far we can take it. I wouldn't consider being involved if I didn't have confidence in her detecting abilities. She has such an analytical brain."

"That's because she spent so much time in analysis." Dave did a decent Groucho Marx imitation with his own twitchy eyebrows and a pen.

"I'll be sure to tell her what you said." His boyish sulk sent Kate into a fit of laughter. She had never known a couple with a relationship like theirs, and after thirty-five years of marriage, it improved like fine wine. "Don't pout, I won't tell her. The letters are interesting though, aren't they? Kimberly is alive and someone knows who killed Jack."

"Interesting is a bit of an understatement. Have you decided where to start?"

"We talked about checking into divorces Jack handled that were messier than usual. That could mean anything. I'm not sure if Tracy wants us to call or visit. I suppose a visit would be more effective. You can see their faces and know if they're lying."

"Hey, are you cheating on me?"

Dave's head rose and Kate turned to the doorway to see Tracy wearing an equally effective pout. "Give me a break. Tracy Kendall, gossip columnist extraordinaire, jealous of a simple gardener?"

"Heavens, I don't care if you take him. I don't want him to take you. You know that old song, 'A good girlfriend is hard to find'. Are you ready to go to work? I think I've narrowed things down a bit."

"I'm ready." Kate stood and waved to Dave. "Thanks. It was fun while it lasted." The women left his office arm in arm trying not to smile at his quivering lower lip.

"Your chair isn't nearly as comfortable as the one in Dave's office."

"I told him not to replace the old one with another comfortable chair. No one ever stays in my office longer than necessary."

"You think that's because of the chair?"

Ignoring the remark, Tracy put a long finger on the center of her glasses and slid them up her nose. "I made a few phone calls this morning, not to ex-husbands, but ex-wives. I figured we'd learn more from the women since men aren't good at remembering emotional moments. At least they aren't good at talking about them if they do remember. We have five candidates."

"Who's on our list of top five suspects?"

"The first one deservedly tops the list. Your favorite and our sheriff back then, Ben Crayton."

"It wouldn't surprise me if he did it. He's always had a hot temper."

"And it was even hotter after his divorce. He stormed around town furious at his wife and Jack. We'll have to talk to him along with everyone else, but it won't be pretty."

"We're off to a good start. Suspect number one, retired Sheriff Ben Crayton."

"Next in the lineup is Harold Duffy, the guy who owns the garage on Main Street and Elm."

"I bought the flower van from Harold, and he keeps it happily running. He doesn't strike me as angry or dangerous."

"He's not a hothead, but Laurie told me he acted like a real jerk when she went to see Jack. Then we have our postmaster, Milt Borcilino. Next, we have George Williams who owns the submarine sandwich place, and finally Mad Dog Jackson. You know him I'm sure. He does custom chrome work for motorcycles."

"I know Mad Dog, but I don't remember if I've ever heard his first name."

"It's Maynard, but don't call him that."

"I promise. Why don't we visit him first? I've run into Mad Dog a few times recently and he's been pretty mellow, but on the off chance that he lives up to his name, it will make the rest of the interviews feel like a walk in the park."

A deafening roar greeted Kate and Tracy as they approached Mad Dog's garage. Tracy yelled through the opened door, but quickly recognized the futility. To protect his remaining hearing from the noise, Mad Dog wore a set of fat headphones. She entered the building and raised a hand to tap his shoulder, but Kate grabbed it before she made contact and pulled her back outside. "Don't surprise him while he's working on that machine. Somebody will get hurt."

At Kate's prudent suggestion, they waited until the noise stopped. When they went inside, the Dog, as people knew him around town, had removed the headphones and was wiping his hands on a rag. He stood about five ten with a mass of tight curls that spilled untamed to his broad shoulders. The t-shirt he wore had once been white, but time and grease had taken their toll and it now matched the salt and pepper gray of his hair. A completely gray beard hid the lower part of his face in a similar frenzy.

"Mad Dog, do you have a minute?"

"Hi, Tracy, Kate. Sure." You would expect the sounds emitted from a chest the size of Mad Dog's to be deep. You would also expect them to be loud. The ladder was not true. His soft bass was surprisingly melodious, especially compared to the irritating roar of the extinguished equipment. "I'm guessing that neither one of you needs chrome on your bike. What's up?"

Kate jumped right in. "We're reopening an investigation and want to ask you a few questions about your divorce and your relationship with Jack Vandenberg."

"Have a seat." He located a clean spot on his rag and wiped two of the four folding chairs that populated the garage. Kate and Tracy sat, and without bothering to wipe the chair, he joined them. "I didn't have a relationship with Jack. He worked for my wife. I mean my ex-wife. As far as how the divorce went, it wasn't pretty. I didn't want it and made that known to the whole town. Looking back, I can understand why Lynn wanted out. I was drunk, high, or both most of the time back then. I assume this is leading to you asking me if I killed Jack." He saw their matching nods and added his own. "From what I've heard over the years, he died at eight in the evening. I was usually well on my way to oblivion by then. The straight answer to your question is no, I didn't kill him. I wasn't mad at Jack, I was mad at my ex. I wouldn't have killed her either, even though I did mention wanting to a few hundred times. Honestly, I figured I'd have been a good suspect between being crazy with anger and wasted around the clock. It amazed me that Ben didn't knock on my door."

"He never questioned you?" Kate looked surprised. She agreed with Mad Dog's assessment that he made a good suspect, certainly better than her. She calmed herself with a deep breath and watched the gray curls bounce as Maynard Jackson shook head.

"I know, Kate, and I wasn't one of the Sheriff's favorite people. He hated my guts and let me know it. He might still. He didn't like us long-haired types, especially on Harleys."

Tracy stood and extended a hand but Mad Dog waved his greasy paws to indicate a handshake might not be a good idea. "I heard you remarried."

"Since you're Raccoon Grove's favorite gossip columnist, I'd imagine you did. Terry and I finally tied the knot. She's a great cook, has her own Sportster, and doesn't take any crap from me. It's a good thing. I'm too old to do what I did twenty years ago. I might have been too old then."

"Well, thanks for your time. What are you working on?" Tracy pointed to the highly polished piece of chrome on his bench.

He picked it up and smiled. "It's Terry's birthday. I chromed her Kickback risers."

"Ah," Kate said, without a clue to what a Kickback riser might be. "I'm sure she'll be delighted."

CHAPTER 6

D o we think Mad Dog is telling the truth?"

Kate laid the menu she'd been studying on the table, tapping the words *Alice's Restaurant* under a Picasso-style image. "He does make a good suspect, but I believe him. If it happened near his house or outside the Boar's Head, I'd say he could have gone into a drunken, stoned rage. If he went crazy and killed Jack, how did he make it out there and back without leaving clues or fingerprints on the gun? That took some clear thinking. Besides, despite his threatening name, Mad Dog Jackson is a teddy bear. Can you believe he chromed a part of Terry's motorcycle for a birthday present?"

"I've seen her Sportster. It's a nice bike. Mad Dog does seem easy going, but he wasn't always so sedate. At least his growl wasn't." Tracy cut short her response when a waitress appeared to take their order. Her shapeless gray shift hung to her calves, essential attire for Charleston-dancing flappers. Straight black hair cut in the popular pixie style of the 1920s capped her head, and a lengthy string of pearls hung around her neck. Had she not been writing with a cigarette holder that doubled as a pen, she might have been swinging the beads. Heavy black lines covered her modest eyebrows and she'd drawn a matching outline around her eyes. If those embellishments weren't enough to attract attention, bright red lipstick applied slightly wider than her mouth and the jaw snapping style with which she chewed her gum, would. Kate no longer owned shoes designed to torture her feet, legs, and back, and shuddered as the woman recorded their orders and departed on her four-inch heels.

Tracy, who barely noticed the waitress, wasted no time returning to the investigation. "I agree about Mad Dog not killing Jack, or if he did, he really doesn't remember. His answers were open and honest and he could have told us to take off. I still can't believe no one questioned him. I wonder if Ben talked to anyone besides you."

"I don't know, Tracy. Something I've always wondered is why the FBI wasn't involved since it was believed that Kimberley was kidnapped."

"I asked Ben about that a few months after Jack's death. They stayed in touch for four or five weeks, but when there was no evidence of abduction and no call for ransom, they left it to Ben. The case remained open in their files, but they didn't think it warranted any further investigation at the time. I wish the Gazette had taken a more active part. Once the story caught the attention of the city papers, it made more sense for us to focus on the effect on our community, rather than the crime itself. And, since we were relatively new in town, I wasn't as nosy."

"I didn't know you then, so I won't comment on that. When we talk to Ben, we should find out if he interviewed anyone else. Do you still run into him?"

"Dave and I had the pleasure at the Boar's Head the other night. I'm not sure how much help he'll be. He's been hitting the sauce at a hazardous rate."

"I heard that at Adam's office when I dropped off an arrangement yesterday. I catch up on more gossip in a few minutes there than anywhere else in town, besides from you. Of course, funeral parlors aren't great places to chat."

"How is the good Doctor Collins these days? Dave and I saw him and Elaine in Chicago about six months ago, not long before she started using the wheelchair. We were at the symphony and the lights flashed ending intermission just as we ran into them. We didn't have time to visit."

"He was with a patient when I went in, so I didn't see him, but you couldn't squeeze another person into the waiting room. His practice is doing well from what I could see. It's a shame about their daughter Sara. She's been in and out of mental hospitals for years. I remember her as a happy little girl, but I've heard she was hospitalized for depression."

"That's right. It started right after Kimberly disappeared, but Adam didn't have her hospitalized until she was almost eleven. He didn't want to even then, but he didn't know what else to do." Tracy recalled. "I knew she and Kimberly were friends, but I would have thought Sara was too young to be that devastated by her disappearance. Maybe she had problems and Kimberly's vanishing was enough to push her over the edge."

Kate stirred her iced tea thoughtfully. "I never understood what happened to Sara. I suppose you could be right about Kimberly's disappearance pushing her over the edge, although she's doing okay lately. She's lived with her parents for the last two years and hasn't gone back to the hospital. I see her at the library on occasion. Last time we met, she asked me to recommend my favorite authors and mysteries. Catherine at the beauty parlor said she's seen her around town more often and that she looks great. What do they do in those hospitals? They cost a fortune, but are nothing more than expensive hotels that dispense drugs. Adam probably works as hard as he does to pay the bills."

Tracy was about to agree when the bell at the door sounded and someone entered. "Speak of the devil." She stood and waved at Sara Collins. "Sara, come and sit with us."

The petite young woman approached, thumbs hooked in her back pockets, wearing a smile and clad in standard Raccoon Grove attire—jeans, a tee shirt and white tennis shoes on her size six feet. Short black curls accentuated her pale skin and she directed a pair of steady green eyes at Tracy and Kate. "Hello, Ms Kendall, Ms Chandler, I'm afraid I can't stay. I have to pick up an order for dad's office. No one could get away, so I volunteered. I hope I can take a rain check. Ms Chandler, I'd like to talk to you when you have some time." She went to the counter and wrapped her arms around two large bags of food, nodding at them as she pushed her shoulder into the heavy door and left.

"I have an idea, Kate. Let's have lunch with Sara on the gazebo. She said she wants to talk to you. I'll bet she'd love the gardens. She sounds good, doesn't she?"

"She does, and I like the lunch idea, but before we work on that, should we tackle another suspect?"

"I can't. I have to start my column for the next edition." Tracy, the poster child of good intentions, grabbed the bill and pulled her wallet from her purse. Her chagrined look meant only one thing and without waiting, Kate took money from her pocket and the check from Tracy's fingers.

"I'll take care of the bill. You can buy next time." Between her designer clothes and her wine collection, Kate knew the journalist was willing to spend money, just not carry it.

❦

Five uninterrupted hours in her office gave Tracy time to answer correspondence and create a good first draft of her column. It wasn't until her fingers stopped tapping the keyboard that she noticed a grumble from her stomach. Her progress and the noise from her midsection were ample reason to stop for the day. She had an even easier time convincing her husband.

Of the two, Dave was handier in the kitchen, but Tracy knew her way around well enough to assist. They prepared and ate a pesto salmon and fettuccine of Dave's own creation. At the end of the meal, Tracy took charge of loading the dishwasher and they retired to the long couch in the living room. Dave settled in the corner and she stretched out with her head in his lap. "Tell me about the interview with Mad Dog." His fingers brushed her cheek while she snuggled in to recount the conversation.

"He's really mellowed over the years. Do you remember Mad Dog when we first moved here? Back then, half the town folk were bikers and the other half farmers." Her head barely moved as her eyes shifted to view his face.

"I remember that he could be easygoing one minute and jump all over you the next. The booze and drugs might have been responsible for a big part of that. Of course, in those days, the biker half of town was always ready for a fight, especially come closing time at the Boar's Head. When they said 'last call', a large number of patrons thought they said 'last brawl.'"

She laughed. "You didn't brawl, Dave."

"No, I didn't, but I pulled you out of a free-for-all or two. You spent most of your time with the biker crowd, didn't you?"

"Not really, and I didn't get into brawls. Well, maybe one." Tracy didn't play poker because her face, and often her words, too clearly expressed her feelings. Dave heard a sigh, the prelude to her decent into wistfulness, and patted her shoulder to continue. "We came out here thinking we were two radical upstarts ready to publish a Pulitzer Prize winning weekly. We were in our late thirties and should have known better. As radical as we might have been, or thought we were, compared to the group here, we were conservative suits from the city. I did enjoy the bikers more because I had more experience with motorcycles than tractors. Did you know I rode a bike before I drove a car?"

"You've mentioned that a time or two, but I didn't believe it until I saw you jump on George's Harley and take off." Dave shook his head. "And now, in my golden years, I have this wonderful memory of my adventurous wife roaring down Main Street on a full dress Hog. Mad Dog did great chrome work even back then."

Tracy turned on her side and closed her eyes. "George had a nice ride. I thought he was a little tense when I brought it back. Did he say anything to you?"

"Any conversation George had while you were on his bike, he directed to heaven."

She slapped his thigh and changed the subject to hide her amusement. "Why do you suppose Ben didn't question Mad Dog? He told us he expected him to. Ben made no secret of his contempt for the bikers."

"We should ask Sheriff Robbins for a look at the old reports. They didn't put everything on computers back then, but they might have entered them later. I'm sure Ben won't remember much, and the way he feels about me, he won't tell me what he does remember."

"He's given up, hasn't he? His sole ambition these days is to stay drunk. I suppose that numbs the pain, but if he's still brooding about the divorce, he should have gotten over it years ago."

"I thought about that, Tracy. He was always a curmudgeon, even married, and he was much worse afterwards, but about a year after the divorce, he showed signs of recovering. When Jack died and Kimberly disappeared, he hit the skids again and hit them permanently. Maybe he felt guilty that it happened on his watch, because he wasn't doing his job."

"He lasted another five years, Dave. It took the town council a long time to replace him."

"He did a good job the first dozen years. They wanted to give him a chance. Everyone hoped he'd turn it around."

"I suppose we should be grateful the crime rate didn't amount to much back then."

"It made our work easier. Speaking of work. Did the envelopes or letterheads from the anonymous letters tell you anything?"

"According to the postmarks, one came from Chicago and one from Beecher. Both writers used plain, twenty-pound white bond and I'd guess, printed them on an inkjet printer. I saw nothing distinctive." Tracy sat up. "Why try to stir up interest in who killed Jack after all this time?"

"I would guess people are wondering that about you and Kate."

※

Encouraged by heavy spring rains, Raccoon Grove Creek swelled to within inches of its banks, and although the last days of May brought dryer weather, the water made only a minor retreat. For a brief time in its existence, the slow-moving trickle passed itself off as one of the many streams and rivers that wove through the state.

Ben was familiar with the deception. He'd parked in that same spot for most of his life and had witnessed every season, every mood. This day he saw what he always saw, what he liked to see, woods, water, and no people. It was illegal to build in the forest preserves, so except for changes invoked by Mother Nature, the thick woods outside of town stayed the same. In the town itself, things changed, and in Ben's eyes, not for the better. Raccoon Grove was close enough to Chicago to attract those who needed the city, but wanted to live in the country. That brought money to the community, but it also brought more people and more change.

The brown pint bottle he drew from his pocket was still sealed. He remedied that and took a swig, clenching the steering wheel when the cheap whiskey burned his throat and hit his stomach like molten lava. He ran a sleeve over his mouth and waited for the pain to pass. Kendall was right about the booze. His body couldn't take much more. Getting old was one more inevitable change and he'd downed enough bad booze to hurry the process.

The next swig went down easier and rattled enough brain cells to recall another change someone wanted to make, a change that would have a direct effect on his wallet. He pulled out his phone and jabbed a number. When the familiar voice answered, wrinkles on Ben's hardened face rearranged into something akin to a smile. "I need money."

"I don't know where you plan to get it, Ben. I told you, I'm through giving you money."

"You talk tough considering how much you could lose if I told folks around here what I know. I'm sure you've noticed since the Gazette ran that anniversary piece, people are interested in the Vandenberg case again. Tracy Kendall is telling everyone about a letter she got. That letter came from me. But you knew that, didn't you? If you don't pay up, I can send more details. I know them well. Better yet, maybe I'll use the information to write a best selling book, or a made-for-TV movie. It'd be quite a story, don't you think?" The audible sigh meant victory. "Where do you want to meet?"

"Wait for me at that abandoned trailer on Old 14, but I can't make it until midnight."

"Yeah, okay." Ben raised the bottle in a salute. He had reason to celebrate.

"Meet me behind the trailer. How much do you want?"

"How about thirty grand? It's time I bought me a new truck."

"Are you nuts? Where would I find thirty thousand dollars? I'll give you five hundred. That's it. I mean it, Ben. That's it."

"Sure, five hundred's okay. I just wanted to make sure you weren't holding out on me. I'll see you around midnight." Ben disconnected and took another drink. Celebration or not, he'd have to slow down until he collected his cash.

Dense clouds covered the slice of moon, determined to block all light to the isolated spot on Old Highway 14. Ben's green Dakota all but disappeared in the darkness. Even the silver trailer meant to conceal him was barely discernable with nothing to reflect. Only long time residents knew their way around the unpopulated patch of land after dark.

He kept to his plan and took it easy on the booze to make sure he stayed awake. The problem with that was it left him sober enough to think, and on those rare occasions, he wondered what the hell he was doing. He had no particular sorrows left to drown, at least none that he could remember. He drank because he didn't have any choice. It was as simple as that.

Nobody in town would remember his good years as sheriff. He was lucky they'd let him collect most of his retirement and didn't just can him. If they had, he'd have ended up on the streets and dead long ago. Of course, that might have been better than living like he was, with nothing inside but pickled intestines and a rotten liver. It probably didn't matter much anymore. He had a hunch he wouldn't be around a whole lot longer. Except for an empty bar stool at the Boar's Head, it might take the good folks of Raccoon Grove a few weeks to notice he was gone.

One thing was bugging him. When he sent the letter to the paper, he thought it was just to make sure the payoffs continued. He wasn't big on psychology, but maybe there was something more to it. Maybe a small part of him, a part that somehow escaped the alcohol poisoning, wanted the town to know the truth. He didn't read the local paper. He didn't read any paper, but Dave and Tracy Kendall were the only people in town who treated him better than dirt. If Tracy wanted to find out what happened to Jack Vandenberg that night, maybe he should tell her, even if it meant cutting off his supply of extra cash. There weren't any taverns in hell, and that was where he expected to retire permanently.

The car surprised him. He hadn't heard it drive up. When the vehicle stopped, the headlights disappeared and left only the parking lights to illuminate the unhappy figure. Ben chuckled as he watched him approach and opened the door to swing his legs out of the truck cab. "You bring my money?" The figure said nothing as he drew near. "Let's have it."

"I told you this can't go on. You aren't getting any more money, Ben." A hand flew toward him and he felt something sting his leg.

"Ow, shit. What was that?"

"Why did you write the letter? Why couldn't you just leave things be?"

CHAPTER 7

The large ranch style home Dave and Tracy shared sat on four wooded acres at the eastern edge of town. Most mornings they enjoyed a quiet drive to the office, sipping a thermal cup of coffee to awaken any slumbering brain cells. The scene as they turned onto Old Highway 14, told them it was not most mornings. Police and ambulance lights flashed and a dozen village and county uniforms milled about on the side of the road.

"I wonder what's going on." Tracy rolled down her window and leaned out for a better look. "Dave, slow down. This is more than an accident."

"Can you see anything?"

"Oh, brother. That's Ben's truck fused to a tree." Dave maneuvered into a space between the squad cars and they ran toward a group of officers.

"Is he all right?" A deputy standing near the truck heard Dave's question and gave his head a slow shake.

Tracy spotted Sheriff Robbins in the crowd of uniforms. "Scott. What happened?"

"I just got here, Tracy, but it's my guess Ben finally found a way to put himself out of his misery. I'll give you a holler when we know more."

Something about the position of Ben's truck puzzled her, but when she started toward the accident scene, Scott grabbed her arm. "I'll call you later, Tracy."

"That tree is in a culvert. He couldn't have been going very fast when he hit. I'm certainly not telling how to do your job, Scott, but you might want to check it out."

"I appreciate the help, and the fact that you're not telling me how to do my job. See ya' later."

"It was this way or his liver, Trace." Dave broke the silence they'd maintained since returning to the car. "He's been determined to kill himself for the last ten years."

"I know. He's been on a mission, especially lately, but from where I stood, he didn't hit the tree hard enough to do his body much damage. If he was loaded, which is a given, he would have been relaxed, making it even less likely. I wonder if his heart gave out."

"That's a possibility. He wasn't the healthiest guy in town. Did Scott say he'd let us know?"

"Yes, but if he doesn't call before ten tonight, we won't be able to print the story until next Friday." Tracy tapped her coffee cup to put her thoughts in order. "We need to put an obit together. Ben served as sheriff for seventeen years and at least twelve of them were good. He deserves something."

"Okay, but let's put it on page one and make it a memorial. We can find a picture of him in uniform and push the state fair pictures back a few pages."

"That's a good idea." Neither of them spoke again until they arrived at the paper. "Dave, I've been thinking about the writer who claimed to know who killed Jack."

"What were you thinking?"

Tracy looked about to respond, but instead, twisted her mouth to the side and shook her head. "Never mind. It's too far out even for me."

⁂

A figure stood near the gardens, but Kate walked from the greenhouse and halfway through the yard before she saw and recognized her ex-husband. He had not been to the house since the divorce, and when they ran into each other in town, the meetings were uncomfortable, particularly when he accompanied the woman who replaced her as his wife. "Dirk. Is anything wrong?"

"No." He answered without turning. "Kate, I heard your gardens were beautiful, but I had no idea. I remember when you put in the first plants after the kids moved out." He shook his head and faced her directly. "You're still beautiful, too. You look content."

"Thanks, I feel content. Let's sit. Do you want a glass of water or a cup of coffee?" At his response, she went to the house and returned with their glasses. "What brings you out this way?"

He sat in one of the deck chairs and kept his eyes on the glass he took from her hand. "I wanted to visit. There've been some big changes in my life recently and I've realized a few things I never gave any thought."

"Vicki?" Kate guessed there were problems at home. Dirk was forty-five when he married twenty-year-old Vicki. Now that he was sixty-five, the gap became a chasm. Someone in their forties feared aging much more than someone in their twenties. Lying next to a senior citizen would remind her of her own inevitable aging, and sooner than she liked.

"She moved in with some kid her own age and asked for a divorce. Kate, I didn't realize how dreadful what I did to you was until Vicki did it to me. This apology comes twenty years late, but I am sorry."

"Neither one of us knew what we were doing back then. It's only now that I've grown enough to be a parent to my kids, though they don't know that. They're long gone and I'm still a stranger to them and my grandchildren. Do you feel grown up, Dirk?"

Some questions need only brief consideration, but for a sixty-five-year-old man to reflect on if he was grown up required thought. Dirk took a minute to respond. "More often these days, but once in a while I find that frightened kid lurking inside. You've grown up, huh?" He studied her. "I don't have to ask if that's a good thing, Kate. I can see it is."

"For the first time in my life, I feel it too. Do you suppose everyone takes a lifetime to figure things out and no one is willing to admit it?"

"If my friends are an indication of a sluggish growth rate, I'd say that's true." He returned his gaze to the gardens. "I'm sorry I didn't come to your mom's funeral. I didn't feel right about it. She didn't like me much."

She smiled. "No, you weren't her favorite person, but she wouldn't have minded. Forgiveness came easy to her. She always saw the good in people, even people who didn't see it in themselves."

Kate's calm helped Dirk relax and he leaned back stretching his legs. "I heard you and Tracy Kendall are investigating Jack's murder. She has a way of solving mysteries, doesn't she?"

"She has two under her belt and is hoping to make this the third. By the way, you're not a suspect. Mainly because you wanted the divorce, but also because as hard as we tried, we couldn't find any dirt on you." When her comment registered, his easy smile returned. "Do you know anything about what happened that night, Dirk?"

His white hair had been jet-black and worn combed straight back. He still combed it that way, though a large part of the top of his head glistened in the sun. One thing hadn't changed. Behind his thick glasses, Kate saw the same attractive blue eyes. He was still a good-looking man. He always knew that about himself, but she wondered if he still thought so.

"I went to a card game that night. At least it was supposed to be a card game. Milt and I were the only ones who showed. Poker isn't much fun with two people, so around nine thirty, we decided to forget it and went to the Boar's Head. That's when we found out about Jack."

Their conversation continued for another half hour before Dirk finally sighed and stood. "I have an appointment at the office in a few minutes. Thanks for listening to me, Kate."

"I'm glad you stopped by and I hope you will again. You'll survive her leaving, and you'll get your life back."

"I suppose. I'm glad you've done so well." He kissed her cheek, his face doubtful, and as he walked away, Kate thought he might need a little more convincing about his chances of survival.

❦

Creative visualization, a term popularized in 1978 by Shakti Gawain's book of the same name, is a means of finding solutions to problems by forming a specific image in your mind. Tracy remembered the book as she opened her office door and envisioned the mountain of mail on her desk sorted, answered, and filed. Unfortunately, the mental exercises had no effect. The desk still resembled an Alpine slope. She concluded grimly that the only way to change that reality was to plow through the drifts.

Personal computers hadn't, as promised, decreased her work. Instead, they opened a new avenue of feedback from her readers, doubling their responses. She opted to deal with the snail mail first, and once she'd reduced it to a manageable pile, attacked the comments from cyber parts unknown. Much of the correspondence contained old gossip, and after a long session of sorting, reading, and deleting, boredom forced a break. She leaned back and studied the view from her large office window, which framed the misleadingly quaint main drag of Raccoon Grove.

When she and Dave met at the Tribune, neither doubted they would be together for a while. They shared a commitment to both the newspaper game and each other. They married six months after they met, and fared well as a couple and as journalists. The move to Raccoon Grove promised a peaceful, serene life, very different from the mammoth city. It didn't take long to learn that people were people no matter what size the community. Things moved slower in the Grove, but they moved pretty much the same way. Love, hate, joy, sorrow, jealousy, and greed, brewed equally well in urban and rural caldrons. Age wise, they had no trouble fitting in. Half the population was in their mid to late thirties, and the previous generation and their grand kids made up the other half.

Tracy turned from the window to the picture of her and Dave on the desk. The recently taken photo showed Dave's gray hair and youthful grin. She remembered other pictures that filled the frame and saw them growing older together. Each told a story and most of the stories were good. Theirs had been as close to perfect as any marriage could be, but even they faced a hard time or two.

The first bump came in their eighth year of wedded bliss when Dave had a fling in New York. He met the woman on the final day of a three-day conference. Tracy would never have known, but Dave, surprised and ashamed at his behavior, told her and asked forgiveness.

Her first reaction was to leave. She'd always sworn she would dump any guy who cheated on her. Only it wasn't any guy. It was Dave. Sincere pleas and genuine remorse shattered every barrier her offended ego could build. It took a few months to make the necessary adjustments in her head and heart, but she did, without regret.

The second storm clouds appeared when Tracy felt stuck in her dull black and white life and noticed the rest of the world bursting with excitement and color. They had been in town for ten years, but at that moment, it felt like a lifetime. A break seemed the best solution. She packed a bag and took off leaving only a short note to say she would be back soon. Her unplanned course took her first to Canada, where she checked out Niagara Falls and then Philadelphia, simply because it wasn't Raccoon Grove. It revitalized her to be on her own and doing something different. She felt great.

Her good spirits dissolved quickly when she returned and found that Dave had not slept the entire time. Though relieved to see her, he was furious that she didn't call. For several weeks, he spoke to her only when necessary. His extreme reaction puzzled her until she heard from Kate, whose unrestrained anger came as an even bigger surprise. "Why would you think we wouldn't be worried? Never mind, you didn't think. Tracy, when people love you, it isn't okay to drop out of sight. I've been worried sick and Dave was out of his mind thinking something dreadful happened. Pulling that stunt took selfishness to a new level."

She wanted to argue, but her two favorite people in the world made it clear that she'd screwed up. The trip took care of her needs, but their responses told her she could have made better choices about how she handled the details. She apologized, and never told either one of them how much it pleased her that they cared enough to be angry.

In twenty years of friendship, Tracy learned a great deal from the gardener. Kate would never have believed it. She saw herself as a person in a constant state of learning how to live, and yet the very way she lived, without judgment or expectations, was a lesson in being alive. She once told Tracy that flowers and people grew at their own pace and that no amount of urging or manure would make them grow faster. Tracy feared getting old, but Kate enjoyed it as a time of peace rarely experienced when young. When Tracy became impatient, Kate waited for her to relax and regroup. If she lost her notorious temper, Kate would smile and walk away without a word. Kate, who believed so little in herself for so long, discovered the wisdom many missed and shared it with her friend.

"Enough daydreaming, old girl." Tracy returned to the mail with newfound energy, but stalled after reading the next letter. Its contents brought her to her feet and carried her to Dave's office. "Listen to this. 'Kimberly Vandenberg lives at the address below. She thinks her name is Janet Doyle, and doesn't remember where she grew up. I lived with her for a few years and she sometimes had memories that confused and frightened her. Our relationship ended badly, so we're not in contact. I found the online version of your paper after searching for Raccoon Grove, two words Janet mentioned. When I read the article about the missing Kimberly Vandenberg, I knew it was Janet. She has a ring she wore as a child with the letters KV on it. Please help her.' What do you think?"

"I have no idea, Trace. Could Kimberly Vandenberg be alive?"

"Of course, she could be, but whether or not she is, who knows. It's the same generic bond paper and envelope as the one I received last week. The Gazette would be easy enough to find on the internet. How many Raccoon Groves do you know? I suppose the best thing to do would be to contact Janet Doyle. Let me check something." She pulled the other letter out and held it next to the new one. "The phone number is one digit different. Maybe you were right, Dave. Maybe the person typed it wrong the first time."

"Do you want me to call and ask this Doyle woman if she's ever heard of Kimberly Vandenberg?"

"We shouldn't call to do anything except make an appointment to meet her. If she turns out to be Kimberly, hearing that her father was murdered and that she might be someone else, wouldn't be the sort of message to get over the phone. I'll call from my office and tell her we may have some interesting news about her family. Don't go away."

She returned in minutes. "Janet agreed to see me on Monday. Given what we know about my nurturing skills, I'll ask Kate to come along in case things get uncomfortable. There was one interesting moment at the beginning of the conversation. When I said I was from the Raccoon Grove Gazette, I heard her inhale and she didn't say anything for a few seconds. I hope she's up to hearing our news."

"Do you want me to come along?"

"No offense, Dave, but a six foot five gray-haired stranger in a black suit might not be calming. This will take a lighter touch."

"No offense taken. I'll dig around in the photo morgue and find pictures of Kimberly. They could be helpful to you and Janet Doyle."

"Excellent idea. You do that and I'll call Kate." Tracy hurried back to her office, but before she pushed Kate's number, she answered a call from Scott.

"I have news on Ben, although I'm not sure I understand it myself. His blood alcohol was high, but no higher than usual for him, and he died from a blow to the head. We couldn't match it with anything on his truck. Doc doesn't think there was a problem with his heart and wants to look closer."

"Not his heart. Hmm. Do you think it's possible that someone killed him and set it up to make us think he ran into the tree?"

"Leave it to you to see murder in a simple accident. Actually, after I took your advice and looked at the position of the truck, that thought crossed my mind. If someone from around here did it, they'd figure we'd call it an accident and not investigate. Everyone knows about Ben's drinking habits."

"We're running a memorial for him tomorrow, but we won't mention anything except the car accident. How strange. Scott, can I go with you to Ben's house when you search it? I want to check something."

"I'll wait until after the funeral, but I don't see any reason why not." Tracy said goodbye and pushed Kate's number. She gave her a quick summary of what she learned from Scott, and a more detailed explanation about the proposed meeting with Janet Doyle. Kate was more than willing to go to Chicago, but not quite ready to believe that someone killed Ben.

CHAPTER 8

The sound of her phone at eight o'clock on a Saturday morning surprised Kate. What surprised her even more was her daughter's name on the caller ID. One of the more devastating effects of the stupor she lived in for many years was on her relationship with her children. She had closed herself off from them emotionally. Eventually finding her own peace, she had no idea how to close the gap created by her fear. "Andy. Is anything wrong?"

"No. Does something have to be wrong for a daughter to call her mother?"

The frosty words, though no surprise, had a chilling effect. "Of course not, I'm delighted to hear from you. How are you?"

"I'm fine. Any excitement in the Grove?"

Andrea was not one to chat, especially with her mother, and Kate thought she sounded strange. "Ben Crayton died. They found him in his truck after he hit a tree. Tracy told me they're doing an autopsy because of some discrepancies."

"He got even grumpier after he left the force, but that was a while ago."

"Yes. He'd been drinking heavily, but it's still difficult to believe he's dead." Kate wanted to bring the conversation a little closer to home. "How are the kids? I haven't heard from them in a while."

"Is that a slam?"

"Whoa. No. It's not. Andrea, maybe you should tell me what's going on."

"Why the sudden interest in my life? You never had any before."

Kate took a deep breath and a large sip of coffee trying to find the right response to her daughter's anger. She didn't have any delusions about her kids. She had been a horrible parent. Kate's own mother made her love clear, but Andy and Jeff could not, and would not say the same thing about her. She spoke softly, making every effort to keep anything Andy could interpret as criticism out of her voice. "Andrea, I know we haven't been close, but I am very interested in your life."

Tracy and her mom were the only people she'd confided in about how her sense of inadequacy kept her distant from her children. They both told her the same thing—tell Andrea and Jeffery. Perhaps the time had come to follow their advice. "I understand why you think I wasn't interested. Until I was in my forties, almost everything scared me, including my husband and children. You, Jeff, and your father were so much smarter and better at things that I kept my mouth shut so I didn't say anything dumb. I ended up not saying anything. I'm sure it appeared as though I didn't care, but I promise you, I cared a great deal." Andrea stayed on the line, but said nothing. "After everyone moved out, I tried to figure out what scared me and why. Part of my problem might have been because after my dad died I was terrified to feel anything. I don't want to blame all my mistakes on his death, but I believe it affected me. I was slow to discover myself and slower to figure out what to do with that self once I found it. I'm not explaining this well, Andy, but I want you to know I realize I wasn't a good mother, and I'm sorry if I hurt you. I really do love you."

A painfully silent ten seconds passed. Kate was about to say Andrea's name when she finally spoke. "I didn't know that, Mom. I mean, I didn't know you felt that way, but you're not the only one who handled things badly. One of the reasons I called is because I don't hear from the kids anymore. Brenda sent me an email to say she'd be in England for three months. An email. She couldn't take two minutes to call and tell me she'd be out of the country. I suppose I should be grateful it wasn't a text."

Kate heard the muffled tears and wanted to hold her, another thing she'd done badly. When her children cried, it frightened her. She held them, but never knew what to say. Unable to make them feel better, she withdrew even further emotionally. "Andy, why don't you come for a visit this weekend? I'll fix lunch and we can sit out on the gazebo. I'd love to see you and I'd really like us to talk face to face."

By the end of the call, they'd dried most of their tears and Andy agreed to come the next day. She worked for an accounting firm in Chicago, and she and her husband owned a condominium on the lakefront. The other news she shared was of their upcoming divorce.

Kate had a few hours to work in her gardens and recover from the emotional conversation with Andy before Tracy called. She informed her that they an appointment to talk to one of their suspects, Milt Borcilino. "He said he'd be home around noon and we should come by. Can you be ready in an hour?" Sixty minutes later, they drove to the home of the postmaster.

Milt's wood frame house was a block from the building where he spent his days, and two blocks from the diner where he ate most evenings. He kept the place tidy and painted the

Jean Sheldon

exterior every few years, but, to the chagrin of many of his neighbors, lacked home decorating skills. Kate and Tracy joined him on the porch where he sat in a large, well-worn recliner, with the footrest raised and his hands clasped over his stomach. "Hi, ladies. Have a seat." His intertwined fingers rose a few inches to direct them to a porch swing. In khaki shorts, a Cubs t-shirt, and aged Birkenstocks he looked ready to enjoy his weekend. "What can I do for you on this fine day?"

"We have a few questions about your divorce," Tracy told him.

A lengthy career with the US Postal Service taught Milt, among other things, how to manage his emotions. His involuntary scowl at Tracy's statement disappeared quickly and he kept his tone light. "Why do you want to know about a divorce that happened twenty years ago? We didn't like each other anymore and split. That's why people usually divorce, isn't it?"

"There were rumors you were angry, especially at Jack Vandenberg." Tracy stoked the emotional embers that Milt attempted to keep under control while Kate sat quietly pushing the tips of her tennis shoes on the porch to ease the large swing back and forth. His control wavered.

"I might have been a little angry. Jack had no right sticking his nose in other people's business. He could have talked her into the damn thing for all I know. Maybe that's how he made the Vandenberg fortune."

"Milt, your wife went to him. Attorneys don't go door-to-door to drum up clients." Tracy hoped to get a rise, but it surprised even her to see how little it took to trigger liftoff.

"Look, I heard you two were after Jack's murderer. I'll save you some time. I didn't like him, but I didn't kill him and that's the end of this conversation." He pushed the footrest down, climbed out of the chair, and went inside. The door didn't slam, but the click of the lock told the two women that it wouldn't open again, at least not while they were there.

"So, we keep him as a suspect, then?" Kate asked her astonished partner. It was only as they pulled onto the street that she remembered her conversation with Dirk and slapped her thigh. "Shoot, I forgot that Dirk told me he and Milt were together the night Jack died. They were supposed to have a card game, but no one else showed up. That makes Milt's reaction to your question even stranger. Why would he be that defensive if he had an alibi?"

"When did you talk to Dirk?"

"He stopped by the house yesterday. Didn't I tell you? His wife moved in with her new boyfriend and wants a divorce." Kate liked to keep her eyes on the road when riding with Tracy, because sometimes, when their conversations became too intense, Tracy didn't.

"Give me a few minutes to digest this. Why didn't I know that Dirk's wife not only had a boyfriend, but that she moved in with him? That's gossip, and collecting gossip is what I do in this town. Isn't it?"

"You've been busy on the murder investigation. It's cut into your gossip-gathering time."

Tracy could have offered an excuse of her own, but Kate's was adequate. "Did Dirk mention who else was supposed to be at their card game besides him and Milt?"

"Jack told me he was going, but I'm not sure who else. I doubt if Milt will be much help. I'll talk to Dirk."

"How's he doing? It must have been difficult for him to come and see you."

"I'm glad he did. We needed to talk, although I think he needed it more than me."

"If you've finished filling me in on local gossip, maybe it's time we went back to work. Why don't you pick our next interviewee? It's between Harold Duffy at the garage and George Williams at the sandwich place."

"Let's talk to George. If we make him mad enough to want to throw something, it will be a sandwich and not a tire iron."

Tracy lifted her head as she opened the sandwich shop door and inhaled the delicious aroma. She wondered, not for the first time, what divinely inspired soul thought to mix flour, water, and yeast, and bake them in an oven to produce such an intoxicating smell. She pushed Kate inside and followed with her nose in the air. "Let's split a sub. We can ask George to join us."

"Okay, but I don't want any of that strange, spicy stuff you put on your sandwiches."

"How can anyone grow the variety of beautiful flowers and plants you do and have such boring taste in food?"

They joined the line behind the large 'order here' sign and Kate stayed close enough to watch over Tracy's shoulder. "If I ate what you eat, I'd have to grow ginger and fennel to take care of my heartburn."

Tracy was about to respond when George came out of the back room and headed toward the door. She abandoned the line and hurried to intercept him while Kate took their turkey sub without the fixings to the cash register. She couldn't hear what Tracy said, but as she approached, George's face turn white and then red in rapid succession. His jaw tightened as he launched himself to his feet and sent the chair hurtling backwards. "If that's why you came, you're wasting your time. I have nothing to say about what happened back then. That part of my life is over and you ought to leave the past alone. Excuse me."

Kate put the tray on the table and they both watched George disappear to the back of the restaurant. A few minutes later, his truck squealed onto the street and around the corner. "Tracy, this investigation isn't making us many friends. What did you say to him?"

"Just that I wanted to know about his divorce. He reacted the same way Milt did. Why do you suppose they get so angry? We're talking about things that happened twenty years ago, not twenty days." She shook her head and gripped her half of the sub. "We might as well eat. Did you bring the shaker with the chili pepper flakes?"

"No. Should we visit Harold Duffy and put these interviews behind us?"

Neither the abrupt end to her interview, nor the lack of spices upset Tracy's appetite. She swallowed a mouthful before answering. "If the town gardener is tough enough to take on one more suspect, then the town gossip columnist had better keep up. Thanks for the sandwich. The other person we planned to question was Ben Crayton, and that's not an appointment we'll keep, not on this plane, anyway."

"Harold around?" Tracy spoke as they entered the garage and startled the mechanic closest to the door. He turned his glazed stare from the computer and car engine it monitored, to her and Kate. "I said, is Harold around?" The women cautiously followed his nod around oil spots and tools to the back of the shop and Harold's office. The only thing that distinguished it from its surroundings was a wall with a window and a door. Behind the open door, Harold sat at his desk. "Hi, Harold. You work weekends too?"

"Hi, Tracy, Kate. Just Saturday. What brings you two here?" He stood and removed an assortment of parts and magazines from two worn vinyl chairs. "Kate, don't tell me the van broke down."

"No. It's running fine. We'd like to ask you a few questions if you have a minute."

"I have a minute. Take a seat." He pointed, but Kate remained standing.

"Before we do, will you throw us out if we mention your divorce or Jack Vandenberg?"

"Sit down. I'd be crazy to throw two beautiful women out of this grease pit. How I can help?"

"Who wanted the divorce, you or Laurie?" Tracy asked, checking for oil spots on the chair before she sat.

"At first, it was me. I told her I wanted out, but I sobered up and changed my mind. By that time, she decided she liked the idea. It upset me, but, hey, what could I do?"

"Where were you the night Jack was murdered?"

If Tracy's direct questions surprised him, Harold didn't show it. "You don't forget where you were when someone you know is murdered. Laurie was living at her sister's by then, so a couple of the boys came over and played cards at my place. We did more drinking than card playing and most of the night is a blur. I didn't hear about Jack until the next day."

"Do you remember who was at the card game?"

"Not off hand, Tracy. Give me a few days to see if I can move things around in my brain."

The women raised questions they hadn't asked since their talk with Mad Dog, and Harold answered without hesitation or anger. His face stayed the same color and he didn't clench his teeth. Even so, both women sighed when they finished, grateful the interviews were over.

"What did you think?" Tracy pulled in front of Kate's house and turned off the car.

"He sounded cool and detached enough. Didn't Laurie tell you he was furious about the divorce? Your earring's coming out." She reached over to assist, but knocked the small blue opal to the seat. The earrings were a birthday gift from Kate the previous October. Early Romans believed opals fell from the sky created by lightning. Kate suspected that was how Tracy arrived.

"She said he went ballistic. She came close to asking Jack to help her with a restraining order. Twenty years is a long time, though. Look how much Mad Dog changed." Tracy hooked the earring and checked it in the rear view mirror.

"True. It did bother me that he said he remembered playing cards, but he forgot who was there."

"I hadn't thought about that, but you're right. He should have remembered one or two of the others. Of course, he could have killed those particular brain cells with drugs and alcohol. Harold used to be one of the big partiers. I'll see what else I can find on him. Do you want to go to the lake with Dave and me tomorrow?"

Kate remembered her daughter's visit and shook her head with a broad smile. "Andrea is coming by for lunch."

"Andrea. Why?"

"To visit and chat. I forgot to tell you she called. It surprised me, but I'm delighted. Our conversation went well, better than any exchange I can remember between us. I'd love it if we could become friends. She called because she's going through a hard time at home. She feels separated from the kids, and Mitch told her he wants a divorce."

"Ouch. I'm sorry. This has been a real family week for you, hasn't it? Be sure and tell her I said hi." Tracy saw Kate's doubt about the meeting. "You're ready for this, honey. Perhaps more than you've ever been."

"Maybe so. As I've grown older, something in me seems to have shifted. I respond differently to things. I mean, when I used to think about trying to make amends with Andrea and Jeffery, I felt embarrassed about my own shortcomings, and quite honestly, I thought since they were the kids, they should make the effort. That was my ego talking. Now, having them in my life is more important than any humiliation or rule of etiquette. Does that make sense?"

"It makes perfect sense. You and Andy are going to have a great visit."

"I hope you're right. Ego aside, I have quite a bit to make up for with my kids."

CHAPTER 9

There are those who consider the brewing of coffee a chore, like boiling an egg, done solely to enjoy the labor's results. To the devotee, the process is akin to ritual. Compulsive brewers may go so far as to keep secret the exact number of seconds required to grind the dark beans for a perfect cup. Even moderate fans are superstitious about its preparation—stored in glass, measured with stainless steel, and prepared with only the purest water. These nearly religious practices are responsible for the creation of a beverage that spans all lines drawn to separate people. Rich, poor, old, young, liberal, conservative, artist, bricklayer, all find common ground in coffee. Board meetings, church meetings, family gatherings are the tip of the latte of events that begin with participants huddled around an urn, pot, or other dispenser of the liquid leveler. Coffee calms, yet excites. It begins a long workday and ends a seven-course meal. Its aroma has charms to soothe the savage breast, and it has coursed through the veins of our most inspired writers, artists, and musicians. Uncomfortable events often become manageable when considered over a cup of coffee.

"There's something I've always wondered, Mom." Andrea slid one of the two cups she'd filled in front of Kate.

"What's that?"

"How does it feel to be so beautiful?"

As far back as the pageant days, discussions about her looks made Kate uncomfortable, only a decade ago, such a conversation would have been unthinkable with anyone, no less her daughter. "I never felt beautiful." She raised the mug in thanks and took a sip, recognizing at once Andrea's doubtful frown. "That's a difficult thing to tell people, because they assume I'm lying, or that its false modesty. It's not. I never felt beautiful, at least not until I became eligible for senior discounts."

"Come on. I've seen pictures of you when you were only twelve and thirteen years old. You were drop-dead gorgeous. How did you think you won those beauty contests?"

"I fit the criteria that others used to define beauty, but when I looked in the mirror, that wasn't what I saw. I knew that one day everyone would figure it out. Whoever they were looking at and whatever they saw wasn't there. No matter how many people told me I was beautiful, no matter how many contests I won, I knew by how miserable I felt inside that they were wrong."

Andrea considered her mom's face and her words. "You're still beautiful."

"It's only in the last ten years that I've learned to see beauty in myself. After my dad died, I lost track of who I was, but your grandmother never gave up on me. Between her and the gardens, I finally understood what she meant about beauty coming from inside. She helped me see that my insides weren't nearly as horrible as I'd thought." Kate smiled and squeezed her daughter's hand. "Tell me what's going on inside of you."

Andrea's husband had grown tired of their marriage and couldn't pretend anymore. Too involved with her work to notice the space growing between them, she was also unaware of how little contact she had with her two daughters in college.

"Brenda's email was a major wakeup call. How did I manage to disconnect from my husband and kids?"

"You learned from one of the best. Bring your coffee and we'll visit the gardens. I have a number of new flowers this year."

People who stepped out Kate's back door, or entered through her gate, often needed a minute to take in the splendor. Andrea gasped. "Oh, my, you really have found yourself, haven't you? It's magnificent. You must see beauty in this."

"I do." The women were the same size and shape, with similar coloring, except that Kate was completely gray and Andrea's brown hair showed only a streak or two. Her beauty, though not as arresting as Kate's, drew stares. Kate wrapped an arm around Andy's waist and nudged her forward. "You know you're beautiful, don't you, Andy?"

Moisture that had filled her brown eyes when she told Kate about her family, returned. "No, I guess I don't. People have told me I am, but I never believed them. Growing up around you set a pretty high standard." Kate cringed. "I didn't mean that as an insult. I just always felt that I couldn't compete. It's funny, I never thought of myself as being like you, but I can see that in some ways, I am. If that means I'll find the peace you've found, then I'm pleased."

They continued through the gardens and in between pointing out old favorites and naming new plants, Kate told Andrea her hope that they could be friends. "It isn't reasonable to expect to have a friendship overnight after I pushed you away for so long, but I'd like to try. I truly believe I couldn't have loved anyone until I learned to love myself. I'm just sorry it took me so long to do that." Kate had pinched off a few flowers as they walked and when they reached the gazebo, she arranged them in a bouquet and handed it to her daughter.

Jean Sheldon

"Put them in water. They might make you feel a little better. They've done wonders for me."

"I can see that, and I will. I'm glad I came."

"So am I. I forgot to tell you that your dad came by the other day. His wife moved in with her new boyfriend. She wants a divorce."

"The bimbo moved out. I was surprised it lasted as long as it did." Kate stayed quiet. Most of her life, she imagined that people used the word to describe her. "Will you come and visit me after Mitch moves out? I'd rather you waited until then. The divorce was his idea, but he's made little effort to move and he's angry at me about something. Don't ask me what. He grumbles whenever I run into him. Maybe he expects me to help him pack."

"I'll come by, and I'll wait until he's gone. By the way, Tracy and I will be in your neighborhood tomorrow. Not quite on the lake, but that far north." She told Andrea about the letters and the following day's meeting with Janet Doyle.

"Do you think she could be Kimberly?"

"I suppose anything's possible, but no one believed she was still alive."

❦

"Thank you for seeing us Janet. I'm Tracy Kendall and this is Kate Chandler. I think the easiest way to do this will be to show you the letter we received at the newspaper." They sat in Janet's small living room where she occupied a worn armchair and Kate and Tracy shared a matching sofa. In the limited space between them was a coffee table obscured by the previous days *Chicago Tribune*. The *Arts and Entertainment* section topped the pile. Tracy pulled the letter from her purse and handed it across to Janet who showed no emotion as she read. When she finished, she folded the sheet and handed it back.

"I'm sorry you came all this way for nothing. I couldn't be Kimberly. I'm sure Tim sent the letter. He lived with me here for a short time. I had a few peculiar memories and he thought I should look into them, but I've lived in Chicago my entire life."

"What about the ring your friend mentioned. Does it look like this?" Tracy handed her an enlarged photo of a ring on a child's hand. The photo clearly startled Janet, but she regained control. "It might have been a popular style for girls back then." Her response sounded so final that when she put the photo on the stack of newspapers and left the room, neither Tracy nor Kate was sure if she'd return. Seconds later, she reentered and put a ring identical to the one pictured next to the photo.

Kate examined it briefly. "It could have been popular at the time, Janet, but why does yours have the initials KV on it and not JD?"

"My dad gave it to me. Maybe he found it."

"In the letter your friend Tim wrote, he said he looked for Raccoon Grove on the internet because you mentioned it a few times." Tracy pointed at Tim's letter. "Have you ever been there?"

"No, but my father might have lived there before he came to Chicago. I vaguely remember him mentioning it."

"Where is your dad?"

"He died two years ago. He worked as a janitor until he developed a heart condition. He was in a nursing home for the last six months of his life. I've lived in Chicago my entire life. At least, I think I have. I don't remember much of when I was very young. Dad said I fell on the stairs and hit my head. It made me forget things."

"What kind of work do you do, Janet?" Kate asked.

"I'm an actress."

Tracy held out another photo of Kimberly. "That's Kimberly Vandenberg about six months before she disappeared. Does anything about it strike you as familiar?"

Without taking the picture from Tracy's fingers, Janet gave it a quick look and shook her hand. Then she looked closer. "I remember a pair of shoes like the ones she's wearing, but I didn't have them here. Not with my dad, I mean." She became anxious. "What's going on?"

"Do you have any pictures of yourself as a child?" Kate took the photo from Tracy's hand.

"No. The basement flooded years ago and all our photo albums were ruined." Janet's agitation increased when Tracy asked where her mother was. "I don't remember her at all. Dad said I was only five when she left. He said she wanted to take me, but he wouldn't let her."

Kate shared a brief look with Tracy before asking Janet if her father ever had contact with her mother, or told Janet where she went. The question unsettled her further and Janet took a piece of tissue from a box, twisting it in her fingers as she shook her head. "It doesn't matter who she was or where she went. Herb Doyle, my father, took care of me." She stood, struggling for control. "I am not the person you want and I think you should leave."

Tracy put the photos in her briefcase and as she and Kate prepared to leave, placed a business card on the table. "Call if you want to talk."

Driving in a city the size of Chicago takes practice, but once you've learned the attitudes and streets, you don't forget, anymore than you forget that the red octagon means stop. It was clear, as Tracy rolled through one of the familiar signs and entered southbound Lake Shore Drive that years of driving the less intense byways of rural Illinois had not diminished her skill. She maneuvered into the center lane and leaned back to begin the first leg of their return trek to Raccoon Grove. "So, what's your opinion of Janet Doyle aka Kimberly Vandenberg?"

"We'll hear from her."

"She wasn't very forthcoming during our visit. Why would she call?"

"I can think of two reasons, Tracy. If she's a fake, it will be to reel us in. If she's Kimberly Vandenberg, she'll need our help."

"You think she could be a fake?"

"It's possible. At times, she acted sincere, and at other times I thought she was doing just that, acting."

"We need to find out if there has ever been a Herb Doyle in our neck of the woods. Another mystery. How exciting." Tracy wiggled in her seat.

"You're a strange person, Tracy Kendall."

After depositing Kate at home, Tracy arrived at Gazette and climbed the stairs to the offices where she found Dave waiting. She gave him a kiss, dragged him into his workplace, and sat behind the desk. Her obliging husband snuggled into the guest chair with a groan. "Now I see why people don't want to leave. I should exchange it with the desk chair."

"You have enough trouble staying awake in this one. Do you remember a person named Herb Doyle living here around twenty years ago?"

"Not really, but we'd only been in town a few years. Who is Herb Doyle?"

She filled him in on the conversation with Janet and asked a question she'd been considering. "What if he was Kimberly's real father? I mean, what if Louise got pregnant by Herb before she married Jack, or even after. That would explain why he kidnapped her. Do you suppose Jack would have known if she wasn't his?"

"I don't know. Do parents have that kind of bond with newborn babies?"

"Having never had the experience, I can't answer that question, but the biggest problem with that theory is trying to picture Louise having an affair. That wasn't her style. I didn't know her well, but I did a lot of research on her family after Jack's death. Her dad was a minister in New Lenox and rather strict from what I understand. When he passed away, she lived with an Aunt here in town. Her mom died when she was young and the aunt died shortly after Louise graduated from college. She was an active member of the Methodist Church and pretty straight laced. Of course, if she'd fallen in love with Mr. Doyle, it might have been deep enough to do something out of character."

Dave pulled himself from the chair and stood behind Tracy with his arms stretched over her shoulders and his fingers on the keyboard. "Let's see what we can find."

In minutes, he pointed to a page and Tracy read. "Good job, Mr. Kendall. Herb Doyle lived here for almost six years, which means someone will remember him. We should check city and county employee files to see if he turns up. Half the people in this town work for one of them, and the rest work for the state."

"You're prone to exaggeration, Tracy," he said amid a few more keystrokes. "There you go. He worked as a janitor at the high school."

"See, I don't exaggerate. It's interesting that there was a Herb Doyle who worked at the high school. Janet said her father was a janitor in Chicago. What would his connection have been to the Vandenberg family?" She pushed his arms away and typed. "Louise Vandenberg taught at the high school until she married Jack. Guess what. She gave birth to Kimberly eight months after they married. Maybe Louise was carrying Doyle's baby."

Dave resettled in the guest chair. "She could have been carrying Jack's baby and Doyle wanted to believe it was his."

"True, Dave, but whoever the father was, this information adds support to the theory that Janet Doyle and Kimberly Vandenberg are one in the same. Janet said Herb was the only father she'd ever known."

"Why would he have waited five years to kidnap her?"

"Good question. What if he was in jail?" She shook her head and turned to the monitor. "No, he worked at the high school until, huh, until the year Kimberly disappeared. This is so strange."

"I remember a few events from when I was five. Doesn't Janet remember anything?"

"She said she fell and can't remember her childhood. Maybe Herb didn't know Kimberly was his at first and Louise told him later."

"Or he was deranged and loved Louise from afar. He might have decided that if he couldn't have her, he'd have the next best thing and took her daughter. Maybe there wasn't a relationship between Herb and Louise at all and he just went berserk and kidnapped her child. Boy, this is some wild speculating. We need a few facts."

"Did our research give you one of your 'gotta have a scotch' headaches?"

He threw a hand to his forehead and gave her a pained grin.

CHAPTER 10

Kate remembered a time when people held doors for one another. It was common courtesy, but fashions and conventions change. The person she followed into Doctor Collins's office swept through without looking back, forcing Kate to stick out a foot and stop the door from smashing her or the floral arrangement she carried. Safely inside, she stood at the reception area and waited for someone to notice her arrival. When no one responded, she hefted the weighty display onto the counter with a thud.

"Sorry, Kate, I didn't see you. Things are a little crazy around here these days." Nancy, the receptionist, greeted her warmly despite the chaos. Doctor Collins had an arrangement delivered every week for the waiting room. He believed fresh flowers helped his patients. Kate agreed.

"Nancy, can you locate the blood screen on Mr. Dowling?" The doctor hurried in and was ready to dash out again until he saw the flowers and Kate's face between the blossoms. "They're beautiful, Kate. How are you?"

"I'm great, Adam, but you look a little overwhelmed." She pointed at the crowded waiting room.

"We've been swamped. Everyone either has the flu or thinks they have it. That's not counting the people that stopped by because a television commercial recommended they ask their doctor if they have a disease. I hope you're having a little more fun than us."

Kate wanted to tell him she could be scrubbing floors and having more fun, but thought it unkind. "Tracy and I are involved in something interesting. We talked to a woman in Chicago yesterday who could possibly be Kimberly Vandenberg."

Adam, who had stopped to sign a form one of the nurses stuck in front of him, dropped his pen. He picked it up quickly and finished his signature, handing back the clipboard as he approached Kate. "Do you think she could be Kimberly?"

"We don't know, but her story's interesting. Take care of yourself, Adam. You can't keep this pace up forever. Remember, I know how old you are." As Kate returned to her van, she saw the postmaster, Milt Borcilino, approach.

"Kate, hang on a minute, will you?" She stood with the driver's door open, prepared to jump in and lock it, and held her keys defensively between the fingers of her right hand. Milt noticed and stopped a few feet away. "I want to apologize for my behavior Saturday. You caught me way off guard. I obviously still have some strong feelings about what happened back then, but that's not an excuse for being rude. I'm sorry."

"I accept your apology. Are you okay?"

He stared at his post-office-issue black shoes. "I have more anger about my own behavior back then than anything else. Melanie took care of me when we were married and I didn't think I'd make it alone. What sent me into a tailspin was my damned bruised ego. I'm still a little embarrassed that I was thirty-five going on eight. The night Jack died, I planned to confront him and ask him if he wasn't pushing Melanie to make his fee. A few of us had a card game planned and I decided to talk to him, but he didn't show. Of course, I found out why soon enough."

"I remembered after we visited you that Dirk told me about the game, and that you both went to the Boar's Head. Tracy and I didn't need to bother you. I'm sorry for that."

"It's not your fault. Something's not right if I react that much to such old wounds. That's not anyone's responsibility but mine. My anger at Jack dissolved the minute we walked into the bar that night. Unfortunately, my anger at myself didn't. Melanie was fair about letting me see the kids. She had one rule—if I showed up drunk or high, I couldn't take them. Back then, I thought she was just being a bitch, and I'd yell and make a scene. Of course, she was right. If she hadn't made those rules, I wouldn't have made postmaster. If I didn't stay straight to see the kids, I'm not sure where I'd be today, with them or my job. Mel and I have talked over the years, and she's pleased with her life. I wish I'd known how to make her happy back then, instead of taking so long to grow up."

"I understand completely."

❧

Sara heard her mother call from the kitchen, marked her place and set the book on a table next to the lawn chair. She smiled at their lovely yard. How wonderful it was to be viewing it instead of the dull walls of a hospital. "I'll be there in a minute, Mom," she called over her shoulder. Two years without a serious setback. Could the nightmare be over?

She scanned the yard and noticed the growing number of trees and bushes that needed trimming. Her mom's illness no longer allowed her to do the yard work and she hired a man to come once a month, but it wasn't enough. Sara wanted to take over and hoped Ms Chandler would give her some guidance.

A sudden breeze spread the thick sweet scent of lilacs as it jostled the bushes making them puff their flowery chests in pride at Sara's arrival. She pinched off a few clusters, smiling until she spotted the pink rose bush at the back of the yard. Her blood chilled and the lilacs slipped from her fingers as she felt the demon stir. "Come and eat." Her mom called again, and Sara felt the darkness fade, no match for her mother's love. She retrieved the flowers and turned toward the house, inhaling deeply as she looked at the kitchen window and then to the window above, her room.

For as long as she could remember, she'd had a recurring dream where she stared out that window at her father kneeling at the back of the yard near the rose bush. When he stood and turned, she waved, but he didn't see her because his hands covered his face. He was crying.

She mentioned the dream to various doctors over the years and listened to their interpretations, none of which made sense. Her present psychiatrist, Carolyn Kovecki, suggested that perhaps she had actually seen something, but at such a young age, didn't understand what the images meant. The doctor assured her that in time she would remember and understand the message of the dream. Comforted by the thought, Sara went inside and put the flowers in a glass on the table. "I brought you a present, Mom."

"They're very pretty, dear. Thank you. Come fill your plate. We need to put some fat on those bones."

"Okay, let me make yours first." Sara pushed Elaine's wheelchair to the table and ladled stew into her dish. "This looks great. I feel fatter already."

Thick curls adorned the heads of both Collins women, although the elder was mostly gray and Sara sported an inky black. Elaine, an inch taller than her daughter, was a stocky

Jean Sheldon

solid figure contrasting Sara's slight build. She turned the green eyes they shared back to the stove and studied her. "You don't look any fatter to me, young lady. Make sure you fill that dish and eat every bit."

"I will, Mom." Sara leaned down and kissed her cheek. "Everything is going to be fine."

⁂

Case File: Sara Collins

Primary Physician: Carolyn Kovecki

I've seen Sara for four years, two for inpatient treatment, and two as an outpatient. Her strength and resilience are impressive. At twenty-five, she has spent a large part of her life in and out of hospitals and institutions, starting at the inconceivable age of eleven. She has suffered immobilizing depressions through many of her years, and yet, somehow, maintains a level of optimism.

Our early sessions were often one-sided. I talked and she listened quietly, or offered an occasional nod. I sensed she thought I wanted her to behave that way. Eventually, she understood she could tell me not only what she thought or remembered, but also what she felt about those memories. She returned home shortly after that breakthrough and her outpatient treatment proceeds well.

I've read previous doctors' notes and gone over my own, but have not found a clear cause for her depressions. Her father, Doctor Adam Collins, gave a possible explanation of where they began. A medical emergency called him away, and since his wife was out of town, he'd left Sara alone. Although he went only a short distance from home and returned within minutes, he found her in the living room screaming hysterically at the television. Sara has no recollection of the event.

Doctor Collins is protective of his daughter. In my opinion, more than is healthy for either of them. I attribute the overprotective behavior to his guilt for having left his child alone.

Sara has a wonderful relationship with her mother. After discovering her child was too frightened to attend school, Elaine Collins began home schooling her. She continued the education whenever possible and Sara recently took classes at the community college and passed her high school equivalency exam. Even now, though confined to a wheelchair with Distal Muscular Dystrophy, her mother's unwavering positive outlook is Sara's greatest support.

As for her father, I must admit, his behavior is difficult to understand. As Sara recovers, she finds his actions equally confusing. The great strides she has made convince me she will have the life she desires. I informed her father of my conclusions, but I'm not sure if that was the wisest thing to do. Sara's belief in her success and her mother's support may be enough to deter any of the doctor's unhealthy influence. I wish he would explain his motivation. I'm sure his caution is for Sara's sake, but I see no happy conclusion if he doesn't let her grow strong and healthy.

Sara has recently voiced an interest in learning how to garden and grow flowers. She intends to talk to a local gardener about the possibility of learning the necessary skills. It would be a positive step toward reclaiming her life.

❧

Tracy kept her eyes on the computer screen as she answered the phone, pushing it to her ear with a grunt. "Tracy, Scott here. I have interesting news."

"Hi, Sheriff. What's up?"

"I just read the autopsy report. Ben didn't accidentally meet his maker. Chet found a needle mark in his leg and traces of methohexital in his body. The drug knocked him out and a blow to the head killed him. Whoever did it shot enough of the drug into a femoral artery to knock someone Ben's size out in a hurry. We didn't find what they used to hit him, but the back of his truck showed signs of a collision. Someone might have pushed him into the tree. What I don't get is why. People didn't like Ben much, but I can't imagine anyone would be angry enough to kill him."

"Thanks for the update. You're right. I couldn't guess who'd want to see him dead. Do you know if anyone was recently released from prison that Ben put there?"

"I can check."

"You don't suppose a stranger did it." She answered the question before Scott could respond. "No, that doesn't make sense. A stranger wouldn't have bothered to set up the accident. Okay, Sheriff, what's next?"

"I'm not sure. Have you and Kate made any headway with Jack's murder?"

"You're too young to remember it, aren't you?" In Tracy's mind, Scott Robbins, the man who replaced Ben fifteen years earlier was still in his twenties.

"I remember when it happened. I was in the service, but mom kept me updated. As it turned out, there weren't many updates."

"That's true. I'm glad you called, Scott. I meant to ask you last week if you have records from Ben's cases."

"We have whatever he kept. His police work deteriorated over the last part of his career, so the records are pretty sketchy, but you're welcome to look."

"When would be a good time?" She opened the calendar on her computer and pictured the sheriff at his desk grinning. Not much happened in Raccoon Grove.

"How about now?"

Tracy ended the call and rang Kate. "Do you have time to go to the station and help me check the records from Ben's investigations?"

"Of course, I do. Do you mean this instant?

"Yes, but I'll give you five minutes to wash the dirt from under your fingernails."

"I'm afraid that'd take more than five minutes to accomplish. I can wear gloves if you're embarrassed to be seen with me."

"Be outside. Gloves are optional."

"Will you run anything about our investigation in the next edition?" Kate asked as buckled her seatbelt.

"Yes. Tomorrow's *Tidbits* will contain everything we've learned thus far, which means it will be a short column." From Kate's house to the center of Raccoon Grove was a ten minutes or so walk, depending on her pace and the number of neighbors she met along the way. They'd barely touched on the interviews when Tracy pulled in front of the sheriff's department. "We're here. Are you ready to investigate?"

"Hello, ladies." Sheriff Robbins directed the women to an old metal desk holding an equally dated computer. "You can use this station. I'll help you click into the record files and then you're on your own."

"Thanks, Scott." Two hardback chairs screeched mercilessly as Tracy dragged them across the floor. When Scott found it safe to remove his fingers from his ears, he opened the files and left them to their investigation.

"Look, Kate. This is from the night of Jack's murder. I can't read this bit at the top. He crossed out the first four or five sentences and started a new section. *20:00 Gunshot reported off Timber Lane near the Vandenberg place.*"

Kate took over. "It says that when he went up the driveway he heard screams coming from the house. The front door was open and Louise Vandenberg was standing over Jack's body, screaming hysterically that Kimberly was missing."

Tracy pushed her glasses up and continued where Kate left off. "The rest talks about calling for the ambulance and deputies. He made it back to the station at around two in the morning and filed the report. I wonder what he scratched off at the beginning. By the way, there's a funeral service for Ben tomorrow."

"I know. I have to deliver the flower arrangement later today. I meant to ask if you planned to run a memorial." Tracy nodded. "Will you and Dave be at the funeral?"

"We will, and I'm betting on a big turnout. Death tends to make people forgive and forget. As far as I can see, for the six months before the murder, his reports were at least legible and coherent. The only one marked up is the day of Jack's death. The reports after that become more illegible by the day." Tracy turned to the front desk where the sheriff sat with the Kankakee paper pretending not to be listening. "Could someone have gone in and altered a file, Scott?"

"No. We didn't digitize the older files, just scanned them in as images. What you see is what you get. Did you find something interesting?"

"Let me print this and show you." Tracy sent the document to a nearby printer, but before she took it to Scott, she and Kate huddled over the copy. "Can you read it? Even with my glasses it's beyond me."

"It's almost illegible, but I think he wrote that he was on Timber Lane when he saw something." She squinted. "I can't make out this part, but these two words might say 'dog collar'. That can't be right. The rest of that section he crossed out completely, except for part of the last line, and I'm sure it doesn't say what I think it says, 'check within.'"

Amused by Kate's interpretation, Scott could no longer feign disinterest. He took the report from her hand. "I'll be darned. You're right. It does say 'dog collar', and 'check within'. Maybe the sheriff had a Zen moment."

Tracy imagined Ben Crayton in a meditative pose and shook the thought out of her mind. "If he was on Timber Lane, he was near Jack's house when the first call came in. Who would have been at the station to take the call?"

"Back then, the department used a mobile car phone. Emergency calls were automatically relayed." Scott pointed to the scratched out part on the printout. "If he was out there at that time, he might not have cared to share that information. The whole town knew how he felt about Jack."

"Then why not write a new report?"

"He wrote the second part after dealing with Jack's death, Kimberly's disappearance, and Louise's hysterics. He'd have been exhausted and might have taken a few drinks when he went back to his car. Besides, Ben was the only person who read those reports. He might not have cared." Scott returned the page to Tracy's waiting hand. "If he was drinking earlier, that would explain the poor handwriting. After finding Louise and the mess in the house, he'd have sobered in a hurry. A few more shots wouldn't have fazed him and the lower half of the sheet would be legible."

"Why didn't the county get involved in the investigation?" Tracy asked.

"The only thing I can figure is that Ben told them he'd handle it. His report says they were there that night, but he never mentioned them again. He told me later that the Feds lost interest when no one requested ransom."

Tracy tapped on the copy and chewed her lower lip. "I don't believe Ben killed Jack. Kate, we need to find the neighbor who made the call and the person who helped Louise through that time. She lost her husband and her daughter. She couldn't have gone through it alone."

Kate wasn't as ready to concede Ben Crayton's innocence. "He could have killed Jack. That would explain why he wanted to pin it on me."

CHAPTER 11

Joe arrived in Raccoon Grove hoping to pass himself off as a California boy. He was not. He'd never been there and had no great desire to go. Chicago born and raised, he liked the fast pace and the constant hustle, especially when he did the hustling. He also liked that it was never truly dark in the city. Sure, some of his favorite bars kept the lights low, but even the ally's he used for impromptu business deals had streetlights. Nothing prepared him for the blackness of night in the country as he made his way along the creek.

In one way, it was useful. No one would spot him. It wasn't all that likely they would anyway, not at two in the morning, and not through the ample vegetation on the outskirts of town, but he wasn't taking any chances. He parked the rental car by the creek and hiked a half mile to the Vandenberg property. The moon, an unknowing accomplice, exposed only a sliver of reflective surface as it crossed the night sky. In his black shirt and slacks, Joe was virtually invisible. Unfortunately, so was the landscape. He stumbled through woods thick with gnarled tree roots, persistent weeds, and dense berry brambles. Finally, after what seemed like a trek through the rain forest, he reached the driveway and followed it to the Victorian house, dark and empty since the death of Louise Vandenberg.

Her death brought Joe to town. He frequently scanned legal announcements and obituaries for a chance to run a swindle. When he read the ad Louise Vandenberg's attorney ran looking for relatives, he considered his chances. Of course, he wasn't a Vandenberg. His last name was Miller, but he'd dropped a good chunk of change for phony documents that were supposed to convince everyone he was Joe Vandenberg. It never occurred to him that he'd have to prove his relationship to a particular Vandenberg family. He had to find something in the house to help him create a believable connection. As long as he was there, he'd see if his 'relatives' left any valuables behind.

He'd been there once before. After reading the ad, he drove down to make sure it was worth the trouble. That time he just parked in the driveway and walked around, figuring if someone questioned him, he'd give them the relative story and take off before they could ask too many questions. No one bothered him, but he didn't learn much because the curtains in the house were drawn. He did find an uncovered garage window and guessed by the old Mercedes and new Lexus that Louise Vandenberg had a few bucks.

The driveway was easier to navigate, but no more visible than the path through the woods. He flashed his light for an instant every few steps to find the front door. Once there, he removed a set of lock picks from his pocket and went to work. Joe had a few encounters with the law in his twenty-eight years, but none for break-and-enter. He fumbled with a set of borrowed picks until the final pin slipped into place and the lock opened. Pushing the door slightly, he held his breath and waited for an alarm. After thirty seconds of anxious silence, he went inside and closed the door.

His hand hid most of the flashlight beam and until he made sure the windows were still covered, he didn't try the lights. When he finally flipped a switch on the wall, nothing happened. The electricity was off and that meant no air conditioning or fans. Sweat dampened his shirt, but he couldn't risk opening a window.

In front of him, beyond the large entryway, was a staircase. To the right, a living room and another room that from where he stood, looked like an office. Joe turned in the opposite direction and saw a wood paneled wall covered with photographs. He guessed they were various Vandenbergs and in-laws and stopped to study their faces.

After he'd read the attorney's ad, Joe did an online search for Jack Vandenberg and found an article in the local paper about the murder. It had a picture of the family with the story, the same family that hung on the wall.

He left the photos to climb the polished wood staircase two steps at a time. At the top of the stairs, he entered a room with a white four-poster canopy bed and two matching dressers, one taller with four drawers, and the other shorter and long with a mirror. A pale pink bedspread matched the walls and a collection of dolls and stuffed animals covered the bed. Curtains matching the design on the spread hung over each of the two windows.

It was a kid's room, but Joe knew there hadn't been a kid in the house for 20 years. He guessed it belonged to the daughter and was thinking how creepy it was that the old lady left it that way when he remembered the fake letters. He pulled them from a back pocket to drop in the small dresser's top drawer. They said what he thought were sweet and childish things about how pretty she was and how he wanted to see her again. He signed them Cousin Joe Vandenberg.

A comb and brush set and a small music box with a ballerina sat on top of the dresser. He wound the key and watched the dancer spin, her hinged leg lifting and falling to the soft metallic strains of *A Time for Us*. The combination of warm air, music, and the doll's movement in the dim light mesmerized him. When the song finished, it took him a second to remember where he was, and to notice the air was even hotter and heavier upstairs than on the first floor. He pulled off his shirt and used it to wipe his face and neck before shoving a handful of fabric in his back pocket.

He hadn't expected to find anything of value in the kid's room, but did a quick search through the drawers and emptied a few boxes in the closet before departing to a larger bedroom down the hall. That one looked recently inhabited and he guessed it belonged to Louise Vandenberg. His investigation turned up a jar of change and a few pieces of inexpensive jewelry, but no other cash or valuables. He dumped as much change as he could in a pocket and tossed the jar, reminding himself to focus on finding something that would welcome him into the family.

Twenty minutes later, Joe sat on the bed shaking his head. The only thing he saw that might be remotely useful was a bunch of books that looked like diaries. Reading the depressed memories of an old lady was the last thing he wanted to do, but they might have information he could use. He grabbed a handful and left the stifling heat to head downstairs and cool off. On his way out, he noticed that the curtains were open. His flashlight would have been visible outside. "Oh hell, no one's out there."

As he headed back to the stairway, Joe spotted a painting he hadn't noticed earlier and lifted a corner hoping to find a safe. At the sight of bare wall, he slammed the frame and waved the flashlight angrily. By chance, the erratic stream of light revealed an undersized door at the far end of the hall.

He hurried over and discovered a narrow stairway that at first appeared to lead nowhere. Upon further examination, he saw a rope hanging from a hinged panel, a trap door to the attic. What better place than an attic to stash old papers. He dropped the books, lowered the hatch, and climbed a few steps to poke his head through the opening.

In the dim beam of the flashlight, the exposed ceiling rafters cast long shadows. A fluttering noise overhead sounded to Joe's nervous ears like bats. He shivered and slapped his hand on the floor for balance only to inhale a mouthful of dust. No one had been up there in years, at least no human. Another noise came from the corner and as he redirected his light, something scurried behind a dusty trunk. The thought of crawling around with the present inhabitants dampened his curiosity. He descended, found the diaries and headed for the office on the first floor. If nothing turned up in the rest of the house, he'd come back and search the attic during the day.

The office was another room that probably hadn't changed in twenty years. Two of the four walls held shelves filled with books. Joe assumed they had to do with the law, since Vandenberg was an attorney. As depressing as the diaries might be, he was sure they would be more entertaining than legal cases.

He moved around to the large oak desk and opened the top drawer. Before he had a chance to search it, a light appeared through the curtains on the windowed wall. Switching off the flashlight, he moved the drape slightly and saw a police car in the driveway, flooding the yard and house with light. Joe felt around the desk, found the diaries, and raced through the dining room, knocking into furniture every few feet. When he found the kitchen, he fumbled briefly with the back door lock and slipped out.

It was too dangerous to run through the unfamiliar terrain, so he walked quickly and managed to stay on his feet until he entered the woods. There, thick brambles twisted around his shoes and gravity, unaffected by the lack of light, sent him hurtling forward. The books and flashlight slipped from his fingers as he grabbed a tree to remain upright. Once steady, he dug in the scratchy brush to find the fallen articles, but found only one diary and a mass of painfully sharp thorns.

Lights swept through the treetops, which meant the police car had turned around at the house and started back down the drive. There wasn't time to dig for the rest of the stuff. He had to get back to his car.

As he shoved the book in the back of his pants, Joe felt moisture on his arms, blood from the scratchy undergrowth. He pulled on his shirt and ran toward what he hoped was the creek and his car, arriving at the same time as the police vehicle. He worked to control his breathing as the deputy climbed from the cruiser and approached. The multiple lights from the car made it impossible to see the officer. The female voice caught him off guard. "What are you doing out here?"

"I went into the woods to take a leak."

"You walked into pitch black woods to take a leak in the middle of nowhere in the middle of the night?"

"I'm shy." Joe stretched his arms in the air, faking a yawn to disguise his need for air.

"Let me see your driver's license." Deputy Linda Knowski was a tall, solid woman with short blond hair under her Smokey hat. As she examined the Illinois license, she moved her flashlight beam from the picture to Joe's face. "Joseph Vandenberg. You're the guy who's here to collect the Vandenberg estate. This says you're from Chicago. If you live this close why haven't we seen you around?"

"I moved to Chicago from California last year."

"Why are you out here tonight?"

Joe's breathing steadied and his confidence returned. "Since I'll be living here soon, I wanted to see if the neighborhood was safe. Not much crime from what I can tell."

"No, there's not much crime in Raccoon Grove, Mr. Vandenberg. Not so far, anyway. Here's your license. You were about to head home."

Joe didn't miss the omission of a question mark. "Yes, ma'am. I'll be on my way then. Nice talking to you. Keep up the good work." He returned the license to his wallet and shoved it in his back pocket, not realizing the hurried motion dislodged the diary. He gave the deputy a mock salute and as he climbed in the car, the book fell to the ground unnoticed.

It wasn't until Joe drove away that Deputy Knowski spotted the diary. She was in a hurry to go home and catch a few hours of sleep, but felt duty bound to pick up the trash. She did not however, feel an ounce of curiosity and tossed it over her shoulder to the back seat. Meeting Joseph Vandenberg left a bad taste in her mouth. "It's not a real comfort to think that guy might be a citizen of Raccoon Grove."

Jean Sheldon

CHAPTER 12

Mourners filled he one hundred and fifty seats in the chapel. Those without chairs stood along the back wall and flowed out the open rear doors. Ben had few friends, but everyone knew him and many came to pay their respects. Kate walked to the chapel and was glad to see Dave with an empty seat on either side. "How did you get here?" She whispered as she joined him. "I didn't see your car."

"I walked. Tracy's driving over and it didn't make sense to bring both cars."

It took Kate only a second to scan the crowd. She didn't see the gossip columnist. "Where is she?"

"She supposed to meet me here. She wants to sneak in right before the service starts. Her column ran this morning and she's already received calls and emails from unhappy readers."

"I can't understand why people don't want to know who killed Jack. Besides, it was twenty years ago for heaven's sake."

"A lot of people think the less you know about what's going on, the better off you are."

"Right, they're called politicians." Dave lifted an eyebrow without comment.

The large numbers on the watch Tracy recently purchased to compensate for her declining vision told her she had five minutes before the start of the service. She parked a block away and hurried toward the chapel, thinking she was late enough to avoid confrontation. To be safe, she scrutinized arriving mourners for irate stares. Unfortunately, she missed seeing Edwina dash across the street to intercept her. "Just what do you think you're doing, Mrs. Kendall?"

"Oh, hi, Edwina. I'm here for Ben's funeral. We'd better get inside. I think the service is about to start." Tracy tried to push past, but the librarian planted her comfortable shoes on the sidewalk and blocked an escape.

"I saw the paper this morning. That was a painful time for our community, and better forgotten. What possible good would it do to rehash our darkest hour?"

"Our darkest hour? Edwina, why don't we discuss this another time?" Tracy tried again to slip by without knocking her over, although she was very close to not caring if the cantankerous woman took a tumble.

"Fine. Bring in your overdue library books and we can discuss it then." She spun and hurried away leaving Tracy stunned.

"I don't have any overdue library books, you old goat." She took a moment to regroup and elbowed her way through the standing-room-only crowd to find Dave. When she spotted him and Kate sitting next to each other, she scooted Dave over and parked herself between them for protection.

"Were your fans waiting?" Kate asked.

Tracy checked the back of the room for discontents. "Just one. On top of the phone calls and anonymous mail I've been getting, I have to deal with people stopping me in the street."

"I don't suppose any of the malcontents had anything useful to offer."

"Actually, I did get an interesting email from Karen Penrose before I left. She suggested I shouldn't bring a phony into town to inherit the Vandenberg estate because it wasn't fair to Louise. The inheritance would be a good motive to pretend to be Kimberly Vandenberg."

Kate caught on quickly. "Janet Doyle. Have you learned anything else about her father?" Tracy shared what they discovered about Herb. "So it's possible that she is really Kimberly Vandenberg and the timing of her friend sending the letter is a coincidence. That would be unbelievable."

"What sparked her friend's letter was the Gazette's anniversary article, so it wasn't a coincidence. I just wonder if the story gave Janet an idea for a scam. Maybe the so called friend, Tim, doesn't exist and she sent the letters herself."

"Did you talk to anyone who knew Herb Doyle when he lived here?"

Tracy opened her mouth to report they hadn't, but saw the minister move to the front of the room. "We'll talk later."

Nathaniel Thompson, Jr., who took over as head mortician at Thompson and Sons after his father's death, had done his elder proud. Ben looked good. Perhaps better than he had in years. He still fit in his uniform, which Scott found at the Sheriff's Office, and the cosmetologist successfully subdued the red nose and cheeks he'd developed in the last decade. Burying the ex-sheriff in his uniform might not have been politically correct, but the citizens of Raccoon Grove rarely worried about what other people thought about their town.

The elderly minister, who remembered not only Ben's role as sheriff, but also his difficult youth when the family lost their farm, asked the assemblage to keep in mind the many good years of service he'd given the town. Some would consider the job he did, but most of the younger citizens would remember the stool he occupied at the Boar's Head.

Near the end of the service, Tracy leaned over and handed Dave her car keys. "It's parked around the corner, a block down on Oak." As he stared blankly at the object in his palm, she grabbed Kate's arm and dragged her from the chapel. "Come on. Let's go get your car. We can meet Dave at our house. He isn't going to be happy that we left him to deal with the mob."

"We?"

"You two abandoned me." Dave whined as he entered the Kendall's living room. Tracy and Kate hid their guilty smiles behind wine glasses and looked at each other instead of him. He was not about to be ignored and cleared his throat dramatically. "Weren't you the least bit concerned that I might have been lynched?" He ignored the wine bottle on the table and poured himself a scotch before sitting on the couch next to Tracy. "You're not nice," he told her, and added to Kate. "Neither of you."

When a kiss on the cheek did nothing to melt his icy attitude, Tracy slid closer and wrapped her arm around his shoulders. "I'm sorry, honey. I thought you could handle it, you being the publisher and all."

"I'm not the one who makes the decisions at the Gazette. You would think everyone in town knew that by now." He kissed her cheek, then stood and walked across to Kate and kissed hers. "I forgive you both, though I shouldn't. Do you need anything while I'm up and feeling magnanimous?" Not wanting to push their good fortune, the women shook their heads.

"I'll tell you what I don't understand." Tracy assumed he'd finished his outburst. "The people in this town are usually unflappable. Why would an investigation into a twenty-year-old murder rile them?" Neither of her companions answered. "And another thing that doesn't make sense is the large number of anonymous letters. Everyone around here wants their opinions known and the Gazette has had a policy of not printing unsigned letters from day one. Whoever sent them didn't do it to be heard. They did it to give me a headache."

"They didn't send them to give you a headache, Tracy. They wrote to stop us from sticking our collective noses into the Vandenberg case. Maybe we should we give up the investigation."

Dave recognized Kate's ploy, but Tracy took the bait. "You are kidding, aren't you? Do you really think we should stop because of a little negative feedback? It means someone wants to hide something and has enlisted others to interfere with our search. I'm not ready to stop. I'm especially not ready to be bullied into stopping. Are you?"

"Nope, but I'm not receiving letters from angry people, or being harassed on the street. If you really intend to go on with this, maybe we should pick up the pace. Can we set up interviews with the people who taught at the high school with Louise?"

Dave finished his scotch and rejoined the discussion. "That's a good idea. I can work on that."

"Thank you, my dear, forgiving husband, and I want to find out who helped Louise. First, I have to meet Scott at Ben's house."

"I'll go home and make some phone calls." Kate finished her wine and stood. "I want to see if Dirk remembers who was supposed to be at the card game, and I want to give Harriet Ralston a call. She is the eyes and ears of that part of town. She might even rival you in her volume of gossip." Tracy, obviously preoccupied with her next task, didn't comment.

"Hi, Dirk, it's Kate."

"I saw you and Tracy dash out of the chapel earlier. What was that about?"

"The Gazette is receiving letters from unhappy town folk who aren't thrilled that we're digging into Jack Vandenberg's murder."

"Maybe you shouldn't be, Kate. People could be hurt by reopening that mess."

Her ex's response surprised her. "Who could be hurt? The Vandenbergs are dead, except for a questionable distant cousin from Chicago who's after the inheritance. We don't know for sure if he's even family."

"It wasn't only the Vandenbergs affected by that tragedy. I saw Adam yesterday. He's concerned about Sara. She's finally getting back on her feet, and he thinks bringing up the murder could cause her to have a setback. Whatever happened back then affected Sara in a way no one understands."

"I hadn't thought about that. I can appreciate Adam being worried about his daughter. I'll suggest to Tracy that she shouldn't put anything else in the paper. We can still investigate, but do it discreetly. That way no one will be hurt."

"What's your interest in this, Kate? Is it because you and Jack were an item?"

That remark did more than surprise Kate. It angered her. "Since my life was the farthest thing from your mind back then, I don't know how you would know anything about it. Jack Vandenberg was my attorney, but he was also my friend at a time when I needed one."

"I'm sorry. That was a stupid thing to say. Please forgive a cranky old man."

The intensity of her anger at Dirk's remark surprised her and reminded her of Milt's observation about old hurts. "I understand, and I'll talk to Tracy, but about the investigation, I called to ask if you can remember who planned to be at the card game that night and didn't show."

"Well, I told you, Milt and I were the only ones who did make it. Art Andrews passed away last year, but he usually joined us. Let me think a minute. George Williams and Adam Collins planned to play, and the sheriff said he'd come by if he finished work early. As you know, he didn't. And, of course, Jack."

"Did any of the guys who didn't make it call to say what was up?"

"No. Back then, our card games were at the Legion hall. There was a public phone, but no one kept track of who came and who didn't. And that was before everyone carried a cell phone."

"Thanks. By the way, Andrea stopped by on Sunday. Mitch filed for divorce and she's not feeling very good about her life these days."

"Damn. Poor Andy. You know, Illinois just passed that Companion Act. I used to think it was a good thing Jeffrey was gay and wouldn't have to go through the pain of divorce. Now he's in the same boat as the rest of us."

"You always could give things an interesting, if not confusing, spin."

"Did Andy mention seeing me?"

"She didn't, but I'll bet she'd appreciate a phone call. I told her about Vicki. How are you doing with that? Have you two talked?"

"No. Vicki doesn't think there's any reason for us to talk. She's quite comfortable in her new life. I'm trying to remember that you said I'd survive. I'll give Andy a call, Kate. Thanks for letting me know. Maybe we can put a different spin on our family. We could use it."

Tracy felt uncomfortable entering Ben's house only hours after his funeral. The sheriff was there to find a clue to his death, but she had something else on her mind. Something she hoped wasn't true. "This feels kind of weird," Scott said as he unlocked the door. Although she wouldn't admit it, her anxiety lessened knowing he shared her discomfort.

Fifteen years earlier, the town council finally acknowledged that a drunken sheriff was little comfort to citizens and decided to replace Ben. They chose Scott. He joined the force when he returned to Raccoon Grove after a tour in the Marines. The skills he learned in the service made his transition easy and he quickly became one of their most qualified officers. He'd been in uniform only four years when Crayton lost his job. Because of his background and because the council didn't know what else to do, they made him sheriff. The citizens liked him and approved, even though his dry sense of humor often left people wondering whether he was serious.

Inside the house, Tracy saw that Ben took no better care of his living quarters than any other part of his life. She scanned the room, ordering her brain to stop her eyes if they landed on anything unusual. They didn't. "Does he have any family left in the area?"

"None that I know of, Tracy. I talked to Beth. She remarried a few years after she and Ben divorced and doesn't enter into the picture, but she said most of his family died years ago. Do you intend to tell me what you're looking for?"

She didn't, and avoided his gaze. "I have this weird hunch, but I don't want to tell you yet. If I'm wrong, I'll make up something else."

"Then I'll wait and see."

"Let's check out the rest of the house." She led the way into another cluttered room that appeared to be an office. At least

Jean Sheldon

it had a desk and a computer. "I was hoping we wouldn't find a computer. Can I turn it on?"

"It's a murder investigation, Tracy, and we don't know if there's important evidence in here or not." After a brief discussion, which Scott didn't expect to win, but felt duty bound to undertake, he agreed and pulled out a pair of gloves. He was only mildly surprised when Tracy reached into her purse and withdrew a pair of her own.

She saw his amusement. "I grew up in a high crime neighborhood in Chicago."

"What did you do, volunteer with the scene investigating team after shootings?"

As Scott examined a nearby closet, Tracy sat at the computer. "He has internet access, let's see where he goes." Seconds later, she pointed to the monitor unhappily. "He's a regular at a number of porn sites. I'd say it's a pretty safe bet he doesn't have an accounting program on here." She didn't find anything noteworthy bookmarked or in the history folder and closed the browser to search for documents. Scott finished examining the closet and stood with his arms folded until Tracy released a loud sigh.

"What did you find?"

"What I thought I might find. Ben wrote the letter to the paper that said he knew who killed Jack Vandenberg."

"What?" He read the opened document. "Well, I'll be. Do you think he killed Jack and the guilt finally got to him?"

She opened other files, but found nothing. "I don't know, Scott. Five minutes ago, I would have said there was no way he killed Jack. Now, I don't know. If he didn't kill him, he knew about it right from the beginning. He was there, he found Louise. Why wouldn't he have reported who did it unless it was him?"

"Maybe Louise did it and he was protecting her."

"That doesn't work for a number of reasons, the biggest being that even if she killed Jack, she would never have done anything to hurt Kimberly. Everything comes back to that, doesn't it? What happened to Kimberly?"

"Seems to. Was that your hunch? That Ben wrote the letter to the Gazette."

"Yes, but I hoped I was wrong. Damn." Tracy didn't see any diary or journal where he might have entered personal information. She abandoned the computer to tackle the stacks of mail and papers that covered the remaining surfaces.

"What made you think he wrote it?"

"I figured that unless it was a bad joke, it had to be someone with access to the information, or who knew personally what happened that night. I also thought it was someone the information couldn't hurt anymore. Ben might have believed he fit in that category. He's been behaving like he planned to drink himself to death."

"But he didn't, Tracy. Someone killed him."

The numerous piles of junk mail, magazines, and unwanted sales fliers stacked in the space were daunting. Rather than think about it, Tracy grabbed a large handful to examine. Her fingers, still covered in latex, gripped the outer envelopes, but the rest oozed out from the middle and fell to the floor. "Damn." She knelt to retrieve them and uncovered a letter addressed to Ben. Her expression changed from irritation to puzzlement when she opened the sealed envelope to see ten one hundred dollar bills and a note. "Oh, brother. I think we might have discovered Ben's reason for not turning in the killer. Listen to this. *I can't keep paying you forever, Ben. This has to stop.*"

CHAPTER 13

Tracy moved to the unwashed window where sunlight, impervious to the years of neglect, streamed. She examined the envelope. "The postmark says February 1999. You were sheriff by then. Ben was blackmailing someone, and from the sounds of the letter, he'd been doing it for a while. I'll bet he carried a pile of mail in here drunk and didn't notice this envelope. Then he buried it under more mail. He wouldn't have let a thousand dollars sit around collecting dust."

Scott's disappointment was clear. He didn't want to think the man he'd replaced had hidden a crime and blackmailed a criminal, but Tracy didn't take time to comfort him. "You know what this means? Blackmail is a good motive for murder, especially blackmail that went on that long. If he were extorting money from the person who killed Jack, it explains why the investigation never went anywhere. It also confirms that whoever did it, still lives in Raccoon Grove."

"How does it do that, Tracy? Even if it is a payoff, we don't know if it had anything to do with Jack's murder. If it is connected to the murder, how do we know it was still going on and got Ben killed? We'd have to find a current envelope postmarked Raccoon Grove filled with cash."

"Even drunk, Ben wouldn't lose too many envelopes like this. I wish I knew why he wrote to the paper. Did he really plan to reveal the killer? Why now?"

"I can't guess, but the only thing we know with some certainty is that Ben blackmailed someone in 1999. That doesn't mean he blackmailed someone as far back as Jack's death or as recent as a few days ago."

"Oh, come on, Scott. This has to be tied to Jack's death and maybe even Ben's."

"I didn't say it wasn't, but we don't know anything for sure." The sheriff wore a mix of sadness and confusion. "None of this makes sense. Maybe Ben wrote the letter because he found out he was sick and as he grew closer to meeting his maker, he felt guilty and wanted to tell someone. I wish he'd come to me instead of writing a vague letter to the paper."

"Who was Ben's doctor?"

"Adam Collins. I talked to him earlier. Ben didn't come in often, but he had some stomach trouble a few months ago and Doc told him to take it easy, for all the good it did."

"I don't think Ben was dying. Adam would have known if he had something fatal. Here's how I see it, Scott. Ben knew who killed Jack and blackmailed that person for two decades. At least he did until the killer decided not to pay anymore." She waited for his response.

"I don't know."

"You don't want to believe he would do something like that, but it's likely he did." Tracy didn't push too hard. She often needed cooperation from the sheriff's department. "What if the person being blackmailed knew that he wrote it? I've been telling everyone in town about the letters we've received."

"If that's who killed him, it might explain why he decided to do it now. I just thought of another possibility. What if the person he was blackmailing told Ben he'd had enough? Ben might have sent the vague letter to the paper as a threat that he'd reveal the whole story. He knew everyone in town would hear about it."

"Oh, that would explain a lot. Let me shut down the computer. I assume your office will want the hard drive and this." She put everything back in the envelope and gave it to him.

"What a mess. Come on. I'll take you home."

"No, take me to the paper. My car is there and I need to do some research."

The sheriff stayed quiet on the ride back, but Tracy had no problem filling the dead air. "This Vandenberg kid that came for the estate is too young to be involved, but maybe he really is a relative and Jack did something to his father. He might feel he's owed the estate. Even if that's true, I don't see how it would involve Ben. Unless this kid's father was the person he was blackmailing."

Scott didn't answer until he pulled up in front of the newspaper. "Easy does it Tracy. We don't know conclusively that money was for blackmail."

She knew he didn't believe that and after climbing out, looked back in the car. "Scott, if there's the slightest chance that Ben was blackmailing the person who killed Jack, it means there is a killer living in our town. We have to look at every possibility." She slammed the door without waiting for a reply.

※

"Did you find anything to convince them you're related to the family, Joe?"

"No. I went through a few rooms upstairs and put the phony letters to Kimberly in her room. I also found some diaries that the old lady kept, but my visit got cut short. I was searching the office when a cop showed up and I had to take off." Joe explained his mishap in the woods and his visit with Deputy Knowski. "I must have dropped the diary again on the way to the car. I can't find it. I didn't expect to have to prove I'm related. I mean, how many Vandenbergs can there be in Illinois?"

"It doesn't matter. The estate's worth over two million dollars and they're not going to hand it over just because you claim to be a relative. Don't underestimate the good citizens of Raccoon Grove, Joe. You'd be a fool to assume they're a bunch of hayseeds."

"Maybe, but no matter how smart they are, I'm going to get that inheritance, and I'd like that to happen soon."

"Remember, half belongs to me."

"Sure, I can live on a million bucks for a few years. I'll even donate a few hundred to the town."

"You're a real philanthropist, Joe."

"What's that?"

"Never mind. When can you go back for the diaries? No matter how this thing goes, there might be information we can use."

"Stop worrying. We'll get the money one way or another. By the way, half the town showed up to pay their respects at a funeral today. Some guy named Crayton. Did you know anything about it?"

"Ben Crayton. He was sheriff until he started hitting the sauce too heavy. Didn't you read that stuff I gave you? Why should I waste my time putting it together if you don't bother to read it?"

"I read a little, and I still got all the notes I took when I was out here last week, but I didn't think I needed to know about anybody except the Vandenberg family."

"In a town as small as Raccoon Grove, you need to know about everyone. Read the information, Joe. You don't know what obscure fact will be important."

"Yeah, yeah, I'll read it.

"Let me know when you have the diaries. We can go through them together."

"What have you been working on?"

"Making sure I can salvage things in case you screw up. I'll talk to you later."

Joe leaned back in his car seat and closed his eyes. After he paid off the guy chasing him, he planned to take life easy and enjoy the money. "Maybe I won't split the dough. I'm doing all the work."

❧

Kate finished her phone conversation with Dirk and called Tracy to tell her that Adam Collins wanted them to stop the investigation. "He's being protective of Sara, but he is her father and she's been through a lot. What do you think we should do?"

"I talked to a couple of people earlier today and they said the same thing. Adam must be letting his patients know how he feels about our looking into the past. I don't know how the Vandenbergs relate to Sara's problem, but if Adam's concerned, we can hold off until we have solid information. For the moment, we won't print anything and do our looking discreetly."

"Dirk also told me who didn't show up at the card game. He said Art Andrews, George Williams, Adam Collins, Milt, and Jack were supposed to be there. Ben told them he'd try to come after he finished his shift."

"Art Andrews died last year so we can't talk to him. I wonder why George didn't make it to the game. We'll have to see if we can find out where he went that night. I rather doubt he'll tell you or me. Adam had an emergency patient, if I remember right. Did anyone call to say why they didn't make it?"

"No. They played at the Legion hall. There was a pay phone, but Dirk said they just played with whoever showed up. It is rather odd that out of the seven people they expected, only two of them showed up."

"Did he say if that was unusual?"

"No. I'll try to remember to ask him if we talk again soon. What have you been working on?"

"Our next plan of attack. Do you want to talk to Harriet and a few of the other Vandenberg neighbors with me tomorrow?"

"I spoke to Harriet. She said she'd tell us whatever she could. How many houses were out there twenty years ago?"

"I can't say, but I know that Harriet was there, and she'll point us in the right direction. Dave's searching death notifications in the entire northern part of the state to track down Herb Doyle. Unless he moved out of state to die, we should be able to find the records."

"Tracy, I think it might be a good idea to talk to Sara Collins in person about what happened back then. She could have information she doesn't realize can help."

"What kind of information?"

"Things she might have known about the Vandenberg family that no one else knew. There's still a remote possibility Kim was Herb Doyle's child, or he and Louise had an affair. Sara and Kimberly were best friends and she might have picked up problems between Louise and Jack. If Kimberly was Herb's daughter and Jack found out, that certainly could create problems at home. I'll feel her out before I ask anything and see how she reacts."

"I doubt that she'll remember much since she was so young. You'd have to be careful, Kate. Who knows what innocent remark could stir something up? From what I've seen, though, Sara looks strong."

"She does, and happy. She said she wanted to talk to me about something. Maybe we can do that and ease into a conversation about the past. I'll see how she looks before I mention anything about the Vandenbergs."

"I trust your judgment on that. When do you want to set it up?"

"She's due here shortly."

"Kathleen Chandler. Who taught you to be so sneaky?"

"You have to ask?"

Kate left Sara in the garden and went inside for water, watching her through the kitchen window as she filled the glasses. The various blooms brought a smile to the young woman's face, but as she approached the pink rosebushes, her demeanor changed from fascination to fear. Her body stiffened and her complexion paled even further. Kate hurried outside and set the water glasses on the table. "Sara." Her voice stayed soft, as did the touch of the hand she rested on her shoulder. "Let's go to the gazebo. Is there something unpleasant about the roses?"

"No, I just…. I can't explain it, Ms Chandler." The somber expression didn't belong on Sara's young face. "I felt frightened. I had a similar reaction to the bush in our yard, but I have no idea why. I'm sorry. I'm fine, really."

They settled on the white wooden chairs and Kate squeezed the young woman's hand. "I'm sure you are. There's a tranquil look in your eyes these days that I haven't seen for many years. Your mom must be pleased. How is she?"

"Mom is mom. She has a great outlook on life. She does more to help me keep it together than anything. In fact, that's the reason I wanted to talk to you. I need to ask a favor."

Sara's quick recovery and returning smile confirmed Kate's hunch that she wasn't the fragile figure her father portrayed. "I'd be glad to help with anything I can. What's the favor?"

"Mom hires a gardener once a month to take care of the yard now that she can't, and that's not enough. I thought if you'd consider teaching me, I could do the gardening and yard work. I don't have money, but I could work for you while I'm learning and maybe even after, if I turn out to be any good. I've always felt a connection to flowers, even if I haven't been around them much."

Kate recognized the longing in Sara's eyes. She knew how it felt to be on the outside looking in, desperate to be a part of the world. "I've been thinking about hiring an assistant, and you'd be perfect. It's a wonderful idea, but while you're training, I'll pay you an hourly wage. After that, you can work at a reasonable salary, which we can decide on then. How does that sound?" Sara thought it sounded great. "The first requirement is that you call me Kate."

"Okay, Kate. When do I start?"

"For today, let me take you on a tour through the gardens and the greenhouse. You can see what you're getting yourself into."

The technology of cell phones amazed Kate. From what she could tell, they did everything but cook. Unfortunately, her limited experience and lack of desire to learn kept her clueless as to how do more than make and receive calls. Even then, she struggled to hold the compact device to talk and do anything else. She pushed a programmed button and wedged the phone awkwardly between her shoulder and ear to pour a cup of coffee. Tracy had the good sense not to answer until she'd taken a sip. "Sara's visit yesterday went great. She asked if I'd help her learn to garden and nearly jumped up and down when I suggested she work for me. It'll be wonderful for her, and me. I need the help." Kate took another sip and smiled. "I wish you could have seen her face. She is delighted with the flowers."

"She's not the scared little girl Adam makes her out to be?"

"No, she's not. Maybe he doesn't realize how well she's doing."

"Whatever Adam thinks, you're right, Kate. This is fantastic for Sara, and you sound pretty excited yourself. I can't think of anything more therapeutic for her than growing flowers. Learning from the best flower arranger in the northern part of the state won't hurt. I have news too. Dave's search turned up a Herb Doyle who died two years ago in Chicago. A friend of his at the Tribune promised to dig around for more information."

"Another point for Janet Doyle, possible heir to the Vandenberg estate. How remarkable would it be if she were Kimberly? Everyone in town thought she was dead, but no one wanted to say it."

"I'm still not convinced she's Kimberly, but you're right, things continue to add up in her favor."

"Tracy, were you able to find out which neighbor called about the gunshot?"

"No. I read over the files we printed, but apparently, Ben didn't think the caller's name was important enough to put on his report. Anyway, we still need to talk to Harriet and the rest of the Vandenberg's neighbors. One of them must have called it in."

Kate listened as she topped off her coffee and moved to the kitchen window, but Tracy's voice and the phone crashed to the floor when she looked at her backyard. "Oh, dear, god. The gardens."

CHAPTER 14

Even on the rare occasion when Tracy wasn't in a hurry to get from point a to point b, the 25 mile per hour speed limit in Raccoon Grove bugged her. Since becoming a resident over two and a half decades earlier, she had accumulated enough speeding tickets to support not a small town, but a small country. At the abrupt end of her conversation with Kate, she jumped in her car and floored it, hoping the sheriff and deputies were having breakfast at the diner. She screeched to a halt in front of Kate's house and inhaled deeply before pushing on the back gate.

Kate's gardens were in ruins. "Dear lord. Who would do this? Kate, where are you?" She found her kneeling in the middle of one of the flowerbeds, streaks of dirt under her eyes where she'd wiped earlier tears. "Honey, what happened?" Tracy offered her hand and without waiting for a response, gave it a tug. "Let's sit for a minute and figure out what to do."

She didn't need persuading. Tracy pulled her to her feet and led the way to the gazebo where Kate wiped her hands on her jeans and shook her head at the damage. "It isn't as bad as it could have been. A number of plants were knocked over, but the only broken flowers are where he stepped."

"You're sure it was a man."

"Either that or a woman with very large feet. Whoever did it left a message." Kate pointed to a sheet of paper on the lawn, which Tracy retrieved.

"Mind your own business and leave the past alone." She returned to the chair. "Another warning to stop investigating. Kate, I feel terrible. This is my fault, I'm so sorry."

"How could it possibly be your fault? Unless you wore Dave's shoes and jumped around in my gardens. You didn't force me to become involved."

Tracy dug around in her purse for tissue and pushed it into Kate's clenched hand. "Wipe your face."

As Kate obeyed, a gasp came from the direction of the gate where Sara stood in the same pose Tracy had taken only moments earlier. "What happened?"

Slipping the note in her pocket, Tracy stood. "It looks like some kids threw a party out here. Your boss says it isn't too bad. Will you help her fix this mess?" Sara managed a nod as she scanned the damage. "Good. Kate, can I do anything to help that doesn't involve dirty fingernails?"

"No. Sara and I can handle it. Don't you think, Sara?" Kate shoved the soggy tissue in her pocket and stood to exchange a hug with Tracy. Her young assistant, though still unable to speak, gave another hopeful nod. "You're off the hook."

With one last look at the colorful chaos, Tracy headed toward the gate. "I'm sorry this happened. Don't disturb the footprints while you're repairing things." The gate slammed behind her but she shouted one last remark. "I'm so sorry."

Tracy drove the speed limit and took deep breathes to keep calm, but rather than chanting a mantra, she released a stream of words more common at the Boar's Head than an ashram. They didn't help. At home, she slammed the car door and then the front door, throwing her purse at a table with enough force to launch it off the other side and topple a brass umbrella stand. "Son of a bitch," she screamed at the Louis Vuitton clutch as it burrowed into the carpet.

Her noisy arrival brought Dave from the kitchen. "Trace, what's wrong?"

She ignored him and stomped to the bar. "Is it too early for a drink? I didn't think so." She filled a glass with scotch and fell onto the couch muttering what she might have considered an explanation. "Son of a bitch."

Dave sat beside her and cautiously repeated his question. "What's wrong? I haven't seen you drink scotch on a Sunday morning or heard you swear with that much enthusiasm in years."

"Someone marched through Kate's gardens and destroyed them. They smashed her beautiful flowers."

He took the glass from her fingers and gulped a portion of the contents. "Why would anyone do that?"

"Someone doesn't want us to investigate Jack's murder and that means they're guilty and don't want to be caught." Tracy took the note from her pocket and convinced Dave to trade it for the glass. "You know, Adam Collins has been telling people he doesn't want us investigating. Maybe it's him."

"Adam isn't guilty of anything except worrying about his daughter. I can't see him running through Kate's flower gardens. Tracy, I want to ask something that that might sound insensitive. Could Sara Collins have done it?"

"I don't find it all that insensitive. I considered it myself as I drove to Kate's house, but the look on her face when she came in the yard was complete shock. She was horrified. Besides, Sara's problems were with depression, not violence or psychosis. No, she wasn't involved. Kate said the footprint belonged to a man. Let me see the bottom of your shoes."

"Cute. What about Milt and the others? Could one of them have been mad enough to do it?"

"Mad Dog and Harold weren't angry. George and Milt stormed away before we could talk, but Milt apologized to Kate later. I should talk to them again, I suppose. It wouldn't hurt to find out if their shoes are muddy. Would you like to come along?"

"You want my company?"

"Of course, I do, but I'm taking the rest of the day off. It is Sunday. We can talk to them tomorrow, right after we visit Scott at the station." She kissed him. "Why don't I make breakfast? After that, I'm going back to bed."

⁂

"It must be difficult to see this kind of damage done to your yard, Kate." Sara continued resetting the rows of crooked and bent blossoms.

"It is, but I have enough sense to know that even though these gardens are the most important things in the world to me, to others they're only flowers. I'm sure it's what Tracy said, a bunch of kids drank a few beers and started showing off." She looked around. "Things got a little out of control. That reminds me. Our star reporter said we were not to disturb the footprints. I have no idea what she has going on in the cunning little mind of hers, but since the plants under his print are smashed, there's no hurry to retrieve them."

"These are finished. What next?"

"Why don't you work on the peonies? They're just about done for the season and I want to split them and widen the bed." Kate thought it best to work on restoring the rosebushes while Sara tended the other side of the yard. She felt sure the gardens would go a long way in helping the young woman heal. Of course, Kate believed the gardens could bring world peace.

Her rose bushes suffered little damage. The species was so hearty that horticulturists in some parts of the world claimed plants dating back to the first century. Kate's weren't that old, but if it were up to her, they would be. The intruder pulled a few stalks from the trellises and gave up, probably for a more benign victim. A deep footprint next to the bush suggested he'd tried to smash it in response to a handful of painful thorns. His stomp did no permanent damage to stems that were as strong and flexible as the thorns were sharp. As she finished the roses and joined Sara, she made a mental note to tell Tracy they'd be looking for someone with holes in his hand. "I think we should call it quits for today. I hadn't planned to spend all day Sunday in the garden. Things look good though, don't they?"

The vastly improved gardens restored Sara's good humor and she pulled off her gloves as she stood. "Compared to how they looked this morning, I'd say so. It doesn't surprise me that gardens as incredible as yours wouldn't let anyone destroy them. That's an attitude I need to remember."

"That's an attitude we all need to remember."

"Have you grown flowers all your life?"

"I didn't do much of anything with the first half of my life, I'm ashamed to say."

"I heard you were a beauty queen."

Kate snorted, not a skill learned on the runway. "That's such an awful term. For the first twenty years of my life, I did what ever was easiest. It wasn't as profound as following the path of least resistance. I was just numb. For the next twenty, I played wife and mother, and, unfortunately, not well. After that, I planted my first garden. I was, and still am, grateful to my mom and Tracy for encouraging me." It wasn't until they arrived at the gazebo that Kate noticed Sara had not responded. She handed her a bottle of water. "Are you okay?"

"I'm not glad you went through a hard time, Kate, but knowing that even a person as perfect as you struggled, helps me believe I can have a normal life."

"I can only imagine how awful it's been, but I know it's always easier to see the positive in others than in ourselves. Trust me when I say that none of us comes close to perfect. Some learn to talk the talk and walk the walk. Some don't. The flowers are perfect. They don't need an ego to convince themselves or anyone else of that." As they admired their achievement, Kate, who still hadn't had a chance to ask Sara about the past, searched for a way to do so. Sara saved her the trouble.

"I'm sure you know I've spent a lot of time in hospitals because of depression. I don't want to be perfect. I just want a life."

"I have heard, and I can understand your wanting a life. Have you ever thought about what went on the night Kim disappeared? That was when you started having problems, wasn't it?" Kate worried her question was too direct. To her relief, Sara answered without hesitation.

"I've thought about that a lot over the years, but it's been difficult to make anything clear in my mind."

"Have your mom and dad been able to help you remember?"

"Mom was at her sister's in Iowa that week."

"What about your dad?"

At times, the slightest change on a person's face, a negligible twitch or flush can divulge their emotions. Kate watched as Sara silently admitted to both sadness and confusion. Her eyes focused on Kate, but her thoughts entertained images only she could see. "Dad said my problems aren't connected to Kimberly's disappearance. He told me it was a coincidence that the night she disappeared I watched a movie that terrified me. I don't remember the movie."

"Your dad has been very concerned for you."

"I know. He's afraid to let me even think about the past. For a while, when a picture came into my head that didn't make sense, I'd ask him about it. He told me the same thing every time. The images were from the movie. I've asked him what movie it was, thinking I could watch it again and see why it scared me, but after all these years, he doesn't remember. I'm not sure if that's true. I think even if he did, he wouldn't tell me. My doctor suggested that when I remember something, or become afraid, I not mention it to dad, but call her. He's trying to help, but he doesn't understand that I need to remember even if it frightens me. Otherwise, I'll always be on the edge, ready to fall back in."

Although Kate needed no further convincing, Sara's impassioned response reinforced her belief that she was stronger than Adam Collins believed. "You're doing great, Sara. You're dad will realize that one day. I'm sure your doctor knows what's best for you. You were in South Suburban Psychiatric Center, weren't you?" Kate mentioned the nearby state mental health facility. "Is that where you go for outpatient treatment?"

"Yes. My doctor is Carolyn Kovecki and she's been tremendously helpful. She isn't ready to increase my medication because I become afraid or depressed. She bothers to find out why. She has talked to dad about helping me remember, but he thinks it's dangerous to dredge up the past. Carolyn convinced me to talk to you about learning about flowers. I told her about your gardens and that I wanted to do something for our yard. I know she would love to see them. Would you mind very much if I brought her by?"

"That's a great idea, and I can give her an objective report about how fantastic you're doing working for me."

"No offense, Kate, but that doesn't sound very objective."

Kate laughed. "No, I don't suppose it does. Well, I'll try to be objective. Please ask Dr. Kovecki to stop by." Kate had never talked to a psychiatrist and felt her stomach make a slight adjustment. She forced a smile and decided Sara wasn't the only one affected by old movies.

⁂

The leisurely day in Dave's soothing company, had not completely dissolved Tracy's anger. The calm she'd regained disappeared when she and Dave met with the sheriff on Monday morning. Scott wasn't pleased about the damage to Kate's yard, but offered little support in tracking down the perpetrator. "Why can't you send someone to take a plaster cast of the footprints? There are dozens of them around the gardens. Sheriff, a crime was committed."

"You tell me how I can justify spending money on a mold because flowers were trampled. It's trespassing, yes, but I can't take footprints every time someone trespasses." Scott had enough experience arguing with Tracy to hold his ground, and enough sense to turn away to roll his eyes.

"These aren't just flowers, they're Kate's livelihood, and it wasn't just trespassing, it was vandalism, malicious destruction of property. What about this?" She shoved the note in his face. "It's a threat. 'Mind your own business and leave the past alone.'"

"That's not exactly a threat. It's more in the line of advice, which I'm guessing you plan to ignore. I can't help you with this, Tracy. Our department doesn't have the staff or the money."

"Then give me a bag of the damn stuff, and I'll make the casts myself. Dave, help Scott find the plaster." Dave may not have intended to, but he groaned as he stood from the metal folding chair.

"I can sell you a bag for fifty dollars, or you can buy it at the hardware store for ten. Then I won't have to report to the city council why we're a bag short."

"Fine, we'll take care of it."

Dave raised a finger in the air and was about to comment when Tracy flew out the door. His remaining fingers lifted and fell in a resigned wave as he followed her out. "This should be interesting."

If Scott were a betting man, he would have wagered everything that Dave was right. He would have won. The scene in Kate's yard was indeed interesting. White powder dusted the colorful flowerbeds, slightly reminiscent of a poppy field in Oz where Dorothy and her friends encountered unexpected snow.

At the start of the footprint project, Kate had appealed to the enthusiastic sleuths to keep the plaster to a minimum so it wouldn't affect the soil. She added additional silent prayers as she and Sara followed along scooping up any spills.

It wasn't until the fifth imprint that Tracy thought they had a good cast. She flattened her body on the ground and tested the material to see if was dry enough to lift. Dave, who chose that moment to come through carrying another bag of plaster, didn't see her until the last minute. He stopped inches before tripping over his horizontal wife and lost his grip on the open bag of powder. Several handfuls of plaster covered Tracy's auburn head.

"What the...?" She pushed herself to her knees and looked up at a small stream of powder seeping from the bag. Her brain responded before that of her surprised husband and she waved her hands in front of her face, blowing through her lips to keep from swallowing the dust.

Seconds later, Dave recovered and dropped the bag, stopping the flow. Unfortunately, the sight of his plaster-covered partner tickled his funny bone enough to send him to the ground, gripping his sides in laughter. "Oh, this is too good. Quick, Kate, find a mirror. Better yet, find a camera. You see, my darling, I told you you'd look good with gray hair." He interrupted his comment with another wave of laughter.

A coating of plaster powder did little to hide Tracy's annoyance. "Will someone help me up, or are you all enjoying yourselves too much?" She turned her glare from Dave to Kate and Sara who were having almost as much fun.

Kate tried to control her reaction, but between Tracy's comical appearance and Dave's response, she ended up on her knees in a fit of laughter. At Tracy remark, she let Sara help her to her feet and regained control. "Sara, we'd better help her up." She nodded at Dave. "And if you know what's good for you, you'll stay put. Come on, old girl." Once Tracy was on her feet, Kate gave her a quick brushing and offered her an arm and some consolation. "Come in the house and I'll clean you up. Dave is right. Your hair looks pretty good this color."

In no mood to be consoled, Tracy stuck out her tongue, but it disappeared quickly when she tasted the bitter powder on her lips. She wiped her mouth with her sleeve and glared at the others before opening it again. "You all go ahead and enjoy yourselves. I will have my revenge."

CHAPTER 15

After Kate took Tracy inside, Sara noticed a line of clouds moving in their direction and she and Dave hurried to clean up the spilled plaster. If it started to rain, the chemicals would wash into the soil. When they finished, Sara returned to the footprint where Tracy met with disaster and lifted the cast. "Dave, look at this. I think Tracy was right. This one looks good and I see treads from the shoe. Would you help me turn it over?"

Dave saw as he knelt that the cast had promise. He could also imagine his wife's reaction if her masterpiece were broken. He and Sara turned the large white slab with extreme caution and set it down for a closer look. The results confirmed his confidence in her detecting abilities. "Wow, this is almost perfect."

"Why do you sound so surprised?" Tracy rubbed a towel on her hair as she and Kate returned to the yard. She wore jeans and a tee shirt. Not her usual attire, even if they'd boasted a designer label. Coming from Kate's closet, they did not.

"I thought you decided to leave your hair white." Dave's smile contradicted his protest. He stood and kissed her.

"I'll let it go *au naturel*, dear. I actually didn't hate the way it looked in plaster dust, but that might be a little messy to maintain on a regular basis. I'll have it bleached, or whatever they do while it grows out."

"I forgot how good you look in jeans." This time, the smile was in complete agreement with the words as he stepped back for a better look.

The brooding journalist found her own smile, though doubtful. "Saying nice things won't get you off the hook, Kendall, but the jeans do feel good. I might have to pick up a pair to go with my new look. The footprint came out okay?"

"Perfect." Sara held it for her approval. "I've seen that pattern before."

"Me too," agreed Kate.

Tracy's sullen mood returned as she pointed at the mold. "I have too. It's a Vibram Laramie sole. They're common on the bottom of Red Wing biker boots. Half the men in this town, half the men in this county, wear that boot. Around here, wherever you see mud or soft dirt, you see that imprint."

"The mold was a good idea, Tracy."

Kate knew that Sara's words of encouragement sounded like sympathy to Tracy's uncompromising ear and it would only make her more irritable. She bent for a closer look at the print. "Hey, look at this. There's a gash in the pattern. That should help us narrow it down." She pointed to a thick line that ran through the front part of the sole. The new information didn't improve Tracy's mood.

"You're right, Kate. All we have to do is take the cast to the newspaper, install a glass floor in the front reception area, and have someone wait in the basement to check the soles of shoes when people come in. Then, of course, we'll need to invite everyone in town to stop by. We can give out tickets to the state fair or free copies of the Gazette." She walked away, applying excessive force on the towel.

"Is she kidding?" Sara was new to Tracy's sarcasm.

"Yes. She's kidding. That's how she handles disappointment." Dave finished wrapping the footprint in newspaper and stood. "I'll take her to the paper and lock her in her office. She'll perk up."

Once again, Dave's prediction proved accurate. After only an hour absorbed in her column, Tracy's mood improved considerably. In fact, she had enough distance from the misadventure to find it almost humorous. She didn't plan to share that with anyone, but answered the phone wearing an amused grin. "Hello, this is Tracy Kendall."

"Mrs. Kendall, this is Janet Doyle from Chicago. You came to see me last week."

"Yes, Janet. I hope we didn't upset you too much." Tracy remembered Kate's assurance that Janet would call and wondered if it meant she was real or fake.

"What I'm upset about are vague memories I've been having since we spoke. Could I meet Kimberly's family, or see where she grew up?"

"Louise Vandenberg, Kimberly's mother, died a few weeks ago and there's no other family, except a supposed distant cousin in town to claim the estate. No one's living there so a visit to the house might be possible."

"Maybe seeing it will help me sort through some of these images. I've been having a dream about my father in a fight and there was a loud noise. I'm afraid I don't remember anything else. If I am this Kimberly person, seeing Raccoon Grove might help."

"I hope so. How old are you, Janet?"

"I'm twenty-five. Is that how old the Vandenberg girl would be?"

Jean Sheldon

"Yes. Do you have your birth certificate?"

Janet didn't answer immediately. When she did, it was softly. "I found the document in my dad's things, but I don't think it's the hospital copy and it looks, well, it doesn't look right. I think someone made changes."

"Kate, my little skeptic, you were right on the money. Janet Doyle called and wants to visit our little town. She said she's been remembering things and wants to take a tour of the Vandenberg house to see if it helps. She'll be down Thursday or Friday."

"So, we know she's either a smooth operator or Kimberly." Kate repeated her earlier idea. "Did she say anything else?"

"I mentioned the cousin trying to claim the estate, but she didn't comment. She did say she found her birth certificate and it looks altered. If Janet Doyle is Kimberly, then Joseph Vandenberg won't be excited with the news."

"No, since he's counting on inheriting the house and property. The ironic thing is he's been trying to prove he's related. If Janet is Kimberly, she could help him prove that, but she'll inherit the estate. Boy, she could be Kimberly Vandenberg, couldn't she? Did Dave hear any more from his friend about Herb Doyle?"

"Not yet. How are the gardens?"

"They're fine. Sara is a tremendous help. I shouldn't be surprised, but she's a natural with the flowers. Were you able to remove the plaster dust from various parts of your body?"

"Eventually, but when we stopped to tell Scott what we found, he chuckled and asked Dave if I'd started using cocaine. They both found that extremely amusing."

Kate thought it would have been if there had still been plaster in her nose. "What do you have planned?"

"We'd better visit Harriet and some of the other neighbors tomorrow. We've put that off long enough. What do you say we start first thing in the morning?"

"Hang on a second." Kate walked to the back garden and pulled the phone from her ear. "Sara, would you mind if I left you to work alone for a while tomorrow morning?" She shook her head. "You're sure you'll be okay?"

"I'm positive. Go detect. You like that almost as much as your flowers."

"Not even close. I'm sure we won't be long." She put the phone back on her ear as she walked to the house. "My assistant said she can handle things. My assistant, isn't that a hoot."

"Hi, Harriet. How are you?"

"Old and cranky, and I find it quite irritating that neither of you are. Old I mean." People who saw Tracy and Kate together couldn't help but compare the differences. On this occasion, the ex-beauty queen wore her usual garb, jeans, a tee shirt, and sneakers. She'd pulled her shoulder-length gray hair back and wrapped it in a bun. The gossip columnist sported a pantsuit with beige Fermani Italian leather pumps and her styled chin-length auburn hair accentuated her long face. Tracy wore only light makeup and Kate didn't wear any, but they both looked good enough to annoy friends in the same age bracket. "Tracy, I heard you're ready to let your hair grow out and join the rest of us aging boomers. It's about time. Do you want to come in, or did you just drop by to ask about my health. I'm not infirmed yet, as you can see." She held the door and waved them into her living room.

"Harriet, I know I haven't been here in a while, but I don't remember this décor. You've remodeled and redecorated. It's wonderful."

"Thank you, Kate. Yes, I was so bored with the old stuff I want to sell the place. Redecorating made more sense, especially in this economy. The only thing missing is one of your floral arrangements, but since you won't sell retail, I'll have to wait for my funeral. You better do something special for me when I go, girlfriend."

"You bet, assuming my fingers still move when I'm ninety-five."

"Okay, enough sweet talk. What do you two want? I follow the Gazette and know you're looking into Jack Vandenberg's murder. I'm glad someone is. I don't mean to speak badly of the dead, but Ben Crayton should have retired right after his divorce."

"You're right that we're investigating Jack's death and about Ben. Harriet, you weren't the neighbor that called about hearing a shot, were you?" Tracy asked.

"Nope, wasn't me."

"Huh. There weren't as many houses out this way back then, and you're one of the closest. What do you remember about that night?"

"There were only a handful of us, and with all the trees, you couldn't really see anything. You could hear something that loud, though. I heard two sounds, which at the time I thought were backfires. Of course, after I heard what happened the next day, I knew they were gunshots and called Sheriff Crayton. He said he had enough witnesses. Regina, on the other side of Jack's wasn't the one who called either. Like me, she called after she found out the next day. Ben told her the same thing."

"Wait a minute. You heard two shots?" Harriet nodded. "The police report said there was only one shot reported."

"They were ten or fifteen minutes apart. Maybe someone called right after the first one, or only heard the second."

Tracy remembered the blackmail money. Harriet's words confirmed that Ben had not only known who killed Jack, but helped in the cover up. "Kate, we need to talk to Regina." She turned to Harriet. "Is she home during the day?"

"Yes. She's retired and probably out in her yard working on her new garden. Be kind to her, Kate, she hasn't a clue what she's doing." Beside her reputation for gathering gossip, most Grovers knew Harriet for her quick and sometimes less than kind sense of humor. "If she asks for advice, you might suggest she order some of those silk flowers that won't die."

Regina's house was only two properties from Harriet, but Tracy, who wasn't dressed for a hike through the woods, insisted they drive. As they climbed from the car, Kate smiled at the colorful flowerbeds filling the yard around Regina's small brick ranch house. The owner, working in the front garden, climbed from her knees at there arrival, a little embarrassed by the presence of Raccoon Grove's local flower expert. "I'm still a beginner, Kate," she said with an apologetic wave. "I have a ways to go before they approach the beauty of your gardens."

"You're off to a wonderful start, Regina. I can see you did some studying before you planted."

Two bright spots of pink, the color of a nearby Clematis, highlighted Regina's otherwise pale cheeks. "I did. I took books from the library and learned about what to plant when, and which plants help each other."

Tracy had been enjoying the flowers, at least until she heard the word library. The mere mention of it brought to mind her adversary. "I suppose the old bat was there."

"If you mean Edwina, of course, she was there. She's the only librarian we have. I heard you two didn't see eye to eye."

"We might, if she could see. She's practically blind and deaf, and doesn't know if and when people return their library books."

"Oh, I see." Regina kept further comments to herself and turned to Kate. "I'm glad you like the yard. Working with the flowers is very soothing."

"Don't spread that around. I'll be out of business in no time. You'll do great, Reg. Try to keep it small the first few years until you see what works best in your soil and with your exposure. It can overwhelm you to try to do too much at once."

"Thank you, Kate. I'm guessing you two didn't come to give me pointers on my garden. You two sit down and I'll get some lemonade."

While Regina went inside for their drinks, her guests settled into lawn chairs. Patience had never been Tracy's strong suit, but over the years, some of Kate's serenity rubbed off. She sat comfortably admiring Regina's flowers and wondering if she might try growing some herself. The words 'when hell freezes over' jolted her back to left-brain mode and the moment Regina sat down, Tracy fired a question. "Harriet heard two shots the night of Jack's death and thought you did too. Do you remember?"

"Yes, I do. I heard two shots and when I tried to tell Sheriff Crayton, he told me they didn't need more statements." She threw her hands up and fell back in the chair. "How can you have all the information you need if you have an unsolved murder and a missing child?"

"Do you remember how far apart the shots were?" Kate set her glass on a small wrought iron table.

"Nearly twenty minutes if I remember right. I heard the first one around seven-forty-five, and the second one wasn't until a few minutes after eight. As thick as the trees are between the houses, gunshots and backfires are the few things we can make out. I thought someone might have been scaring off an animal, but dusk is a dangerous time to shoot at anything."

"You don't know who called the police the night you heard the shots?" Tracy asked.

"No. Harriet and I talked to most of the neighbors back then and they heard what we did, but no one called it in. No one we talked to anyway. Gunshots aren't unusual out here, but you do remember them. After I heard what happened, I felt bad about not reporting it that night, although I'm not sure it would have made much difference with Ben on the job. I'm sorry I can't be more help, especially after you shared your expertise, Kate."

"Kate loves to share her expertise." Tracy winked at her smiling partner. "Did you know Louise well?"

"I taught with her, and the teachers at the high school all got along, but she quit when she married Jack and became pregnant right after. Probably on the wedding night, at least that's what those of us who count those kinds of things figured. Kim was born three weeks early. She was healthy, just ready to come out. The poor thing couldn't have guessed what lay in store for her. Once Louise wasn't at school everyday, I only saw her around town doing chores and things. She was always friendly."

"Was anyone from the neighborhood close to her after the tragedy?"

"I believe Anna Patel spent time with her back then. You remember she passed on a few days before Louise. Her daughter, Dana, still lives at the house. Maybe her mom told her about their conversations."

"Did you know a person named Herb Doyle when you taught at the high school?"

Regina thought for a minute. "He wasn't a teacher. Like I said, we all knew each other. Oh, I remember. He was a janitor years ago. He took a job in Chicago, I think, but I'm not sure when."

"Do you think it's possible that he and Louise were having an affair?"

Regina almost fell off her chair. "You're kidding, right? Louise? She was the last of the old-fashioned girls and believed in saving herself for her husband. What would ever make you think that?"

"Something I heard, but you know how people love to share gossip, and how unreliable it can be."

"That I do." Regina stood when Kate and Tracy did. "Thanks again for the tips, Kate. Maybe you can stop by when you're in the neighborhood and let me know how I'm doing."

"I'd be happy to, but won't need anyone to tell you how you're doing. There's a great story my mom told me when I was a kid." Kate saw Tracy check her watch. "A great short story. It's about a little girl playing on the beach. She'd dug a hole in the sand and started bringing buckets of water from the lake to pour in the hole. Every time she returned with another bucket, the water was gone, but she refilled it. Finally, someone sitting nearby asked her what she was trying to do. 'I'm putting the lake in this hole,' she said. 'You won't be able to put the lake in there, honey,' he told her. The little girl didn't answer and brought more buckets of water. A short time later, the stranger told her again that she wouldn't be able to put the lake in the hole. She gave him a puzzled look and finally said, 'I already did put the lake in the hole. You didn't think I meant the whole thing, did you?'"

Kate saw the blank looks on Tracy and Regina's faces and smiled. "When mom first told me that story, I had the same reaction. She explained that people would try to judge and measure my life by their experiences and expectations, but only I could decide whether I failed or succeeded. Only I could know what I set out to achieve and whether or not I achieved it. Keep it simple, Regina, and your garden will do great. You'll know how well you're doing by how good you feel about what you've done."

Jean Sheldon

CHAPTER 16

I like your mom's story." Tracy commented as they drove to Dana Patel's house.

"It's great, isn't it? I only regret that it took so many years to really sink in."

"Consider yourself lucky. For one, your mom shared it, and for two, eventually it did sink in. You're a wise person, Kathleen Chandler."

"It still amazes me when someone wants my guidance, or thinks of me as an expert. You must have people asking for advice all the time."

"I do, but it doesn't amaze me. I'm a wise person with a lifetime of information to share."

"You're an old gossip."

"For your information, I wasn't always a gossip columnist. Before we moved here, Dave and I were political journalists."

"Not a big change, I wouldn't think."

"No, it wasn't a big change, and believe it or not, the gossip I cover today is far less abysmal."

"There's the Patel's driveway. Oh, she has a beautiful blend of bulbs along here." Tracy saw her passenger hang half out the window for a better look at the flowers and slowed as they went up the drive. Before they reached the house, Kate pulled her head in with a question. "Didn't Louise do some investigating into what happened to Jack and Kimberly?"

"Yes. Not right away, but in recent years I remember talking to her a few times and she questioned Dave on an occasion or two. I wonder if she kept notes."

"If she did, and we can find them, they'll make our job a lot easier."

"Tracy, Kate, it's good to see you. How are Raccoon Grove's super sleuths?"

Dana Patel's comment, along with her wiggling eyebrow, prompted a grin from Kate and a reply from Tracy. "You gotta love this town. We're fine, Dana. Can we intrude on a little of your time?"

"Certainly, come on in. How can I help your investigation?" She tossed the dishtowel she'd used to dry her hands to the sink and joined them at the kitchen table while Tracy explained their visit.

"We stopped by to talk to Regina and she told us that your mom spent time with Louise Vandenberg after Jack's death. We wondered if she talked to you about their conversations."

"She did. Right after it happen, Mom said if it weren't for Louise's religious beliefs she would have done something drastic she was in so much pain. I honestly don't know how she lived through those first years, but she did. Then, about five years ago, she decided to find out what happened that night. Mom wasn't sure she'd be able to, but looking into it brought her out of the horrible place she'd been in for so long. Neither of them told me what she discovered, but shortly before she died, mom told me that Louise had her witness a new will. She said she'd found a little peace and hoped to salvage at least one life out of the tragedy. I thought she meant her own, but when I suggested that, mom shook her head."

"A new will? Salvage at least one life? What does that mean?" Tracy wanted answers, not more questions.

"Maybe you can find the notes Louise made. Whenever I saw her, she was writing in notebooks. They looked like diaries actually. According to mom, she kept dozens of them."

"I wonder what she learned and if we can retrace her steps. Do you know if she hung on to the diaries?" Tracy's voice lost its annoyed edge.

"I'm sure she did. Is there some way you can check her things at the house?"

"I'll have to ask the sheriff or her attorney. Did you or your mom hear or see anything odd out here the night of Jack's murder?"

"I was at school and mom was with Louise at a church meeting, but dad was home. I don't know if you remember how desolate it was in this part of town, but if there was a car on the road, you could hear it for miles. Dad said George Williams turned around in our drive about seven thirty. He knew it was George because of that stupid submarine sandwich on top of his truck cab. He didn't know if it meant anything, but thought he should let the sheriff know. When he called, Ben said…."

Tracy held one hand in the air and put the other on her forehead. "We know. The sheriff told him he didn't need any more information."

"Right." Tracy's dramatics didn't faze Dana. "Ben told everyone the same thing. Mom and dad always wondered who called in about the shots, because no one they talked to did or knew who did."

"I always wondered why Louise remained in the house for all those years. I struggled for a few years adjusting to my empty house without a fatal tragedy. It must have been horrible to be constantly reminded of Jack and Kimberly." Kate had considered selling the house after her divorce was final, but didn't want to give up her new garden.

"Louise left things as they were because she wanted to be reminded of them. That helped some, just as the investigation did, but she never recovered completely, although I don't believe she killed herself intentionally."

"Maybe if she did discover what happened, having some kind of closure made her think it was time to join Jack and Kim." Kate said thoughtfully.

"No. She believed she wouldn't see Jack and Kimberly again if she committed suicide."

"Did she tell Anna what happened that night?"

"It took her a while to tell mom what happened after she'd dropped her off, and even then, she could only share it a little at a time." As Dana repeated Louise's description of finding Jack, Kate shuddered and looked out the window to the yard where colorful hummingbirds darted about drawing nectar from an arching daylily. The view and a few deep breaths helped her tune back into Dana's conversation. "Jack's car was in the drive and Louise thought he must have gotten home early from his dinner and sent the babysitter home. She didn't see anyone, but the front door was ajar. When she pushed it, she saw Jack on the floor with a pool of blood under his head. She ran upstairs and found Kimberly's bedroom empty. Sheriff Crayton showed up just as she got back to Jack's body."

"Did your mom stay with her that night?" Tracy asked.

"No. They took Louise to the hospital in Kankakee and kept her overnight. They had to sedate her. The next morning, she remembered that Adam planned to drop Sara off because she and the girls were going to make cookies. She thought they'd taken Sara too, but found out, to her relief, that Adam had an emergency and phoned Jack to tell him they wouldn't be by. The appointment might have saved Sara's life."

Close friends rarely find it necessary to fill the air with polite conversation, especially when the situation calls for reflection. Tracy stopped her car in front of Kate's house and they sat in the same silence they shared on the drive home. Tracy finally spoke. "Besides being heart-wrenching, this is a lot of new information."

"There's a part of me that doesn't want to find the diaries."

"I know what you mean, but I'm more determined than ever to find out what happened that night and Louise's notes are going to tell us. I'll stop by Peter's office tomorrow and see if he'll give us permission to look around."

"Okay. Sara is bringing her doctor to visit the gardens tomorrow morning. I'm sure Dr. Kovecki will be pleased to see how well she's doing. I thought I might ask her what she thinks about Sara meeting Janet Doyle if she turns out to be Kimberly."

"I hadn't thought about that. Okay, you talk to the doctor, I'll talk to the lawyer, and maybe Dave can talk to the Indian Chief."

"Huh?"

"You know that old movie with Betty Hutton, 'Doctor, Lawyer...'. Never mind."

⁂

"Thanks for seeing me, Peter. You're looking good. How's that herd of grandkids?"

"They keep their grandpa hopping, that's for sure. Does your arrival mean I'm being sworn in to help with the investigation?"

"I suppose that depends on what you have to offer. I can't just go deputizing every feisty old resident in Raccoon Grove. You're handling the Vandenberg estate, aren't you?"

"Yes, I'm handling it. That makes me more than just your average feisty old citizen. What do you need, Tracy?"

"Where do things with the estate stand right now? I mean with the arrival of this supposed relative from Chicago. What's his name?"

"His identification all says he's Joseph Vandenberg, but there's a little confusion as to whether or not he's a relative of Jack or his family. I'm also still investigating Louise's will. She hadn't changed the document I have on file that left everything to Kimberly."

That surprised Tracy after what she learned the previous day. "Dana Patel told us that Louise wrote a new will and that her mom witnessed it."

"Louise told me she had, but she didn't bring it in to be filed. That's another good reason to believe her death was accidental. I would have thought she'd take care of business before…, well, before she died. You're positive she'd written the new one?"

"Yes. Dana told us Anna witnessed and signed it."

"She would need two signatures. Do you know if someone else signed it?"

"No, but we'll know that when we find the will."

"I'd say it's time to do that, especially with young Joseph Vandenberg breathing down my neck. He's not a congenial person."

"Has anyone gone through the house?"

"No one that I've authorized. I can empower someone I trust to look through the place to expedite settling the estate. I wonder if I could find a local person to do that."

"Do you trust me?"

"Completely. Let's give the Vandenberg kid a few more days to come up with information to prove his ancestry. If it turns out to be his house, I'd feel a little guilty about letting even you go wandering through the place. If I don't hear from him soon, you can snoop to your heart's content."

"And Kate?"

"Of course." His smile revealed a mouthful of sparkling white teeth, the work of a dentist rather than a deity.

"What about this Joseph Vandenberg? Could he be up to no good?"

"He said his father told him they were related to the Jack Vandenberg family in Raccoon Grove, but he has no evidence I've seen. His father died and his house burned, taking with it proof of his lineage. He's anxious to settle this. He said he's late on his mortgage payments, laden with credit card debts, and they repossessed his…." Peter stopped mid sentence and whacked his desk, scattering the stack of papers in front of him and sending Tracy back in her chair. "Sorry about that. I just realized I can find out if that's true by checking with the credit bureau."

"That's a good idea. It won't prove he's not related, but it will prove if he's lying. Will you let me know what you find?"

"I'll call for the information right away and we should know before the end of the day. Boy, your detecting skills must be rubbing off on me."

"Here's another mystery to practice on, and it might also affect your client's property. Kate and I met a woman in Chicago who could possibly be Kimberly Vandenberg."

"What? She shows up after twenty years and only when everyone who can identify her is dead. Sounds a little suspect to me. Did she contact you?"

"I'm not completely sure. We received a letter from a supposed friend of hers after I ran the story on Jack's murder. Janet Doyle, the woman in question, denied she'd ever lived outside of Chicago. Even with her lack of cooperation, a number of things point to it being possible."

"Boy. How about that. A decades old mystery gets even more mysterious. Joseph Vandenberg won't be happy if this woman turns out to be Kimberly. Tracy, I'm confident if anyone can solve it, you can."

"Thanks Peter. I'll talk to you soon." Tracy waved on her way out, but she didn't take time to savor his compliment. Her thoughts were on her next appointment at the salon, where they were going to hide the color that hid the gray. "Do I want to do this? Yes, I do, don't I? No, I don't. Yes, I do."

Jean Sheldon

CHAPTER 17

Two people entered the yard as Kate left the greenhouse. One she recognized as Sara, who shouted an introduction while she latched the gate. "This is Doctor Kovecki."

Kate barely had time to remove her gloves before Sara's doctor hurried across the yard, grasped her free hand, and introduced herself. "Please, call me Carolyn. I'm delighted to meet you." She and Sara were about the same height, a good half foot shorter than Kate's five feet ten inches. She wore a dark blue pantsuit, the tailored jacket covering a crisply ironed white blouse that almost glowed in the bright morning sun. Thick waves of pale blond hair hung to her shoulders in a youthful cut, but carefully applied makeup made her age difficult to estimate. Kate guessed her at around forty, and after the enthusiastic handshake and broad warm smile, liked her at once.

"It's nice to meet you, Carolyn."

"Sara tells me you are teaching her gardening and flower arranging. She's delighted to have a chance to work with you, and from everything I've heard, she should be." She took in the surrounding menagerie of color. "Thank you for sharing your beautiful gardens."

"I'm glad you could come. I'm proud of them, and of Sara's work."

Sara heard the comment and blushed as she approached. "Why don't you show her around, Kate? I just remembered something I have to finish in the greenhouse."

Sara didn't have any work in the greenhouse, but since showing off the gardens delighted Kate, she didn't argue. After the tour, she brought out a carafe of coffee and she and Carolyn sat in the gazebo. "I'm pleased by how well Sara's doing. Ten years ago, most people in Raccoon Grove believed she'd spend the rest of her life needing special care."

"I didn't know her then, but when we met four years ago, I leaned in that direction. Even then, a light in her eyes gave me hope. The difficulty is that somewhere in her psyche is terrifying information. Her struggle was, and is, to find the missing pieces and deal with them. Has she ever talked about it with you?"

"Until she came to work for me, we'd only chatted at the library on occasion. Is there anything I can do to help? Maybe give you some insight into the Raccoon Grove of twenty years ago. If she's thought of something about the town or people and can't remember, I could supply the missing details."

"I can't think of anything off hand, but it's nice to know you are there to help if something comes up. She really is happy working with the flowers, isn't she?"

"I'm no doubt prejudiced, but it's the best therapy I can think of, besides yours, of course."

"Let's hope they both help, but if it turns out to be the flowers, I'll still take some of the credit. I'm glad to have had a chance to see the place Sara finds so fulfilling. It's hard for her not to know how everything fell apart. She has said a few times that she believes Kimberly Vandenberg's disappearance somehow holds the key."

"I can't imagine how they're connected, but that reminds me of something else I wanted to bring up. We've been in contact with a woman in Chicago who might be Kimberly. We're not sure yet, but if that proves true, would it be dangerous for she and Sara to meet?"

The news of Kimberly's possible resurrection widened Carolyn's pale blue eyes. "After all this time, Kimberly resurfaces. Does anyone know why?"

Kate explained the Gazette's anniversary story and the death of Louise Vandenberg. Sara had told Carolyn about Louise, and mentioned the article in the paper. "I suppose there's a chance she's Kimberly and only beginning to remember what happened."

"You don't sound convinced, Kate."

"I'm skeptical, but this woman, Janet Doyle, showed us a ring that Kimberly wore as a child, and the story about her father seems credible. If it turns out that she is Kimberly, it will be quite a shock."

"I can see how it would be, to everyone. Have you told Sara about Ms Doyle?"

"I haven't said anything specific about Janet, but she knows that Tracy Kendall and I are investigating Jack Vandenberg's death. She didn't appear bothered."

Carolyn leaned back to consider the information. "I would like to be there when and if Sara and this person meet. She should have all the support we can give her."

※

Hi, Dave, how's the hardest working publisher in Raccoon Grove?" Tracy gave him a kiss before sinking into the guest chair. "Big news day?"

His eyes stayed focused on the computer screen. "Hardly, although, your phone has been ringing off the hook. What kind of trouble have you been scaring up?" When he turned and saw her newly colored hair, he jumped to his feet and hurried around the desk. "Tracy, it looks sensational."

"This is where you say I don't look a day older. Better yet, tell me I look younger."

"You look terrific. How do you like it?"

She opened her mouth to answer, but held her words as Dave spoke to someone in the doorway. "Hello. Can I help you?"

When Tracy saw who it was, she stood and pushed him aside. "Janet, what are you doing here? I thought you were coming tomorrow or Friday." Janet stared blankly until Tracy remembered why. "It's me, Tracy Kendall. I stopped coloring my hair." She wondered why she felt the need to explain her actions to a complete stranger.

"I'm sorry to drop in unexpectedly. I know we hadn't planned to meet until later in the week, Mrs. Kendall, but I've been remembering things. I hoped that seeing the town would help."

"It's not a problem." Tracy nodded toward Dave. "This gorgeous hunk is my husband, Dave Kendall, editor and publisher of the Raccoon Grove Gazette. Dave, this is Janet Doyle, the woman I told you about."

Dave shook her hand. "Has being in town helped you remember anything?"

"I don't know what I've remembered. When I drove down the main street, it felt familiar, but things are a blur and I'm more confused than ever. Can I see the house where this Kimberly Vandenberg lived?"

"You can't see the inside just yet, but if you'd care to see the town, I can give you the ten cent tour." Tracy picked up her purse and waved to Dave before hooking Janet's arm. "I'll show you parts of town that haven't changed much over the years, and we'll see if they look familiar. Dave, could you let Kate know I won't be there right away."

Dave caught Tracy's wink and when they walked out, he dialed Kate's number. "Hi, Kate, is Sara with you?"

"Yes, is something wrong?"

"No, but Janet Doyle just showed up. Tracy wanted me to let you know."

"What's she doing here? I thought she was coming Thursday or Friday."

"That's what Tracy said. We'll keep you posted."

"Would you like to stop for coffee before we begin the tour?" Tracy pointed across the street to Mike's diner.

"No, thanks. Quite honestly, I'm anxious to understand what's going on."

Janet's sudden arrival meant Tracy hadn't had time to organize her numerous questions. As she pulled onto the street, she realized that might be for the best. Janet was either very stressed or good at acting stressed. It made sense to get to know her a little better. "I can understand that. How was your drive?"

"It's one continuous rush hour these days. Traffic didn't lighten up until I passed Lincoln Highway. Of course, by then, I was nearly here. Can we drive to the Vandenberg's house, Mrs. Kendall?"

"Sure. Please call me Tracy. I haven't quite adjusted to this gray hair. Prepare yourself for these things, Janet, or suddenly, without warning, they happen."

"You mean going gray?"

"I mean being sixty-four when you're sure you were forty on your last birthday."

Janet showed little interest in Tracy's advice on aging and asked about something completely unrelated. "From what I understand, if I am Kimberly Vandenberg, then Herb Doyle wasn't my father. More than that, he may have kidnapped me and killed my father. Is that true?"

"We don't really know anything at this point, but it's possible that if you're Kimberly, you were kidnapped as a child."

"My father wouldn't have done those things. He was a good man." Janet watched out the window as they drove. Suddenly, she pointed and yelled, "That's it. That's the house."

Tracy pulled over and turned off the engine. "You're right. That's it. Do you want to get out and look around? Better yet, we could go up the drive. I don't think Louise's attorney would have a problem with that."

"Yes, maybe it would be good if we went in a little ways." She turned to Tracy. "This is too weird. Why do I know this? How could I be this Kimberly person and not know? My father wouldn't have hurt anyone." Losing her struggle to remain calm, Janet's voice grew louder and more frightened with each word. She was shouting when she turned back to the house.

"Before we go up the drive, Janet, take a few deep breaths and try to relax a little if you can." As Tracy reached for the ignition, she heard a sharp loud noise, followed immediately by the explosion of a thousand tiny pieces of glass behind her. "Get down." She screamed and pulled Janet to the seat.

CHAPTER 18

Our perception of time changes dramatically in a crisis. A brief event becomes interminable as heightened senses capture each passing moment in vivid detail. We see, hear, feel, smell, and even taste, every morsel of stimuli we might not normally notice. That makes the experience vivid beyond comprehension. It is for our own safety that we don't perceive our daily lives with such awareness. Walking out the front door would quickly cause a sensory overload.

They heard only one shot, but Tracy continued to shield her passenger. She moved her hand slowly along the seat and felt glass everywhere. "Stay there, Janet. Don't move." She had no idea how long they embraced the upholstery, but a siren announced an arriving squad car and seconds later, she recognized the sheriff's voice.

"Tracy. Are you okay?" She unwound her body to sit up and helped the young woman do the same. "Tracy," Scott called again and when she turned, his jaw dropped. "Oh, my god, your hair turned gray."

Despite their situation, and her increasingly cranky mood, Tracy smiled. "I had it done earlier. Who shot at my car?"

"Hard to say exactly, but I'd guess it came from the Vandenberg property. That's the only place they'd have that clear of a shot."

"From the amount of glass in here I thought they shot out all the windows." She looked around. "Just the rear passenger's side, but it's all over the place."

"The side windows are made of tempered glass. They design them to explode into a bunch of tiny pieces so they won't cause any serious damage...."

Tracy held up her hand to stop the lesson on auto glass. "Thanks, Scott."

"Who's with you?" He leaned in. "Is she the lady who might be Kimberly?"

Tracy saw Janet's surprise and explained. "It's a small town. Let's head back to the paper."

"I'll give you a ride and have your car towed." Scott backed up and held Tracy's door. "There's glass all over the place and it'd be a little breezy with that missing window."

"Good point. I wouldn't want to mess up my new do, but I have a better idea. Drop us off at my house and I'll pick up Dave's car. Otherwise we'll have to call you for another ride when we finish at the paper tonight."

"No problem either way. I was thinking about adding magnetic signs to the squad cars, Raccoon Grove Sheriff's Department and Taxi Service." The squad car was one of only three owned by the department and shared by the sheriff and five deputies

"Come on. Janet. We'll ride with the local sheriff slash cabbie."

Tracy turned off the alarm as she entered the garage and lowered herself into Dave's BMW, pushing the garage door opener clipped to the visor. Once outside, she used the remote to reset the alarm as Janet climbed into the passenger's seat.

"Nice car," she admired the leather upholstery and wood accents.

"It's one of Dave's many toys, but one of his favorites. I can't be too critical. I have plenty of my own. How are you doing?" Tracy asked as they drove back to the paper.

"I've done enough sightseeing in Raccoon Grove for today. I want to go home and crawl under the covers for a few days. I'll call you when I come out."

"That might be a good idea. I'm considering doing the same thing. Will you be able to drive?"

"Yes. Pray there aren't any snipers on the overpasses. I should be fine."

Dave stood at the top of the stairs when Tracy entered the building. She'd called on the way to the office to let him know that she was okay and would explain their adventure after she dropped Janet off at her car. "What happened? I heard there were shots fired out by the creek."

"One shot. I took Janet to the Vandenberg house, which, by the way, she identified without prompting. We were about to pull in the drive when a bullet shattered the side window. I don't think it was a confused hunter, though lord knows we have enough of them." She raised a few strands of hair and chuckled. "Scott thought it turned me gray, and Janet scrambled into her car to drive back to the safety of Chicago. It might not be a good idea to show people around our quiet little community."

"Tracy. I heard someone shot at your car." Kate ran up the stairs to give her a hug and stopped to stare. "Did the shots turn your hair gray?"

"No, I had it done earlier, but if people keep reacting that way I'm going to put an announcement in the paper. Janet identified the Vandenberg house and I pulled over to let her look. That's when someone shot at the car."

"This has gone way beyond someone suggesting you stop the investigation."

"Yes, it has, Dave. Should we stop?"

"Since you're not really asking, I'll go on to the next logical question. How do we intend to find out who wants you to stop?"

"We should talk to our angry ex-husbands again." She looked at Dave. "Dana told us her dad saw George Williams turn around in her driveway around seven thirty the night Jack was shot. We should talk to him first."

"And you want to bring along a little extra muscle?"

"Not just muscle, David, but calm, cool and damn good-looking muscle."

"God, I'm so cheap."

With his wife on one arm and Kate the other, the threesome entered George's sandwich shop and stood a few feet back from the counter where he worked. It took him a few minutes to realize they were there. "I told you, I have nothing to say to you. What happened to your hair?" He stared at Tracy.

"I'm making a fashion statement. We want to talk to you, George."

He peeled off his gloves and tossed them to the back counter. "Don't tell me they've dragged you into this, Dave. I'd have thought you had enough sense to leave things alone."

"George, why don't we find a private place to talk?" Dave folded his arms and looked every bit of the calm, cool, and muscular character Tracy required. "I'm guessing this isn't a conversation you want to have out here."

The shop grew quiet as customers became more interested in the dialogue than their sandwiches. George grudgingly led the group to the back room but didn't offer them chairs.

They stood in a circle in the middle of a great deal of disarray. A quick glance at her surroundings convinced Kate that she would never eat another sandwich from George's store, and she blanched slightly remembering the ones she'd had in the past.

Tracy ignored the filthy sinks and opened packages of food, many of which were marked 'perishable'. She was there to interrogate. "George, you were seen around Jack's house close to the time of his death. What were you doing out there?"

"Who told you that?" He jumped in Tracy's face, prompting Dave to slide between them until he backed away.

"You were seen turning around in the Patel drive at around seven thirty the night Jack was killed."

Tracy's unwavering glare seemed to spark a memory in George's brain. "Oh, yeah, that's right. I went to pick up supplies in Kankakee and when I got out by Patel's place I remembered I didn't have the list and had to go back to the store."

"You were on your way to Kankakee to get supplies at seven o'clock on a Friday night?" At his surly nod, Kate pointed at his boots and asked another question. "Are those Red Wing boots, George?"

The question caught him off guard. "My boots? Yeah, they're Red Wings. What about them?"

"Mind if I look at the soles?"

"As a matter of fact, I do mind. Look, I answered your question. I went for supplies. I have a business to run here. Why don't you leave me alone?"

Kate not only wasn't buying his food anymore, she also wasn't buying his story. "George, I may be a gray-haired old gardener, but I spent enough years in the beauty pageant circuit to develop an amazingly accurate bullshit detector. What were you doing out by Jack's that night?"

After surveying their faces, George dropped in the chair behind an overflowing desk, studied the floor and pushed his hands through his hair. "I was coming home from Kankakee, but I didn't go for supplies. I stopped for a few beers with a friend."

"You were supposed to be at the card game." Kate remembered the list of players.

"I didn't want to play cards. I wanted to drink. Anyway, I was heading home when Jack passed me on his way to his place. I'd been trying to talk to him alone for days, but there were always other people around when I saw him. I slammed on the brakes, turned around in Patel's driveway, and chased him down. When I flashed my lights, he pulled over and walked back to my truck."

"What did you want to talk to him about that you needed to do in private?" Dave asked.

They waited as George took a deep breath before answering. "I wanted him to tell Linda I couldn't pay her as much alimony as she wanted and I didn't want everyone in town to know my business. I'd hocked everything to open the store. I told him it would only take a year or so and then I could pay her more."

"What did he say?" Kate asked.

"He said I should talk to Linda. I should tell her the situation because she wanted to be fair and he only represented her interests." The confession drained his remaining energy and George slumped further to mumble the rest of his answer. "I accused him of messing around with Linda and he laughed and told me to grow up. When he turned to go, I grabbed his shoulder and spun him around to take a swing. I must have had more to drink than I thought because I missed and ended up on the ground. By the time I made it back to my feet, he was driving away."

"Did you follow him?"

George shook his head. "No, Dave. I'd made a big enough ass of myself. I didn't need to do anything else stupid. I went home and went to bed." He stood. "I may be a jerk sometimes, but I'm not a killer and you guys know that."

"Do you own a rifle, George?" Tracy knew he did.

"Of course I do. Who in Raccoon Grove doesn't own a rifle? I didn't take pot shots at you earlier, if that's why you're asking. I've been here at work, and a half a dozen people can vouch for me."

"Did you destroy my gardens?" He shook his head again, but didn't look at Kate. "Here's my last question, George. What did you do to your hand?" She pointed at gauze wrapped around the palm of his right hand.

He stared at the bandage as if he didn't know it was there. "I must have cut myself doing something around here. I do that a lot."

Kate shivered at another good reason for swearing off subs.

"Can we hear your thoughts, oh mighty bullshit detector?" Tracy asked Kate as they walked back to the paper.

"I don't believe George killed Jack, but I do think he trashed my gardens and cut his hands on the rose thorns. What I can't understand is why. Even if he wanted to stop us from investigating, stomping on my flowers is a weird way to go about it. By the way, I'm not eating in or carrying out from that restaurant ever again."

"I know." Dave shuddered. "Every time I saw something move, I forced myself not to look. I was afraid I'd see a rat."

Tracy had been following the conversation up until the last exchange. Her ability to focus sometimes rendered her oblivious to events beyond the object of her attention. "Was it bad?"

CHAPTER 19

In a garden, especially one as magnificent as Kate's, the visual impact of the flowers can depend on the space provided for viewing. Just as impressionist painters represent a scene by revealing not the color of objects, but the effect of light on those colors, a carefully planned viewing space allows visitors to absorb the range of shades and fragrances as the artist intended. The following morning, Tracy joined Kate in the gardens' focal point, her fourteen-foot Jefferson gazebo.

Along with her reputation as a master gardener, Kate enjoyed a measure of notoriety for her rich dark coffee. She and Tracy shared a cup as Tracy revealed her latest news. "Peter wasn't able to find anything on Joe Vandenberg. I mean he wasn't able to find any evidence that the Joe Vandenberg he spoke to lives in Chicago."

"What does that mean?"

"It means he could be a phony. Peter is looking into it. It might be just that he never changed from his California address, but he's beginning to smell a rat. He also said, until he sees more evidence in her favor, Janet Doyle doesn't have a viable interest in the settlement of the estate. That makes sense. Anyway, he said we can check the house if we want."

"Great. When can we get the key?"

Tracy pulled a set of keys from her pants pocket and jingled them in the air. "Are you ready?"

"I'll let Sara know."

"I think someone messed with this lock. There are nicks in the metal and I'm having a hard time with the key." Tracy's persistence paid off. The tumblers aligned and she pushed the door into the darkened hallway.

Closed since Louise's death, the house felt dank, and both women found the stuffy environment depressing, but Tracy was, as usual, the first to take action. Kate quickly joined her drawing curtains and opening windows. Surrounded by large old trees, the house cooled considerably once air moved through. They went to work. "What are we looking for?" The unpleasantness of the task slightly overwhelmed Kate as she scanned the rooms.

"That's a good question, my fellow sleuth. Since it doesn't make sense to reinvent the wheel, we should find out what Louise discovered and how she discovered it. I'm guessing that will be in her diaries, so the first thing would be to look for those. I told Peter we'd also keep our eyes open for the new will. Do you want to split up, or search the floors together?"

"Let's stay together, Tracy. It's a little creepy being here. We should start upstairs. That way if we're worn out after one floor, we only have to crawl down."

"You're a born detective."

"I'm an old detective."

Tracy turned to the staircase, but stopped when she noticed a wall of photographs. "Look at these. Here's one of Louise with Kimberly and Sara dressed in their Sunday best. Look at all those flowers. I wonder where they were."

"Probably in the yard. Louise kept a beautiful garden before everything happened. Oh, look at this one of Kimberly, Louise, and Jack. They look so happy." Kimberly had her father's brown hair and eyes, while Louise stood out from the group with her red curls and fair complexion. "This picture was taken shortly before Jack's death."

"Kate, can you tell if Janet Doyle is Kimberly?"

"No." She sighed. "I can't tell from this. They were a happy-looking family, weren't they? Looking at these photos I'd say there's not much doubt that Jack is Kimberly's father."

"I agree. If Herb Doyle kidnapped her, it wasn't because she was his child."

A thick runner on the oak staircase muffled their climb to the second floor. Kate thought she had prepared herself for any emotional response the house might arouse, but she entered Kimberly's room and gasped. It was, as Dana had described, unchanged. "I can't imagine how Louise suffered. I'm sure she left things this way hoping Kim would come home. How sad." After a final involuntary shiver, Kate lifted the lid on the music box and awakened the sleeping ballerina.

Tracy, who was kneeling in the closet to examine boxes and bins, heard the unexpected refrains of the theme from *Romeo and Juliet* and called over her shoulder. "Did you find anything in the drawers?"

"I haven't looked yet." Kate replied as she sat on the bed. Determined to maintain her composure, she opened the top drawer of the small dresser and withdrew a bundle of letters, untying the pink ribbon that secured them. "Tracy, these are notes written to Kimberly and they're signed Cousin Joe Vandenberg."

"What's the postmark?"

Jean Sheldon

"There aren't any envelopes that I can see, just letters. Didn't Peter say Joe Vandenberg claimed that he used to write to Kimberly?"

"He did. That's a point in his favor. We can't take anything out of the house, but let's remember to tell Peter about them. It would be an amazing coincidence if another Cousin Joe wrote to Kimberly."

"That's true." She scanned a few of the sheets and looked puzzled. "There's something wrong with these. A five or six-year-old couldn't have written them. Maybe Kimberly's Cousin Joe is a few years older. Do you know how old Joseph Vandenberg is?"

"No. Put them back in the drawer and we'll let Peter figure it out." Tracy backed out of the closet on her hands and knees. "We won't find anything in here, Kate. We need to go to Louise's bedroom and check for the diaries. If there not there we can try the office downstairs." As she climbed to her feet, Tracy pointed back to the closet. "Someone's been through here. They left the boxes uncovered and tossed things around. Louise wouldn't have done that. What would Kimberly have had that anyone wanted?"

"If it was a burglar, they were looking for anything valuable. I'm not sure what they'd expect to find in a child's bedroom." As they left the bedroom and walked down the hall, Tracy stopped to straighten a crooked picture while Kate went to an open door at the end of the hall. "I wonder if that's another room or a linen closet." She found her answer when she peeked in and saw the open trap door. "Oh, these stairs go to the attic. One of us should check it out."

"How much did you pay for your jeans?"

Kate wasn't sure she saw the point, but gave the question some thought before she answered. "Around thirty dollars, I guess. Why?"

The point, which Tracy attempted to clarify by waving at her pantsuit and rolling her eyes, was money. "This suit cost four hundred and fifty dollars, plus alterations. And don't get me started on why women pay extra when men get them free." Most *Tidbits* readers knew Tracy's views on the inequities of life. Kate averted her eyes and climbed the ladder before her friend saw anything she could mistake as interest on her face.

Two small windows supplied enough light to identify various objects. "I see dust and spider webs covering some boxes and trunks." She relayed her observations and made a cautious descent, refraining from further conversation until she stepped off the stairs, brushed her hands together, and pointed back to the hole. "Someone was up there, but they didn't go any farther than I did. There was a handprint next to the opening. As far as I can tell, the current inhabitants are squirrels. Whoever has been nosing around must have left this open."

"That doesn't mean we should." Tracy unhooked the cord and released it, letting the springs slap the overhead door closed.

Kate left Tracy to do her good deed and entered Louise's bedroom. She caught sight of a shelf lined with books. There were no markings on the spines so she removed one and flipped through the pages. "Tracy, come here and look at these."

"What are they?"

"Louise's diaries."

"Dana was right. There are dozens." Kate took a few books and sat on the bed to examine them, but after reading only a few pages, gave up. "I can't read this. It's her private pain. I'm sure she didn't intend to share it with others."

Tracy joined her with a diary she'd pulled from the other end of the shelf. "There's something in these. Maybe we'll find more about the investigation in the later ones. The answers are here. I'm sure of it." She opened the one in her hand and read. "*December 14. Ben is the key. He told everyone he didn't need their evidence, and yet he told me he had none.* She thought Ben knew. See Kate, the answers have to be here." Tracy dropped the book to her lap and scanned the shelf. "Since we can't take anything, we'll have to make a few trips to read them all. Can you handle it? If not, I can give it a shot."

"If it means we'll find out what happened, I can do it. They appear to be in the order she wrote them. I agree the later ones will probably have more answers. I'll check the dates and next time we come, we can figure out where to start."

"It's a little discouraging that she thought Ben knew everything and we can't ask him."

"Even without Ben, I think you're right about these, Tracy. Her diaries will tell us. Should we look for the will?"

"I can't. I left Dave with his hands full. Normally I'm okay with that, but for some reason, today I'm feeling a tad guilty."

Kate checked the first date in every book to make sure they were in order. "The earliest is June 2006, that was her first one. I don't see any for the last few months, but by the dust, or lack of dust on the shelf, four or five were removed."

"Whoever broke in could have taken them. If those were the last ones she wrote, they could have the solution. Maybe Jack's killer knew about Louise's investigation and took them after her death." Tracy sighed. "Let's hope we can get them back, or the mystery may go unsolved for another twenty years. When we come back, let's search the house from top to bottom. If

Louise solved the case in those last books, she might have put them in a safe place."

※

"Did you find anything interesting?" Dave smiled as his wife sat in front of his desk.

"Yes. We found Louise's diaries. They look promising. One said that Ben was the key, or at least Louise thought so. We'll go through them a little at a time and see what else we find. We also discovered that someone's been looking around the house and Pete said no one should have been in there. How did your day go?"

"It was fairly productive, and I even had a little extra time to do some sleuthing of my own."

"And what, my dear Sherlock, did you uncover?"

"I phoned a number of teachers who worked at the high school at the same time as Herb and Louise. They all agreed there was no way Herb Doyle and Louise Vandenberg had an affair. Not only because of Louise's ideas about marriage, but popular opinion holds that Herb was a quiet, down-to-earth person who kept to himself."

"Don't they say you have to watch the quiet ones?"

"I'm quiet."

"That's why I watch you every minute of every day."

"Would that were so, my sweet. Anyway, no one ever remembered seeing them together and two of the teachers vaguely remembered that Herb lived in a trailer out near the Forest Preserves with his girlfriend."

"If that's true, there would have been gossip and I might have information in my files. We were new here back then, but the rumor mill ran seamlessly. Regina said the same thing about our love affair theory involving Herb and Louise, it didn't happen. Didn't you say you were going to ask your old friend Armando at the Trib what he could find out about Doyle?"

"Yes, I did, but I haven't heard from him. I'll give him a call."

"I'll be in my office unburying my desk. Can you do without me?"

"Only for a short time, dear one."

"Gooey. You are so gooey."

❧

"What the hell were you thinking? How is shooting at Tracy Kendall going to help you find a way to prove you're part of the Vandenberg family?"

"Hey, lighten up. I stopped at the bar and heard a couple guys bitching about her sticking her nose into some business that she shouldn't. Two of them were pretty pissed and didn't care who knew it. I figured she'd think they took a pot shot at her. I just wanted to scare her. Slow her down to give me time to figure stuff out." Joe eyed the ceiling and switched the phone to his other hand. "I'm a good shot and no one got hurt. What's funny is when I went to the diner people were talking about some terrorists out in the woods. I could barely keep from laughing."

"If you'd hit Tracy Kendall, you wouldn't be laughing."

"She wasn't hurt and it didn't even slow her down. I saw her and another lady at the house today. I don't know what they were doing, or who told them they could go in. Maybe they're writing a story about my inheritance for the paper. I should let her interview me."

"You should keep your mouth shut and worry about making sure you get that inheritance."

"I'll go back and find the diaries I dropped, but I have to be careful. There's getting to be a lot of traffic in the area, day and night." Joe ended the call, put the phone on the table, and leaned on the headboard behind him. He'd taken a room at the cheapest motel he could find. It was close, but not too close, to Raccoon Grove. "If those diaries belonged to Louise Vandenberg, they might talk about private family stuff that I could use to prove I'm related. Between them and the letters I stashed, that should be enough to convince the attorney. If it ain't, we'll have to switch to plan B." Joe looked up when someone knocked on his door. "Go away. The room don't need cleaning." A large, angry man ignored Joe and opened the door without touching the knob. Another much smaller man with a gun followed.

"Hello, Joe."

CHAPTER 20

Kate and Sara's hard work paid off. The gardens recovered from their recent abuse and were their colorful thriving selves. Tracy and Kate leaned back in the two deck chairs with their coffee. "Where's Sara?"

"She took her mom for a treatment. I'm so used to having her here I get lonely when she's not."

"That's nice, isn't it?"

"Very nice." Normally, it was Tracy who jumped from topic to topic at a blinding speed, but recent events left Kate with numerous questions. "Tracy, if Janet Doyle isn't Kimberly, how could she know the things she does, and where did she come up with the ring?"

"Maybe someone here in town gave her the information. They could have supplied pictures of the house, or maybe she's been out here before. Kate, the house has been empty since Louise died, but we know someone was inside. Maybe Janet broke in and took the ring."

"What about Herb? With what she told us, her story about him could be true."

"All the information isn't in on Herb, but you're right, it is compelling evidence. Who in town could she be working with?" Tracy interrupted herself for a sip of coffee. "She hasn't mentioned the inheritance, but that could be intentional. She knows there is no other family and that Joe Vandenberg hopes to inherit the estate. If she's not Kimberly, she could be waiting to see what happens and trying to learn as much as she can about the Vandenberg family."

"I suppose. What does Dave think?"

"He finds it hard to believe she's Kimberly, but not impossible. He did make one interesting point. When we were driving by the house, Kimberly identified it from a good distance. It's supposedly been twenty years since she's seen it, and she was five at the time."

For a moment, Kate didn't see anything interesting. "Oh, I get it. How would she have recognized the house? The trees and everything else have twenty years growth and the house is almost invisible. Twenty years ago, you could see some of the house from the road. Is that what he found interesting? I suppose she could have sensed the area was familiar."

"He doesn't think she would have recognized the place if she hadn't seen it recently. By the way, he talked to the rest of the teachers from the high school. They said the same thing Regina said. There was no way Louise Vandenberg and Herb Doyle had an affair."

"That was speculation anyway, but he still could have kidnapped her. Remember he left town at the same time she disappeared."

"That's something Dave asked his friend, Armando, to investigate. He's going to check with the Chicago Board of Education and see when and if Herb Doyle worked for them. Dave said he'd call and remind him. He also said many of the teachers he talked to couldn't imagine Herb as a kidnapper. Two of them remembered that he might have lived with his girlfriend. If that's true, I could have information in my old files."

"Why do you have time to visit me and my flowers? You said yesterday you had a ton of work to catch up on, and a husband to appease."

"I still have a ton of work to catch up on, but the paper came out this morning and I'm supposed to rest for a few days. It doesn't always work out that way. Dave and I, and our beloved press operator and his assistant, stayed until about three this morning. That's the newspaper game and I love it."

"Are you still getting letters from disgruntled readers?"

"Yes, and they're still anonymous, which I find extremely frustrating, especially since I've stopped mentioning anything about the case. They could have the decency to sign their names. If you have something to say to me, say it."

Kate knew a number of people in town who wouldn't confront Tracy, no matter what the topic. "No one I talk to has written and most people say they're glad we're looking into it after all these years. They agree with Harriet that the sheriff did a lousy job."

"It may be only one person with something to hide. Scott doesn't think the letters warrant an investigation by the sheriff's department. Of course, Scott doesn't think most of my complaints warrant an investigation by the sheriff's department."

"He's wrong this time. The letters are a form of harassment and someone shot at you. That should be investigated."

"He is investigating the shooting, but the letters were addressed to the newspaper, and that's considered fair game. At least that's what Scott thinks, and don't tell him I said this, but he's right. You couldn't possibly investigate every nasty letter that a newspaper receives, even one as small as the Gazette."

Kate took a closer look at her guest. "I like the gray. Have you accepted your natural look yet?"

"I'd better learn to soon. I almost have a heart attack every time I walk in front of a mirror. I'll adjust I'm sure, and I'll be glad not to have to color it every few weeks. I'm not surrendering to old age yet, but I will concede to some of the inevitable changes."

"When should we go back to the Vandenberg house?"

"How does Monday sound?"

"Like I'd better enjoy my weekend."

※

Sara pushed Elaine's chair down the ramp to the yard and sat on a lawn chair beside her. "Well, Mom, do you approve?"

"You've done a beautiful job. Kate's as good a teacher as she is a gardener, and you're a good student." She squeezed her daughter's hand. "I'm proud of you, and delighted you want to do this."

"I'm having fun."

"I'm glad." Elaine could see that Sara had something to say and she suspected what would be forthcoming.

"Mom, tell me about what happened back then. You weren't here when Mr. Vandenberg died and Kimberly disappeared, but you must have heard things. Even I know how bad gossip is in this town."

Elaine pushed the curls off Sara's her forehead and looked in her eyes. "As thrilled as I am to see your work out here, Sara, I'm even more thrilled to see life in your eyes again. You've been in the shadows far too long. You are ready to hear about it, aren't you?" She gave her hand another squeeze. "People didn't want to talk about it, back then, because they were afraid I suppose. There were no fingerprints on the gun, not even Jack's, so they knew he hadn't killed himself. As far as what happened to Kimberly, no one knows. She vanished. Poor

Louise nearly lost her mind. Nothing could console her. Our lives changed after that. Louise and I were friends, but not as close as your dad and Jack. He was your dad's best friend, and Kimberly yours. After Jack died, he poured himself into his work, but you didn't have work and were still a child. It was harder for you. I wish I'd been here for you that night, Sara." Tears filled Elaine's eyes.

"You've always been there for me, Mom. Please don't blame yourself. Did Daddy ever talk about it with you?"

Elaine's shrug was more an unconscious reaction than an answer. She sorted through explanations that she had considered over the last two decades. How could she explain something she didn't understand? "When Kimberly disappeared, your dad feared something would happen to you. He didn't tell me what made him afraid, only that he wanted to make sure you were safe. He was never one to talk about his feelings, but I believe he blamed himself because he went on a call and left you to watch a frightening movie."

"I can't remember the movie. Sometimes I think it was about a little girl riding in a car, but as hard as I try, I can't remember. Doctor Kovecki says I shouldn't worry about remembering for right now. I should focus on staying strong. She's happy I'm working with Kate in her gardens, and so is Kate."

"I'm sure she is. I like Dr. Kovecki, Sara, and I agree you shouldn't strain to remember. If the memories need to return, they will. I want you to be happy. You deserve that, child." She smiled. "Tracy Kendall called and told me you doubled up in laughter when Dave poured plaster over her. I wish I could have seen that. I mean both your laughter and Tracy covered in powder."

"I wish you could have too, Mom. She looked hysterical, and very unhappy."

At Raccoon Grove's local watering hole, The Boar's Head Inn, conversations rarely included world events. If there wasn't a ball game on television, the jukebox offered a wide range of tunes—from Waylon Jennings' *Honky Tonk Heroes* to Lynyrd Skynyrd's *Free Bird*. A customer unhappy with a particular selection simply gave the old Wurlitzer a shove until the record rejected. After 1980, no one bothered to replace the records and most Grovers liked it that way. Tavern regulars paid less attention to headlines and world events than to local gossip and lottery tickets that might change their destiny. The Boar's Head had yet to claim a big winner.

Harold entered and tipped his head as he sat at the bar. Mad Dog, sitting two stools down, nursed a soda in the otherwise empty inn. "I don't see you in here much these days, Mad Dog. Don't tell me the new wife is keeping the reins tight."

"How ya' doing, Hal? No, Terry doesn't care if I go out. I just like spending time with her and I like being sober. Well, that's not exactly right. I like not having hangovers and a continual pain in my gut. How are things at the shop?"

"Not bad. I have a hell of a time keeping up with the equipment to work on these new cars. They're nothing more than a computer on wheels and I can hardly find mechanics who know what to do with them. What I wouldn't give to manually adjust the air intake on a carburetor."

"I'll bring my '65 Chevy pickup in, and let you take a walk down memory lane."

Harold chuckled and took a ten from his wallet. "Let me have a draft." He turned to Mad Dog. "Has Tracy Kendall been asking you about Jack's murder?"

"Yeah, she and Kate came by a few days ago. Of course, I didn't remember much, but they were as surprised as I was that Crayton didn't bring me in for questioning. You remember what a wreck I was. Did they talk to you?"

"I don't remember your behavior being any worse than mine, but since I was usually wrecked myself, that ain't saying much." Harold emptied half the glass before he continued. "I don't know why Tracy can't leave things alone. Doc Collins isn't pleased. He's afraid it will be hard on Sara."

"To tell you the truth, Harold, and I'm not trying to be a hard ass, but I don't understand how Sara got so screwed up after Jack's murder. Kimberly and her were friends, but they were only five years old. They couldn't have known each other for more than a year or so." Mad Dog twisted the gray hairs on his mustache in a thoughtful pose. "I don't know. It's weird."

"What I thought was weird back then was how so many of the unmarried chicks split and how most of our wives suddenly decided they wanted a divorce. How come they all chose Jack as their attorney?"

"I said that to Terry a while back. She told me the ladies were tired of our shit. If you remember, we were still behaving like teenagers. We drank and rode our bikes, or drank and worked on our bikes. After the first divorce, which might have been Abe's wife, Rita, there was a sort of chain reaction. The rest of them decided they were tired of babysitting. Jack was Rita's attorney and she told the others she liked him, so they went to him. You can't blame Vandenberg."

"Yeah, I suppose. It just seemed like everything changed that year." He finished his beer and ordered another. "I heard there's been a woman in town who might be Kimberly. She says she doesn't remember much of her childhood. It's funny how her and that cousin no one ever saw before showed up when the estate needed to be settled." Mad Dog's shrug prompted

Harold to take another drink. "You and me did our share of partying, that's for sure."

"We certainly did."

"Do you remember the night Jack died? Were we partying together?"

"We could have been, Hal, but I haven't a clue." He turned on his stool, puzzled. "Don't tell me you don't remember where you were either."

No one had come in since Hal, but he glanced around and leaned closer to Mad Dog, his voice barely audible over the television. "I had a few of the guys over for a card game, but we did a lot of drinking and Danny brought some good weed. I don't remember leaving the house, but I must have and I must have been really wasted, because I woke up the next morning in my car over by the creek."

"At least you were smart enough to pull off the road. Or did you run off?"

"I don't know, but I found blood on my hands and shirt. There wasn't any damage on the car, so I wasn't in an accident. I didn't think much about it then and just figured I was in a fight. When I heard about Jack, I checked for cuts or bruises. I couldn't find any." Hal turned to rest his elbows on the bar. Few people ever saw the sparse hair on top of his six foot six inch frame. It was clearly visible when he held his head in his hands only inches above the bar.

Mad Dog whistled softly. "Are you saying you think you could have killed him?"

"I don't think I could have killed Jack or anyone else, but what if I did? What happened to Kimberly?" Harold didn't look at Mad Dog when he lifted his head. He looked at the bartender and ordered another beer and a shot of tequila. For the next hour, he continued to order more of each.

"Harold, let me take you home. You've knocked ten years off your liver's life expectancy."

When Mad Dog dropped Hal off, he made a call. "Hey, do me a favor will you and ask around if anyone remembers being with Harold the night Jack Vandenberg was killed. Yeah, I know it was twenty years ago, but see what you can find out. He's in a bad way."

By ten o'clock on Monday morning, Kate had everything ready for the arrangements Sara would make that day. She still selected many of the designs and flowers, but knew her young apprentice would soon be ready to work completely on her own. Since Sara wasn't due to arrive for another half hour, Kate was about to go in to refill her coffee cup when a voice startled her and she saw Mad Dog come through the gate. "Good morning, Kate."

"Good morning. To what do I owe the honor?"

Mad Dog, like most visitors, needed a minute to take in the gardens before he answered. "I haven't been out here in years. Your gardens are still as beautiful as you."

Despite the attainment of a level of inner peace and self-confidence, the unexpected comment brought a little color to Kate's cheeks, but she was quick to respond. "Such high praise on a Monday morning, this promises to be a good week. Something tells me my gardens are not the reason for your visit."

He faced her. "No, you're right. I came to ask about your investigation."

"If you plan to suggest I tell Tracy to drop it, don't bother. She intends to find out what happened back then, and, to tell you the truth, I agree."

"That's not it. I was wondering if you thought it was possible that one of the local guys killed Jack. I mean, a couple of us weren't happy about how well he did his job."

Kate took his hand and led him to the gazebo. "I suppose anything is possible. Why are you asking?" She didn't think his hesitance was a fascination with the flowers. "What is it, Mad Dog?"

"I'm sort of working on a problem for a friend. What if, hypothetically, someone couldn't remember where he was when Jack was killed? How do you suppose this person would go about finding out, so they could be sure?"

"Sure that they didn't kill Jack?" She watched him nod, still fixed on the garden. "Are you talking about yourself?"

"No, I don't know where I was, but I doubt I killed anything but brain cells. I just mean, what do you suppose a person could do to find out where they were on a particular night twenty years ago?"

"I suppose if it was me, I'd try to contact everyone I knew personally who was in town at that time and see if anyone remembered seeing me, even people that moved away. I've also heard that if you can recreate a scene from your past, I mean the place, the time of year, the state of mind he was in, things like that, the memory might surface."

"I'm not sure my friend would want to recreate his state of mind back then, but checking with everyone makes sense. Thanks, Kate." He stood. "I'm glad you guys are looking into the murder. Those of us that somehow managed to survive would like to know what happened back then."

Kate walked him to the gate. "Mad Dog, why did you come to me instead of Tracy? She certainly has more information than I do and she's always willing to share."

"You're the less intimidating of Raccoon Grove's investigators, and I'm a chicken."

She let him out shaking her head at the improbability of two women in their sixties scaring an old biker like Mad Dog. Her cell phone rang.

"Kate, it's Nancy over at Doctor Collins's office. Do you think you could bring a new pot for the floral piece? The other one was broken, but the flowers are fine."

"Sure, Nancy. I'll bring it right by. What happened?"

"I don't know. I was getting out of my car to come into work when I saw Adam arguing with someone in the waiting area. We weren't open yet, so it wasn't a patient. As I went in, I heard a crash and saw the woman come out in a hurry. I found Adam standing by the broken flowerpot. He went to the back as soon as he saw me."

"Who was the woman?"

"Well, I'm not completely sure because I only saw her once before, but I think it was Sara's psychiatrist from the hospital, Dr. Kovecki."

CHAPTER 21

Afther calling Tracy to explain why she had to delay their visit to the Vandenberg house, Kate found a replacement pot and left for the doctor's office. The waiting room was, as it had been earlier in the week, filled. She waited for Nancy to finish with a pile of forms before greeting her. "You sure do pack them in. I'll stay out of your way. Where are the flowers?"

"Hi, Kate. In the sink in back. I'll show you. There's a counter you can work on. I hope you don't mind arranging them. I'm not very good at that, and as you noticed, we're a little busy."

"I don't mind. How did the pot get broken?"

Nancy looked back at the door and then moved closer. "I didn't want to say on the phone, but I'm almost sure Adam pushed the pot off the counter. At least that's what it looked like through the door. Whoever the woman was, she was already on her way out when I heard the crash. He was as white as a sheet and looked absolutely furious."

"Do you know why she was here?"

"I have no idea."

Nancy returned to the front leaving Kate to arrange the flowers and wonder what had transpired between Adam and Carolyn, if it was Carolyn. As she was about to leave she heard raised voices. Sara and Adam were arguing in the next room.

"Dad, how could you?"

"Sara, honey, I just want you to be safe."

"I might as well be in the hospital. That's the only place you think I'm safe." Kate heard a door open and the sound of what was probably Sara running out of the building.

She nearly bumped into Adam as she left the room with the pot. As surprised as she was by his sudden appearance, what surprised her even more were his words. "Kate, I don't want Sara working for you."

She stepped back into the room and placed the flowers on the counter. "What are you talking about, Adam? She's happy, and very good with the flowers."

"She's not safe working with you. I know she's not."

Kate had known Adam Collins most of her life. He was a kind and sensible man. Something was very wrong. "I'm sure she's safe, Adam, and she enjoys the work. I haven't seen her this happy in years."

"Dr. Collins, we need you in exam room three." Nancy interrupted before he could respond. When she saw the anger on his face she backed away, but instead of yelling, he grabbed the clipboard and left. "What is going on with him?"

"I don't know, but I'm going to get out of the line of fire. I'll see you soon, Nancy." Kate put the flowers in place and hurried out. She found Sara sitting in the van crying. "Are you okay?"

"I'm okay. I heard Nancy call you earlier. I should have taken care of the flowers but I was so angry with Dad I couldn't concentrate. Did he tell you he doesn't want me working with you?"

"He did. What do you want to do?"

"You know the answer to that. I don't like to go against his wishes, but I have to this time. Do you still want me to help with the flowers?"

"Of course. Was Dr. Kovecki here this morning?"

"Yes. I told her he didn't want me working for you anymore and she came to talk to him. She knows how good it is for me and she wanted to make him understand. I guess it didn't go well. I overheard them talking. He told her he has a friend at the hospital who he plans to ask for help in having her removed from my case, and maybe the hospital."

"Oh, dear. Do you think he can do that?"

"I don't know. I've heard of Dr. Carter. I think he's Caroline's boss, but I can't believe Dad would really do that. Maybe he just said it in anger. He might realize what a mistake that would be when he calms down.

Kate wasn't too sure about that. "Maybe so. Do you want to get a cup of coffee or something?"

"No. I'd better let mom know what's going on. I'll come by later this afternoon. Thanks, Kate." She reached in a pocket for tissue. "I'm not sure what Dad is afraid of, but he'll see I'm fine."

When Sara left, Kate phoned Tracy and accepted her invitation to drop by the Kendall home for a recuperative glass of wine. One of the reasons Dave and Tracy loved running the Gazette was their ability to make impromptu executive decisions. They kept Monday as an optional workday. If on Monday morning, both Kendalls felt the need to extend their weekend, they took the day off.

Dave escorted Kate to the living room where Tracy waited until she sat before placing a large glass of red wine in her hand and asking the obvious question. "What's with Adam Collins these days? Everyone in town is talking about how great Sara looks. Why would he think she isn't safe working with you of all people?"

Tracy directed the question at Kate, but Dave responded. "He's been protecting her all these years. Maybe he can't see that she's more than capable of making it on her own. I wish we knew what happened to her twenty years ago. And what happened to him."

"I don't know what's going on with Adam, but there was no mistaking the daggers in his eyes when he saw me. He kept repeating that he wanted to keep her safe. I think he meant from you and me." She lifted her chin at Tracy who made a face before responding.

"He's not thinking straight. Do you think he'll want you to keep making the flower arrangement for his office?"

"I wouldn't be surprised if he no longer required my services. He was incensed."

"What's important is how Sara is handling the stress. It must be difficult for her to be at odds with her father." Tracy let her head fall back and closed her eyes. "I still believe Louise's diaries will solve this case. They may already have." Her head popped up. "Dave, Louise died of an overdose, right?"

"Yes, but they weren't sure if it was accidental or intentional."

"If I remember right, it was prescription sedatives. I have to agree with Peter and Dana. A woman wouldn't wait twenty years after she lost her family to kill herself. It could have been an accident, but what if it was something else."

"Tracy, are you thinking someone killed Louise?" Kate asked.

"What if she figured out what happened and confronted the killer? Someone took those diaries. We need to talk to Louise's doctor. Let's hope it's not Adam, because he won't tell us anything."

"I'll find out. Did you two notice any medications in the house while you were trespassing?"

"I didn't see any medications and we weren't trespassing. We were assisting Peter in his estate investigation. Which reminds me, I'll pick you up in the morning to go to the house, Kate. Dave's loaning us his car."

❧

"Hi, Mom."

"Hi, Andy. Don't tell me, Mitch finally moved out."

"No. Not yet, and I'm not up to fighting with him anymore. I'm staying out of the way. That's the reason I called. I came up with a brilliant idea that will help me and might help you and Tracy."

Kate hesitated before asking the obvious. "What's the brilliant idea?"

"I'm going to spy on Janet Doyle for you."

"You're going to do what?"

"I'll sit in my car outside her apartment and see what she does, where she goes, who visits her, that kind of stuff. It'd be easier for me up here, and more importantly, it will get me out of the house until Mitch is gone. I did a little research on how to do surveillance without someone spotting you, and I read all those female PI books. My car's perfect for this work. It's so plain I can't find it in the parking lot. What do you think?"

"Give me a minute, Andrea. I haven't adjusted to myself as an investigator yet, now I'll have to squeeze you into the picture. What about your job?"

"I'm useless at work. I've decided to take a few of the two hundred and some vacation and sick days I've accrued over the years. I'm actually looking forward to being away from my desk. How strange is that?"

It delighted Kate that her workaholic daughter wanted to take time off from her job. "I'm guessing if I said no, you'd sit in front of Janet Doyle's apartment in your invisible car anyway, wouldn't you."

"Yes, but I'd rather you agreed and we worked together as partners."

"I would too. Do you promise to be careful? I'm sorry that sounded patronizing. How about this? Be careful or I'll come up and slap you silly."

"You've been spending far too much time with Tracy Kendall." Andrea laughed. "Don't worry, I'll be careful, and I'll call you with a report in the next couple of days. How exciting."

Kate groaned softly and remembered Tracy making a similar comment. She gave her daughter Janet Doyle's address, and as soon as they disconnected, punched in Tracy's number. "Andrea's going to do surveillance on Janet Doyle's apartment and she'll report what she finds in a few days."

"Kate, that's a fantastic idea. I'll bet she wouldn't expect anyone from down here to be keeping an eye on her. What made you think of it?"

"I didn't."

"Okay, so it was Andy's brilliant idea, and judging by your brief, and none too chipper answer, you're not overjoyed. She'll be fine. Don't worry. What could go wrong?"

"Please don't say that."

Tracy arrived at Kate's house the following morning to find her waiting at the curb. She disliked when people sat on the street and honked, something that Tracy had no qualms about doing. "Dave's car is cozy after driving my huge van." Kate commented as she climbed in. "Have you heard when your car will be fixed?"

"I haven't, but it shouldn't take too long. I hope they get all the zillions of pieces of glass picked up. I'll be finding them for the next five years."

"When was the last time you kept a car for more than three years?"

"It could happen, but won't if I find glass. I like this car too. Dave suggested I hired the sniper and paid him to shoot out the window because I wanted to drive the beamer. I told him it was simply fortuitous."

"Not many people would call sniper fire fortuitous. Tracy, who do you think they were aiming for?"

"What do you mean, who were they aiming for? I assumed it was me because I seem to have irritated so many folks. No one knows Janet."

"You said Scott knew who she was when he looked in the car. What if someone else who wanted the estate knew that was her."

"Joseph Vandenberg?" Kate nodded. "Peter said he was a sleaze ball."

"She'll have to be careful, whoever she is. I'll be glad when things are settled. Sara was fine this morning. She didn't talk to her dad again yesterday, but she's determined to get on with her life. I have no doubt that working with the flowers will do wonders."

"I'm sure the flowers help, and I bet you're doing a lot for her yourself, Kate. You're an easy person to be around."

"Yesterday started with a compliment and went quickly downhill. Tell me something rotten."

"Who complimented you yesterday?"

"Oh, I forgot to tell you that Mad Dog stopped by." Kate explained their conversation and her amusement at intimidating the old biker. "I told Andrea when I talked to her last night. She thought it was funny. I can't believe she's excited about doing surveillance."

"What made her decide to do it?"

"Part of it is to avoid Mitch, who is having a hard time leaving. Another part might be because she'll be involved with her family. Dirk called her and she said they had a good conversation. Maybe everyone's growing up."

"Not me."

"Everyone but you, Tracy."

They reached the house and went straight to Louise's bedroom where Kate opened a drawer on the nightstand and reached for a bottle of pills. "Don't touch it." Tracy yelled and pulled a pair of gloves from her jacket pocket. "It may not be necessary, but why take a chance of messing something up."

"Do you usually carry these around with you?" She held up the gloves.

"The simple answer is yes."

After twenty years of friendship, Tracy still surprised her. Kate wrapped one of the gloves around the bottle to remove it from the drawer then dropped it into the mate. She wrapped them together and pushed the package into her pocket. "Let's see what we can find in those diaries."

Louise had taken an astonishing number of notes. The last books on the shelf were from four months earlier and the women agreed that the missing ones were probably from the months prior to her death. "Before we start, Tracy, I want to see exactly how many books are missing."

"How will you do that?"

Kate grabbed a handful of diaries from the other end of the row and put them where the lack of dust showed the missing ones should have been. "Looks like the last four were removed. Which ones should we read first?"

"Let's start with the latest. That's the one I read that said Ben had the answers." Tracy pulled it from the shelf and indicated they sit on the bed. "This is dated last December. *I'm pleased that Sara is doing so well. We visited for a while today, and she's a charming girl. I love her almost as much as I love Kimberly. Soon, that poor child's devils will be gone, I know it."*

"I wish Louise could have at least seen her prophesy come to light. We should ask Sara what she and Louise talked about the last time they met. Read some more, Tracy."

"I stopped at the sandwich shop and asked George what he was doing in the Patel's drive that night. At first, he denied being there, but then he said he needed...." Tracy stopped reading and cocked her head toward the door. "Kate, did you hear something downstairs? I don't think I locked the door behind us. Maybe one of the deputies saw the car."

"I'll go check."

"We'll both go, just in case it's not a deputy." They stepped into the hallway and heard a crash, but it wasn't the noise that alerted Tracy's brain. A smell wafted into her nostrils, familiar but out of place. "Hey, something's burning." Her words met a cloud of smoke rolling up the stairs toward them. "Go back," she screamed.

CHAPTER 22

Career journalists can encounter situations that test their wits and survival skills. Tracy was no exception. That didn't lessen her terror, but experience taught her to think on her feet. She shoved Kate into the bedroom and slammed the door. "Soak some towels and put them at the bottom of the door." Smoke poured in through the cracks.

As Kate wet towels and blocked its entrance, Tracy tore the sheets from the bed and ripped them into strips to tie together. "We'll have to climb out the window. Help me slide the bed to the wall." Together they pushed the heavy wooden frame under the window and Tracy tied a sheet to one of the posts.

"The door is on fire," Kate's voice rose and her panic increased with the incoming smoke.

"We're going to drop this out the window and slide down." Tracy grabbed her hand and closed it around the sheet. "You go first. Hurry. When you're close enough to the ground to jump, let go. I'll be right behind you."

Kate's jaw quivered. "I can't."

"You don't have a choice. If you don't hurry, neither one of us will make it out. Hold on tight and don't look down until you've gone a ways." Kate didn't move. "You can do it, Kate. It's only about a twelve or so foot drop and your body's half that. Go." Tracy pushed her to the window and helped her turn on the sill. "Grab hold of the sheet like this and use your other hand to grip it here." She positioned Kate's hands and gave her an encouraging smile and a nudge. "Slide as quickly as you can and use your feet against the wall to walk down. That's it. Keep going. You're doing great." Tracy looked over her shoulder at the encroaching flames. "Hurry, honey," she said quietly. "It's getting a little warm up here."

When she was close enough to jump, Kate released her grip and hit the ground with a thud. Tracy climbed out, slid halfway down, and let go. After an unladylike landing on her hands and feet, she rolled on her back to gulp deep painful breaths. Above her, flames lapped at the bedroom window frame and she watched the burning sheet drop to the ground. The wall blazed.

"Tracy, come on. We have to get away from the house." They helped each other to their feet and staggered across the yard. Kate dug out her cell phone and called 911, unaware she'd dislodged the pill bottle.

Once they had distanced themselves from the blaze, the women collapsed against the trunk of a large oak and watched in horror as the house disappeared in smoke and flames. Sirens announced the arrival of fire engines and ambulances from two of the three stations that covered the thirty-five mile area. Volunteers quickly brought the inferno under control, but not in time to save the house.

A youthful red haired paramedic led the women to an ambulance to check their vitals and supply oxygen. They gratefully accepted his help, the air, and the bottled water. Kate escaped without injury, but the throb in Tracy's left ankle suggested a problem. The medic wrapped it in a brace and gave her an order. "You need a picture taken of that cute little ankle, Tracy. Keep the brace on until you do."

Jean Sheldon

She wasn't pleased with the prognosis. Damaged body parts at her age tended to heal very slowly, or not quite right. Under pressure from the medical technician, she crossed her fingers and promised to go for an x-ray. The familiar sound of a Harley interrupted her half-hearted pledge and she almost fainted to see Dave, who was terrified of the two-wheeled vehicles, pull a long leg over the seat and wave feebly at Mad Dog as he departed.

"You had to be pretty worried about us to ride out here on that." She nodded at the bike and hugged him.

"I was worried about my car, but I'm glad you're okay." Dave straightened both his jacket and his sheepish grin. "I really am glad. What happened?"

"We didn't realize there was a fire until the smoke made it to the second floor. We had to climb out a window and shinny down a sheet." She pointed to her ankle. "In my zeal, I let go too soon and twisted my ankle."

Dave's attention to Tracy's exciting saga drifted as he looked around the property before finally interrupting. "Um, you didn't park the car in the house, did you?"

"It's on the other side of the detached garage. I tried to park it where I didn't see a lot of bird poop."

The answer earned her a kiss on the cheek. "You're a good wife. Do you know how it started?"

"No, we heard someone downstairs and then saw the smoke. Oh, damn." She turned to Kate. "The diaries."

"I thought about them after we climbed out, but I knew better than to mention it. You would have tried to shinny back up."

"I couldn't have climbed back if I wanted to. Are you okay?"

"Yes, just a little shaken. I used my feet on the wall and slid the sheet in my hands the way you showed me, but I felt like I was moving in slow motion. Was it my imagination, or were you getting a little nervous?"

"Me, nervous? Never. You did great, and the important thing is we made it."

"We did, and in good shape, mostly." She pointed at Tracy's newly acquired brace.

"I'm sure the ankle's only twisted. I'll be fine by tomorrow. Come on. Let's go to the Boar's Head. I'll buy you a beer."

Entering a bar in the middle of the day requires a few mental and physical adjustments. Nostrils accustomed to inhaling fresh air can experience momentary shock when accosted by stale smoke, alcohol, and various cleaning products. Pupils contracted to allow less sunlight grow rapidly in an effort to identify barely visible images in the dark setting. It took a minute for Dave to see Sheriff Robbins when he, Tracy, and Kate, entered the Boar's Head. "What are you doing here in the middle of the day, Scott?" He asked. "I thought lawmen weren't supposed to imbibe in uniform."

"I heard from one of the firefighters that you folks were headed this way." The sheriff tipped his hat at Tracy and Kate. "It's as good a place as any to fill out an incident report. This," he indicated the glass of dark liquid, "is root beer."

The morning had been a challenge, and Kate bordered on overload. The last thing in the world she needed was a drink. "Tracy, would you mind taking care of this. I want to go home and check on Sara."

"Give her a call."

"No. I'll just go. I want to clean up a little. Do you mind?"

"Not at all." As she turned, Tracy caught sight of their reflections in the mirror behind the bar. "What I mind is that even after our adventure, you look good and I look like

I jumped out of a burning building. Sometimes it's difficult being your friend, Kathleen. How will you get home?"

"Walk."

Kate gave both Kendalls a kiss on the cheek and waved goodbye, leaving Tracy with a not completely formed pout. "I wonder if I should go home and clean up." Not waiting for Dave's answer, she beckoned the bartender. "Could we have two beers, please? Oh shoot, I left my purse in the car."

When Scott cleared his throat, Dave put money on the bar and waited for Tracy to drain a few ounces of cold beer. "Okay, Sheriff. I think she's ready for you now."

"Thanks. Tracy, I heard you and Kate climbed out an upstairs window to escape the fire. You were lucky you only ended up with a sprained ankle between you. Did you climb out of many burning buildings in your old neighborhood?"

"I never had to make the climb, but I was ready if the occasion arose. My father was a Chicago firefighter. We all knew how to escape from a burning building, whether we wanted to or not."

"You're sure you heard someone downstairs?"

"We did. We went to check and saw the smoke. Neither of us paid attention to anything after that, except making it out alive."

"Do you think someone's trying to hurt you?"

Her eyes rolled in exasperation. "You're kidding. Haven't you been listening to me for the last three weeks? Yes, someone's trying to hurt us. That, or scare the hell out of us hoping we'll stop the investigation. These last two scares have been a little too close."

Scott passed her the clipboard. "Sign here. Tracy, I wouldn't consider telling you what to do, but if I were so inclined, I might suggest you and Kate leave it alone. If you're right, and someone does want to hurt you, I'd rather that didn't happen." He picked up the clipboard, checked her signature, and tipped his hat as he left.

"It would be easier to ignore him if he was a jerk."

"You'll ignore him anyway, right?"

"Yes, but it would be easier."

"Tracy, Mad Dog stopped by the office with a concern. He was there when the call came in about the fire and offered me a ride. By the way, were you impressed to see us come up the drive? Vroom, Vroom." Dave sat on the stool next to her with his hands raised to rev the fantasy throttle on the handlebars of an equally imaginary motorcycle.

"Shocked, but glad. Mad Dog went to see Kate. What's he concerned about?" She spun on her stool to face him.

"Harold Duffy told him he couldn't remember where he was or what he was doing the night Jack was killed."

"Kate said he asked a hypothetical question about a person not remembering something, but she thought he might have been talking about himself. Does he think Harold killed Jack?"

Dave shook his head. "Harold woke up in his car the morning after the murder and found blood on his hands and shirt. He'd either pulled or driven off the road near the creek. He said when he saw the blood he figured he'd been in a fight, but he didn't have any bruises."

"That is a concern. What did Mad Dog think you could do?"

"He knew you and Kate were investigating and stopped by to talk to you, but I was the only one around. The Dog doesn't think Harold killed Jack, but he's concerned that it's making him crazy thinking he did. He's become best buds with the bartenders and his mechanics at the shop are close to quitting on him. Mad Dog hoped that while you were doing your investigation you could keep an eye or ear out for information that might explain what happened to Harold. He's put the word out to his buddies to see if anyone remembers anything."

"Sure I will. I can picture Harold and George doing countless stupid things, but not murder. I'll see what I can find out." She turned back to her beer. "Who's running the paper?"

"Bill brought the last bit of advertising in and set it up. He said he'd cover things. The good news is we'll break even again this week."

"Another successful week at the Gazette. Let's go home and celebrate."

"Right after we stop at the clinic to have your ankle x-rayed."

She lowered an eyebrow. "You weren't there when the paramedic told me to do that."

"Kate told me."

※

"Hi, Sara. Sorry I was away so long."

Sara stood and pulled off her gloves. "That's all right. What happened to you?"

Although Tracy's comment about her appearance had been kind, it was inaccurate. Kate's soot and mud-covered clothes told Sara she'd had an adventure. After a brief attempt to brush off her jeans, she explained the morning's activities. "Except for Tracy's twisted ankle, we're both fine, but it scared the heck out of me."

"I heard the sirens earlier. How did it start?" Sara dropped the gloves and hand shovel, and folded her arms.

"We think someone started it. They're going to investigate. Sara, I know you're aware that we have been looking into the Jack Vandenberg case. I don't want you upset. If you don't want us to continue, tell me and I'll pull out. I hope that Tracy will too, but I wouldn't count on it."

"I don't want you hurt, Kate, but I wouldn't dream of asking you to stop. I want to know what happened here twenty years ago as much as you do. If you find out, I might remember what happened to me."

"I'll make a deal with you. No matter what the reason, if you want us to stop, you tell me and that's the end of it. Have you talked to your dad?"

"I went over to his office a little while ago and we talked some. He said the same thing he always says. He wants me safe. I'm worried about him, Kate. He spends most of his time working and he and mom don't talk. He doesn't look well."

"I've seen how busy his office has been lately. Could it be he's just tired?

Sara sat in one of the deck chairs and Kate followed. "I suppose. I wish I knew what was wrong. His friend at the hospital told Carolyn that dad asked him to help have her removed as my psychiatrist and from her position. I don't understand what he's trying to do."

The more she heard, the less Kate understood Adam's motives. She fell back in her chair with a sigh. "What did Carolyn say?"

"She said even if they fire her, she'll continue to see me in her private practice. She's concerned about her other patients, but said if they want to control how she treats them, it wouldn't make sense to stay. She also said she doesn't want me to lose ground because I've come so far. I don't want to lose ground or her as my doctor. Who I see is out of dad's hands, but I'm afraid that Carolyn will lose her job."

Kate rested her hand on Sara's knee. "Whatever your dad or the hospital decide to do, Carolyn wouldn't drop you as a patient unless that was what you wanted, and you can count on me to do whatever I can to help. I wish your dad could see how much better you are."

"I do too. Maybe he will eventually. I don't know what else I can do to make him understand."

Sara's biggest struggle would be making her father realize he could let go. "I'm sure he's doing this because he's afraid something will happen to hurt you."

"That's what mom said. But, it won't, and he'll come around. I'm sure of it." She stood. "He did say he still wants the floral arrangement every week. If you'd rather, I can deliver it."

"That might be a good idea. A better idea might be if you made the arrangements for his office."

"I'd like that." Sara returned to work smiling, but Kate remained in the chair. She wanted a shower and to change her smelly clothes. Instead, she watched her joyful assistant and wondered what dark secrets the pink roses held.

CHAPTER 23

You look thoughtful." Dave sat in the chair in front of Tracy's desk.

"If that's a polite way of saying I look cranky, you're right. I'm not happy."

"I can see that."

"Dave, it's never been our style to let public opinion push us around. Kate and I are convinced that our investigation won't hurt Sara. Let's run what we have on page one and ask everyone to think about where they were that night twenty years ago—where they were and who they were with. Maybe someone will remember being with Harold. We can ask anyone in touch with people who have moved from here to explain the case and find out what they remember. Our local Facebook and Twitter users can spread the link for the online addition. This entire town should help discover who killed Jack Vandenberg. In fact, the headline could be 'help us solve the murder.'"

"Where do you want to move when the paper comes out?"

Dave's comment earned him a grin and a pinched cheek, but Tracy wasn't ready to take his pessimistic view. "We'll have to wait and see how the good folks of Raccoon Grove react. Some people I've talked to are glad to be involved. We'll print the facts we've gathered so far and compile a list of everyone's whereabouts that night. As many people as we can, including you, me, Kate, the deputies, everyone in any way connected with the Vandenberg family. I also think we need to publish the story on how Ben mishandled the case twenty years ago. He's one person who won't show up to punch our lights out, and maybe we'll find out who called in the shot. We can mention the arrival of Joe Vandenberg and that we've been talking to someone who might be Kimberly. Half the town already knows about that."

Both Kendalls looked up at the out-of-breathe gardener who ran through Tracy's office door waving a camera. "Hey, guess what I have."

"Is that your first camera, Kate?" Dave stood, offering her his seat.

Kate's preoccupation with her news enabled her to ignore his attempt at humor. He knew she'd had the camera for a while. "Tracy, can you download a picture? Is the cast of that shoe still here?"

"Dave, why don't you grab a bottle of water for our guest and I'll see what has her in such a state." Tracy plugged the camera into a USB port and browsed the file. "What picture do you want downloaded?"

"You'll know which one when you see it."

"I didn't know you took pictures of the vandalized gardens."

"Sara suggested it. I thought it was a good idea."

Kate had been right. Tracy knew which picture it was as soon as she saw it. "Well, I'll be. Where did you take it?"

"Behind the sandwich shop. Where's the footprint cast?" Dave brought it from where it leaned on the wall to Tracy's desk.

"You did a good job. It sure could be from the same boot. Did you see who left the print?"

"George. They'd drained something disgusting behind the restaurant and George stepped in it. Then he walked on the concrete pad on his way back inside. I remembered the gash in the sole on the mold you made, pulled out my camera, and took it. It's the same boot, isn't it? I knew it."

"I'm sure it's the same. How did you happen to end up behind the sandwich shop with your camera in hand?"

Kate directed a faintly amused look out the window. "After our conversation with George, I was sure it was him in my gardens and thought I could prove it."

"You did well. Now we have a good idea who wrecked your flowers, but not why. We need to find out, although I'm guessing George isn't going to talk to any of us."

Dave leaned over Tracy's shoulder to view the screen. "We could run an article about the damage done to the gardens on an inside page using Kate's photos and include the photo of the footprint. Even if it isn't George's, someone won't be happy to see it in the paper. We can tie it in with the front page story about the investigation."

Tracy agreed, but Kate was confused. "What story about the investigation?"

⁂

"Did you find the diaries, Joe?"

"No. I haven't had a chance to look. I got bigger problems than finding the damn diaries. That guy I owe money paid me a visit, and Igor, his bodyguard, beat the shit out of me. I'm sure I have a couple of cracked ribs. I need to get this inheritance in a hurry. He said he's giving me a week to pay him his money or I won't survive the next visit."

"You won't have that money in a week, no matter what happens."

"When I'm sure I'm gonna get it, I'll tell him I can give him double if he'll wait."

"I want what's mine, Joe. You pay him out of your share. When will you go back for the diaries?"

"Yeah, well, that's the other piece of bad news. I found out this morning the house burned down. They think someone set it on fire. There might not be nothing for me to inherit."

"The place had to be insured and they'll pay the new owner. See what you can find out from the attorney. You didn't burn it for the insurance, did you?"

"No, I didn't burn it. It happened in broad daylight. I wouldn't take a chance on someone seeing me setting a fire. Damn, there were like thirty diaries, and they might have had something I could use."

"I thought you said you dropped some outside the house. They might still be there."

"I did. In the backyard, but I'm going to have to lay low until the police get through. If someone did start it, there'll be an arson investigation and the place will be crawling with cops."

"Will they find the diaries?"

"I don't think so. I was twenty or so yards behind the house near the woods when I dropped them. The grass and weeds were thick back there. Besides, the police are more interested in the house. If everyone clears out, I'll head back tomorrow. I'm still hurting and I couldn't run from anyone if I had to."

"Do you know if Kendall and her friend saw the letters you planted?"

"I have no idea."

"What do you intend to do?"

"Someone beat the shit out of me. My eyes are swollen and I can barely see. I plan to sleep until I feel a little better." He sighed and held his ribs. "I'll try to find the diaries tomorrow. If that doesn't work, we'll have to make sure we're a little smarter than our two old lady detectives."

"When you find the diaries, bring them here and we can read through them together."

❧

"Hi, Mom."

Kate hadn't looked at the caller ID and when she recognized the voice, she pulled the phone from her ear and stared. She didn't want to make the mistake of asking her son if something was wrong because he called. She took a breath. "How are you, Jeff?"

"I'm okay. Mark and I split up. I'm living alone again."

"I'm sorry."

"It was my idea. He's been drinking and I don't want to deal with it. I helped him too many times. Anyway, I called because I talked to Andy and she told me what she's doing for you and Tracy. I wanted to help, so last night we staked out Janet Doyle's apartment together."

Kate mouthed 'staked out'. "How did it go?"

"We followed her to a new Thai restaurant and ate a great dinner, but she went right home and didn't leave again."

"Sorry it was boring for you."

"It wasn't. Besides finding a terrific new restaurant, Andrea and I enjoyed our visit. We haven't spent that much time together in years. Since we both found ourselves at the end our relationships, we had a lot to discuss. I know we were never a close family, but we drifted even further apart over the years. I'm sorry for my part in that. She also told me how you felt when we lived at home. I thought you were distant, Mom. I didn't know you were scared."

"I didn't know for the longest time, Jeff. I was a wife and a mother and I wasn't supposed to be scared, but I was." She didn't feel embarrassed telling her son her shortcomings. She found it liberating. They talked a while longer about Jeffrey's work and her gardens, and Kate shared how she and Tracy climbed from the second floor window.

"Boy, I'm having a hard time picturing my mom sliding down a sheet to escape a burning building."

"I still don't believe it, but Tracy knew what she was doing." As the conversation continued, Kate felt a fulfillment she'd not known anywhere but in her gardens. When they finished, she wished him luck on his stake out, and told him she loved him.

"I love you, too, Mom. Bye."

Kate hung up smiling and welcomed the new and unusual sensations. Then she laid her head on her arms for a surprisingly good cry.

🌿

Not much remained of the house, but the smell of its destruction hung thick in the air. Kate and Tracy sat in the BMW, their eyes drawn to the ashes and their minds recalling the near fatal experience. "In a way, it's a fitting end for that house and the family's tragedy. All that's left are the ashes."

"That's true, Kate, but Louise wanted some finality for her family, and I intend to see she gets it." She turned to her passenger. "Speaking of families, you've been having quite a bit of communication with yours lately. I'll bet it feels good."

"It feels wonderful."

Kate said nothing more, but Tracy watched her pleased smile. One of the few desires her friend expressed over the years was for a relationship with her children. Tracy wished nearly as much as Kate did that she would find a way to make that happen. "Let's go look around. We better not go inside, it doesn't look stable." At the center of the vestiges stood the charred stairway, barely proof there had ever been a second floor. "That was a gorgeous staircase."

"Yes, it was." Kate sighed as she stepped toward the house and felt something crunch under her foot. She pulled a pair of balled up latex gloves from the grass. "Tracy, it's the pill bottle. I must have dropped it when we ran from the house. I'd forgotten all about it." She shook the bundle and heard the muffled rattle of pills. "I never thought about it after the fire. Should we take it to Scott?"

"Eventually." Tracy took it from Kate's hand and dropped it in her purse. "Let's see what we can find out about them before turning it over to the sheriff. It won't make much difference if we wait a day or two. They would have burned."

Kate found the surroundings depressing. The empty house and neglected yard looked dismal enough before the fire, before they scrambled out of a second story window. "Let's look in the backyard first. Some of Louise's gardens might be in bloom. I can use a floral perk." As they walked to the side where the fire started, Kate spotted a Queen Anne's lace growing amid the ashes. "Tracy, look at this."

"It's pretty."

"Not the flower. Look at the footprint next to it. That's George's boot, or at least it looks like the boot, gash and all. George isn't a volunteer fireman."

"No, he's not. He could have started the fire. Boy, I really can't see George as a killer, but this doesn't look good. The paper came out this morning. Maybe the photo of the shoe print will get a reaction."

They rounded the corner to the backyard and discovered, to Kate's delight, a handful of plants had survived the rubber clad feet of firefighters and the smoke and water that only days earlier flooded the area. The sparse examples of nature's endurance added an eerie touch of color to the ashen remains. Kate's fascination ended at the sound of a twig snapping in the nearby woods and the sight of a figure coming toward them. As soon as he became aware of their presence, he ducked back into the trees. Kate grabbed Tracy's arm. "Should we chase him?"

"You go ahead, I'll wait here." Tracy caught a handful of Kate's shirt as she turned, apparently not recognizing the sarcastic tone in her voice. "I'm kidding. Don't even think about." She looked at her brace. "Even if my ankle was one hundred percent, I wouldn't chase him. We solve puzzles. We don't pursue criminals."

When the stranger moved out of sight, they walked to the end of the yard near the woods where Tracy's brace snagged in a tangle of weeds. She bent for a closer look at the obstacle and picked up a diary. "Kate, look at this." There were two others in the brambles. "These are Louise's missing diaries, but there are only three."

Kate knelt and gathered the other two books. "Why are they out here I wonder?" She held one to her nose. "They must have been here before the fire. They don't smell smoky. Of course my nose hasn't cleared yet." Their voyeur, who was obviously not a boy scout, signaled his return by snapping another branch. "That guy is watching us again. How's your distance vision? Can you see what he looks like?"

"No. Let's call him over and see if he'll talk to us."

"I like your idea of us not pursuing criminals better, Tracy. Let's get out of here."

Tracy pointed the BMW toward town as Kate flipped through the diaries to check the dates. "They cover the first few months of this year. The person we saw might have come for them. You know, Tracy, I've been thinking. Do you think he could be Joe Vandenberg?"

"I suppose. I'll ask Peter for a description."

"Whoever he is, maybe he was the one who left the diaries."

"That would mean he went in the house. Why would he take the books from the house, drop them in the yard, and then come back to collect them?"

"I don't know, but these are consecutive from February to mid March. We saw one dated in December on Louise's shelf, so the one that's missing could be from January or it could be from April. That would have been the last one she wrote."

"If Louise figured out what happened, those books have the answers." Tracy glanced at her watch. "Kate, I don't want to, but I have to go to the paper and face the music. This week's edition has been out for over six hours and I can't subject Dave to any more punishment." Tracy shivered at the image of their offices overrun by an angry mob. "If you want, I can drop you off at home, but I'd feel better if you came along."

"I'll come, but this makes up for laughing at your plaster covered hair."

"No it doesn't."

CHAPTER 24

The phrase 'no news is good news' is not music to a journalist's ear, but it flashed through Tracy's mind as they neared the paper. Between the discovery of the pills and diaries, and not knowing how the town would react to the Gazette's request for help, the women had a great deal to contemplate. When they arrived, Kate found a cloth shopping bag in the back seat, loaded it with the diaries, and hitched it over her shoulder. She held the front door to let Tracy enter first and followed her to Dave's office, prepared for the worst.

"Hi, ladies. Beautiful day isn't it." He sat with his shiny Kenneth Cole loafers resting on the desk and a cup of coffee in his raised hand. "Tracy, you've had numerous calls from people wanting to help solve the case. I fielded as many as I could and left notes on your desk." He was clearly enjoying their baffled expressions.

"I know you printed the story, because I saw it come off the press." Tracy crossed her arms. "Did you decide not to distribute the paper?"

"It went out as usual. You were right. Most people do want to help solve the Vandenberg mess. Putting in the piece about Kate's gardens and the hate mail was a good idea. We heard from people on our side. Kate, most of the people that called expressed their sympathy about your flowers. I also heard from Adam Collins this morning. He wasn't pleased with the articles, but he wanted to know about the unidentified woman. He called her Kimberly, and insisted I tell him if I thought she was really Kimberly Vandenberg. Is he okay?"

"Kate said Sara was concerned about him. What do you mean is he okay? He's always been protective of Sara. Is he going even farther overboard?"

"He said if she was Kimberly, Sara would be safe." Dave took his feet off his desk. "He sounded stressed, and I had no idea what he meant."

"Sara told me he wanted her psychiatrist removed from her case and the hospital," Kate told them as she pulled in another chair from outside Dave's office. "Dr. Kovecki's been the best thing to happen to Sara in years, and she doesn't want to lose her, but as Tracy said, she's worried about her dad."

"That poor kid." Tracy tapped a finger on her chin. "You know, since no one's beating down the doors to bash in our heads, let's call it a day. Where are the diaries?" Kate held up the bag. "Let me put them in my brief case. We need to read these things and the gazebo is the perfect place to do that." Kate agreed. "Oh, I forgot. Will Sara be there?"

"She should be, but that's not a problem. I've talked to her about the investigation and she knows what's going on."

Sara smiled when Kate, Tracy, and Dave came into the yard. "Is this week's paper making it dangerous to stay at the Gazette building?"

"No, it's been surprisingly calm, but that might be the type of calm that comes before a storm," Dave told her. "Since those two intend to do a little reading, maybe you could show me the green house. I didn't get to see much during the foot print adventure."

"I'd be delighted."

Tracy and Kate went to the gazebo and chose the most current diary to read first. Tracy read aloud. "*I'm afraid of what will come of this. Secrets have a way of hurting the people that keep them and innocent others. All these years of trying to find the truth and I see only more sadness. At least I can help one poor soul, even if only a little. My heart is heavy because I think I know what happened. If it's true, I need to face him. I will never forgive what he did, but part of me understands.*" Tracy closed the book and put it on the table. "That's the last entry. Kate, that doesn't tell us anything. Do you think the missing book is the last one she wrote?"

"I've been checking the dates and the latest one in these three diaries is April 15. Louise died in mid May. I noticed at the house that the diaries aren't each a month long. Some are six or seven weeks, some only two or three. It depended on how much information she found. The January notes may have been in the December book. I didn't check the dates at the end, only the beginning. I think the one we're missing is the last one. Maybe that guy in the woods dumped these and kept that one because it holds the solution."

Damn. I'm sure that's it." She tapped the cover. "Louise planned to confront Jack's killer. Let's go backwards and look at the others. Maybe we can figure out what happened the same way she did."

The other two books summarized the legwork she'd done in February and March. She continued to run into brick walls, particularly when she questioned the retired sheriff. Ben did nothing to help and told her she should leave things alone. She didn't. Tracy and Kate were surprised to see how closely their inquiry paralleled Louise's investigation. She'd spoken to the ex-husbands and wives of Jack's clients, visited the neighbors, and tried to make Scott listen to the fact that there had been two gunshots instead of one. She wrote that she regretted having waited so long to look into things because many people had moved or passed on. Others forgot.

"Louise may have run into snags, but I have a feeling she found out what happened." Tracy looked at Kate. "Did she to talk to you?"

"She did a couple of times, and as recently as late last year. She didn't say why, but her questions had more to do with the night Jack died, than the flower gardens. She wanted to know what time he dropped me off. Dirk told me she talked to him too, and he felt as I did, she deserved to know whatever we could tell her. I'm sure everyone in town felt that way. Almost everyone."

Dave and Sara approached. "Any luck?" Dave asked.

"We think we're missing the last one." Tracy explained their plan to discover what Louise might have uncovered.

"That could work, but do you think you can start tomorrow. I'm ready to call it a day, Tracy. Waiting for the rioters at the office wore me out completely. I do want to go in for a few hours tomorrow. Maybe everyone hasn't read it yet and I'd like to be around if the good citizens should rise up angry."

"I'll go in with you. I don't want to be stuck out at the house, even on a Saturday."

"Why didn't you just get a rental?" Dave asked.

"Because then I wouldn't have been able to drive the BMW." She grinned, but it melted quickly. "If I don't hear about my car soon, I'm buying a motorcycle. You'd ride on the back, wouldn't you, Kate?"

"I'd do many things for you, Tracy, but riding on the back of a motorcycle isn't one."

"Chicken." She turned to Dave whose head shook rapidly. Sara followed suit. "Fine, I'll ride alone. Then I won't have to buy an extra helmet. Good night, Kathleen, Sara. Let's go home, uneasy rider." She grabbed Dave's hand and pulled him to the gate.

"Tracy's a unique individual, isn't she?" Sara said as she and Kate watched them leave.

"She is, with a good attitude about life. I admire her for that."

"You have a good attitude about life."

Kate was about to argue, but stopped herself. "I do, don't I. Are you about done for the day?"

"I finished the arrangement for dad's office. Do you want to take a look?"

Sara made great arrangements and when Kate stepped into the greenhouse, she expected something nice. That didn't prepare her for Sara's creation. She hugged her apprentice and took a closer look. "You've outdone yourself. You are a gifted floral designer. What do you think?"

"I like it. I'd like to take a picture if you don't mind. I want to show mom."

"I'll grab my camera. Your dad will be pleased." Kate realized that might not have been the best thing to say. Adam's behavior lately made it difficult to know what would please him, except for Sara to be safe.

⁂

"Carolyn, can we talk?"

Dr. Kovecki looked up from her desk at someone she had once considered a friend. She removed her glasses and leaned back. "Did you come to give me my pink slip, Jonathan?"

"No, I came to talk if you'll let me. I'd like to start by apologizing. I didn't research Sara Collins before I told Adam I'd help." She waved him to a chair.

"Have you researched her now? If you did, you didn't talk to her doctor."

"Look, Adam Collins is more than an old friend. I wanted to help him."

"Even if that help could destroy his daughter?" Unsure if she could contain her anger and disappointment at Jonathan's behavior, Carolyn held back further comments. Jonathan was her senior in the department, but he'd never asked her about the case before he approached the head of the hospital with Dr. Collins's request.

"I took Adam's word for the state of his daughter's health and that working wasn't healthy for her. He loves her and thought you were making her worse by insisting she work." He adjusted uncomfortably under Carolyn's gaze. "I wanted to talk to your first, but he pressured me to start proceedings right away. Look, Carolyn, he helped me through medical school. He and my dad were friends, and when dad died, Adam stepped in. I felt I owed him. I've gone through Sara's case files and I can see she is doing well. It's not her I'm worried about. It's Adam. What has Sara told you?"

"She's worried about him too, more than about herself. She's strong. She still has battles to fight, but she's ready to face them. Jonathan, I swear, I won't let anyone take that from her, even if it means my job."

"I don't want to take anything from her, and I don't want you to leave the hospital. Sara isn't the only person that depends on you. Adam called me this morning to say that he's convinced Kimberly is alive, and if that's true, there's no need to have you removed because Sara is safe." Jonathan wove his fingers together and rested his elbows on the arms of the chair. "I'm at a loss as to what to do for him."

"Do you suppose he'd consider talking to one of the other doctors here? You and I wouldn't be effective."

"I'm sure he doesn't realize how strange he's behaving."

Carolyn felt her anger fade. "How can I help?"

※

Saturdays at the Kendall house usually began after nine or ten. Tracy could work until all hours of the night, but mornings offended her, as did morning people. "Did you change your mind about going into the paper this morning, sweetie?" Dave leaned close and stared at his sleeping partner's face until she growled and opened an eye.

"What are you doing?"

"I'm admiring my beautiful wife."

"You're ticking off your beautiful wife. What time is it, five a.m.?"

"It's eight o'clock. If you don't want to go to the paper, then don't. When you finally do make it out of bed, you can have a bowl of cold cereal. If you do decide to join me, I'll make your favorite breakfast and a fresh pot of your preferred dark roast. Do you want to see if you can maneuver that gorgeous body into a vertical position and find the shower?"

Tracy put the pillow over her head. "You're a vicious taskmaster."

"If that were true, we could stay here for three or four more hours and I'd practice some creative mastering."

"Yuck."

Tracy made it vertical and to the shower. She dressed, blew dry her still unfamiliar hair, and went to the kitchen to find an English muffin laden with bacon, an egg over easy, and a thick slice of sharp cheddar cheese. Dave learned early on in their marriage that the quickest way to motivate his bride was to tempt her taste buds. Two cups of coffee later, they loaded into the BMW and took a leisurely ride to the paper, arriving at nine-forty-five.

"See, I knew you could do it. Remember we have no idea if today will be as peaceful as yesterday. Be ready for anything."

"I can be ready even if I'm not awake. Throughout our years together, Dave Kendall, I have never understood how you could open your eyes and hit the floor running. It's not your most endearing trait."

Dave unlocked the front door and pulled it open to let Tracy enter. "Oh, oh," she said.

"Don't say oh, oh, that way, Tracy. It makes me nervous." He stepped in next to her. "Oh, oh."

CHAPTER 25

Acertain amount of disorder is natural in any busy newspaper office, but what greeted Tracy and Dave wasn't confusion, it was chaos. File folders, yanked from drawers in now empty cabinets, covered the floor. One of the large metal storage units that previously lined the wall of the entrance lay on its side, gutted, its bottom drawer bent in an unhealthy position.

"We'd better check our offices." Tracy suggested and they climbed the stairs to examine their respective workspaces. "Shit." Her response echoed down the hall an octave lower. "Who did this?" She shouted. When Dave appeared in her doorway, she continued. "This isn't just willful destruction. They were looking for something. What would we have to provoke this?"

"I can't imagine, but I agree. They wanted something, and I'd guess they didn't find it. I'd better call Scott."

As Dave left, Tracy's office phone rang. She located the flashing light under scattered sheets of paper and answered in a daze. "Hello."

"Tracy, you won't believe what I found."

"Someone broke into the paper, Kate."

"What?"

Tracy took a deep breath. "We just got here and found everything torn apart. They were looking for something, but I can't imagine what."

"If that guy in the woods saw us pick up the diaries he could have followed us to the paper and thought we left them there. Maybe he does have the first diary but he needs the others for some reason."

"What reason? Who is he and what does he want?" When Dave came in and sat, Tracy conveyed Kate's theory about someone wanting the diaries and watched his head bob slowly up and down. "He either agrees or he's nodding off. Listen kiddo, since you have them, you need to be extra careful."

"Don't worry, I will. Do you want help?"

"No, we'll call the cleaning guy, although Dave and I may have to spend the next two years filing. At least most of the current files are on computers or backup drives. Kate, why did you call?"

"Oh, right. I found Louise's new Will in one of the diaries. She'd folded it and tucked it in the back pocket."

"I wonder why she didn't take it into Peter."

"That I can't tell you, but Anna Patel and Doc Crawford signed as witnesses.

"So, Henry was the second witness. Who's the beneficiary?"

"Are you ready for another strange twist to the case? Louise left everything to Sara Collins."

"Why do you suppose she made Sara the beneficiary?" Tracy and Dave sat in his office. When the janitor finished cleaning his space, he asked Tracy to vacate hers while he worked.

"I'm sure the diaries will have that information. Will you and Kate have time to read them this afternoon?"

"Yes. I want to work on my files for a while this morning. I'll go over later. Did you plan to join us?"

"No, I'd feel strange reading Louise's diary. It's not a guy thing."

"Maybe the world would be a better place if guys read women's diaries, or better yet, kept their own."

"You may be right, but I can't see that happening. I'd better start going through those." He pointed to a cabinet bulging under stacks of paper. "Scott won't come by until Monday. Since nothing's missing, I didn't think it mattered. We've been seeing a great deal of the sheriff lately."

"Unless you're the sheriff's wife, that's not a good thing."

"Tracy, be careful. This thing gets more explosive every day."

Before she could answer, a voice came from the doorway. "Your office is as ready as I can make it, Tracy. You two have a bit of work on your hands. Did someone not like the yesterday's paper?"

"Thanks, Barney." Tracy turned in the chair. "We appreciate you coming in on such short notice. It does have the feel of an unhappy reader wanting to stop the presses."

"That it does. Don't thank me. I'm glad you called. My wife wanted me to wash windows and this was a much nicer fate. Besides, she doesn't pay much. See ya." He waved his dustpan and departed.

"I'll be in my office." Tracy gave Dave a peck on the cheek. "You be careful, too. People know we're a team."

Her office no longer looked disastrous, merely disheveled. She could deal with that, but as she studied the amount of filing that loomed, it struck her that music would make the job easier and put on a CD. Her glasses in place, she sang along with an original Joan Baez tune, *Diamonds and Rust*, surprised to find she remembered most of the words. "*We both know what memories can bring. They bring diamonds and rust.* Right. Diamonds, rust, and irate readers."

Dave was right about the situation getting explosive, and she wasn't the only one who could be in danger. Kate, Dave, and possible fringe associates were at risk. She hoped those involved understood they could drop out of the investigation if they wanted. Well, Kate and the others could. Dave didn't have that option.

Hard as she tried to focus on the filing job, her mind drifted back to the case. She gave up and phoned Kate. "Could you pick me up at the paper in a half an hour? I want to leave Dave the car and I still haven't picked out a motorcycle." She waited for Kate's chuckle and agreement. "I have to drop off ad copy at the bank and I'll meet you outside the front door."

Tracy hadn't been out of the building five minutes when Adam Collins appeared in Dave's doorway looking exhausted and upset.

"Dave, I want to talk to you."

"Adam, most of the town wants us to continue the investigation into Jack's murder. Even Sara is glad about it."

"Yes, yes, I know. I want to talk to Kimberly." Adam ran his hands through his tousled white hair and scanned the office as if she might be there.

"Do you mean the woman we spoke to about Kimberly?"

"She's Kimberly. She must be. Let me have her phone number. I'm sure she'll talk to me."

"It wouldn't be ethical for me to give you her number, Adam, but I will do this. Next time we talk to her, we'll give her your number and the message. If she wants to talk to you, she can call."

"Can you call her now?"

Dave dialed Tracy's cell and she answered on the first ring. She'd just dropped the copy off at the bank and was standing outside the paper. "Hi, hon. Adam's here."

"I saw him come to the building and stayed inside the bank until he went in. Sorry I'm such a chicken."

"I forgive you. He wants us to give his phone number to Janet Doyle and ask her to give him a call."

"I suppose that would be all right. Let me call right now and she can decide whether she wants to talk to him or not. I'll wait in the bank until he leaves, so chase him out."

Dave put down the phone and nodded at Adam. "Tracy said she'd call Janet and tell her you want to talk. How does that sound?"

"That's good, Dave. That's very good. I'm sure she's Kimberly. I can help her remember things. I knew her when she was a little girl."

Adam ran out the door, leaving a bewildered publisher in his wake. "He wants Janet Doyle to remember everything, but he doesn't want Sara to remember anything. What's going on in his head?"

The county wide inter-library loan system gave people in rural Will County access to a great number and variety of books. Kate received an email saying that the titles she'd requested were at the library. She stopped to retrieve them before picking up Tracy.

"Yes, they came this morning, Kate. I have them here." Edwina, the head and only librarian of the two-room Raccoon Grove library lifted a handful of books from beneath the counter. "I see you have one here on investigative procedures. Are you planning on becoming a private eye?" She wore a wary smile.

"No. I like gardening, but I've been working with Tracy on the Vandenberg case and I was curious about how real investigations were done."

"I heard that and hoped it wasn't true. Why do you have anything to do with that woman?"

"What's wrong with Tracy, Edwina?" It didn't take Kate long to realize she shouldn't have asked. Edwina eventually finished her lengthy outburst on the problems of Tracy Kendall and caught Kate up on the considerable gossip that reached the library. "Thanks, Edwina, but after nearly three decades, Tracy hardly qualifies as a smart mouth girl from the city. She's as Raccoon Grove as you or I."

"She's been here for a while, but she's still a city girl. Be careful hanging around with her. She has overdue library books and swears up and down that she brought them back. If she'll lie about that, she can't be trusted."

That, Kate knew, was Edwina's biggest gripe. 'The smart mouth girl from the city' had overdue books. She smiled as she walked out and saw Tracy leaving the bank. She was still smiling when they both climbed in the van.

"What are you grinning about?"

"Edwina thinks you're arrogant, pretentious, and completely lacking in manners. On top of that you have overdue library books."

"I do not have overdue library books. That woman is losing her grip."

Kate didn't have to look at her passenger to picture the annoyed look on her face. "She also told me the latest scuttlebutt. Do you want to hear it?"

"Of course."

"A few people think Ben killed Jack, although Edwina made it clear that she doesn't. I didn't tell her about the money you found at his house, but maybe we should start a rumor about him being a blackmailer. At least people would know he wasn't a murderer."

"Just a blackmailer. Does that put him in a better light? He knew who murdered Jack and covered it up so he could blackmail him."

"Yes, I suppose that's possible. I think Edwina was fond of Ben."

"That's only because he spent all his time in the Boar's Head and never had any overdue library books."

"I saw Adam leaving the paper. I hope he wasn't too upset."

"I don't know how upset he was. I hid in the bank, but Dave tracked me down on my cell phone." She filled Kate in on Adam's strange request. "Did you say anything to Sara about Louise's Will?"

"No. We should take it to Peter and let him do his job. Speaking of Sara, I wonder if she started on that Thompson arrangement. I'll give her a quick call and let her know we're on our way."

Kate called just as Sara finished gathering the flowers she would need for the Thompson order. After assuring her boss that everything was fine, she went to the greenhouse to begin the arrangement and realized she'd forgotten to select the pot. At the rear of the glass-roofed building, a row of metal shelves carried a variety of sizes and types of pottery. She found the one she wanted on a bottom shelf and knelt for a better grip. As she lifted the vessel, a noise behind the storage unit caused her to look up at the gray metal shelving. It, and the rows of pots it held, toppled towards her.

CHAPTER 26

Sara, I'm back," Kate and Tracy entered through the back gate and scanned the empty yard. "She's probably in the greenhouse. I'll let her know we're here." Surprised not to find her at the worktable, Kate stepped inside and heard the sound of metal scraping on the cement floor. She turned to see her assistant crawling out from under a shelf. "Oh, my god. Sara, are you all right?"

"I'm okay. It just knocked the wind out of me."

"What happened?" Tracy came in and she and Kate pulled Sara to her feet.

"I'm not sure. I heard a noise and looked up to see the shelf falling. Someone was in here. I heard footsteps."

The row of metal shelving units stood two feet from the wall to eliminate having to empty a shelf if they needed a pot from the back. Kate examined the space. "They might have been standing behind here and pushed it on you. Do you want to go to your dad's office and let him check you over?"

"No. Please don't tell him what happened. I'm fine, and I don't want him to have another reason to worry."

"We'll have to tell the sheriff, and sooner or later your dad will hear about it."

"Let it be later. Please, Kate."

"Okay. If you're not hurt, you two stand the shelf up and I'll pull it back where it belongs." The large shelf unit, although not heavy, was awkward to move. Kate kicked away pottery shards and pulled it in line.

"Could the shelf have been top heavy?" Tracy asked Sara.

"We don't put anything on the top shelf for that reason. Besides, Kate might be able to reach it, but I'm only five four. It didn't fall, if that's why you're asking, Tracy. I agree with Kate, someone pushed it. I can't imagine why."

"We've been wondering that far too often lately. Let's call the sheriff and then look at those diaries. Kate, I want you to know that if at any time you want out of this investigation, I understand."

Kate ignored her. "I'll grab the diaries. I bet that's what the intruder was after. He didn't find them at the paper and made this his next stop. Since the van was gone, he might have thought it was okay. Tracy, you should check your house."

"We have an elaborate alarm system protecting all our toys, but you're right. I'll call Dave and let him know what happened." She left a message for Scott and called Dave at the office. When he didn't answer, she tried his cell. "Where are you?"

"I'm home. The alarm went off. The company sent out security people and called me. The back office window showed signs of tampering, but no one went in. He or she heard the alarm and changed their mind."

"Someone visited Sara in the greenhouse. He knocked a shelf over but she never saw him. Kate thinks it's all about the diaries."

"Kate is probably right."

While Tracy made the phone calls, Kate went to the house and retrieved the journals and they settled in to retrace Louise's investigation. "Tracy, do you remember Louise's handwriting in the first few diaries. It was small, almost illegible. In these, it's large and sturdy, as if she grew stronger as she figured things out."

"Dana said that investigating helped her through much of her pain. She was right that it makes suicide even less plausible. I didn't know Louise well, but I'm sure I would have liked her."

"I agree."

"Hello." Scott entered the yard. "I got your message, Tracy. Is Sara around? I'd like to ask her a few questions."

Kate answered. "She's in the greenhouse. She didn't see whoever did it, so I don't know how much help she can be."

"I just need a statement. Would it be too upsetting for me to question her?"

"Not at all. I just don't know what she can tell you, but here she is. Ask her yourself."

Sara approached and heard the sheriff's question. "Hi, Scott. Kate's right, I didn't see anything except the shelf falling. Then I heard someone leaving. I'm guessing it was a man by how heavy the steps sounded."

Scott asked a few more questions and Sara returned to the greenhouse. He put his notebook in his pocket and eyed the diaries. "What are you two reading?"

"Louise Vandenberg's diaries. We found them in the yard after the fire, but we think we're missing one." Tracy tapped the one she held. "It could hold the solution to Jack's murder."

Scott answered his phone and after a brief conversation shoved it back in his pocket. "I have to take off. I'll check with you later. I want to know about the diaries."

"He won't do an investigation, but he wants to know what we find." Tracy shook her head and read the first passage aloud. "*I'm afraid the investigation had me more worked up than I thought. Last week I didn't sleep for several nights and Doctor Crawford gave me a sedative. Once I had them, I was a little* afraid of becoming addicted, so I stopped. Just knowing that I'm close to finding out what happened will be far better than any drug. Doctor Crawford was pleased, but told me to keep the remaining pills just in case. That's why Henry signed the will. He was her doctor. I'll drop by his office and show him the pills we found. If he knew she quit taking them, it must have surprised him that she overdosed. I wonder if he examined her body. Kate, you read one."

"*Anna told me everyone heard two shots and yet Ben's report mentioned only one. I don't believe he killed Jack, but he might be covering for someone.*" Kate put the book on her lap and turned to Tracy. "She was right about Ben. Has Dave heard any more from his friend in Chicago about Herb Doyle?"

"Not that he's shared with me."

Dave had just returned to his office when the phone rang. "Is it always this busy on Saturday, or is it this busy because I'm here on Saturday? If a tree falls in the woods and no one is there…Hello."

"Hi, Dave, it's Armando. I have some information about Herb Doyle."

Dave turned on the speakerphone and faced his computer. "What do you have?"

"He left Raccoon Grove to take a job as a janitor for the Chicago Board of Education. BOE listed a few different addresses for him and the owner of one of the apartment buildings said he thought Doyle lived there with his daughter."

Dave stopped typing. "Janet Doyle could be Kimberly Vandenberg. Anything else?"

"Not yet. I'm trying to track down a lead. I'll let you know if I have any luck. Any interesting developments on your end?"

"Lots, but I don't have time to explain it all. Armando, if you do find anyone who knew Herb Doyle and his daughter, ask them for a description."

"Sure, Dave. You people have more fun in your little burg than we do here in Chicago."

"I'm sure it's relative." He ended the call and reconsidered. "Or maybe not."

❦

Adam Collins often came into the office for a few hours on Sunday. With no one else around he could catch up on more paperwork than he did all week. Pleased with his mornings progress, he wasn't perturbed to hear the phone. "Hello."

"Hello, this is Janet Doyle. Mrs. Kendall asked me to call Doctor Adam Collins in Raccoon Grove. She said he wanted to talk to me."

"Yes, that's right. I'm Adam Collins and I wanted to ask you a few questions."

"All right. What is it, Doctor?"

"Where was your bedroom in the Vandenberg house?"

"I don't know if it was my bedroom, but I think Kimberly's bedroom was at the top of the stairs. It was big, and there was a bed with a canopy, a dresser with a mirror, and another tall dresser."

"That's right, Kimberly. Do you remember the music box Sara gave you for your birthday?"

"Please don't call me Kimberly. My name is Janet. I remember a music box. It had a ballerina on top and when you wound it, she danced." She was quiet for a moment and then hummed *A Time for Us*.

"Yes. Yes. That's the song it played," he yelled. "You're Kimberly. You have to be Kimberly. Come back to Raccoon Grove."

"If you don't have other questions, Doctor, I'm hanging up. Goodbye."

"If there's anything I can do to help, call me." When she disconnected, Adam stared at the phone in his hand and smiled. "She's Kimberly."

❦

Kate went to the greenhouse early Monday morning to load completed arrangements into the van. Sara had agreed to make the delivery and Kate was feeling quite spoiled as her assistant entered wearing a pale blue pantsuit. "You look great. I've loaded the van. Are you sure you don't mind making the deliveries?"

"Not at all, if you don't mind that after I finish I have an appointment with Carolyn."

"I don't mind. Is everything okay? Did what happened in the greenhouse upset you?"

"Oh, no, Kate. I mean it upset me a little, but I'm fine. I'd made the appointment earlier in the day because I'd remembered something."

"You don't need to tell me what's going on. I just want to make sure you're all right. I'll see you later."

"Sara, you look quite fashionable today," Carolyn waved her in and saw by Sara's smile that she felt as good as she looked.

"I wish I could say that I dressed to see you, but the truth is, I delivered arrangements before I came and Kate's learned that people prefer we don't show up in dirty clothes and muddy shoes."

"That makes sense. Where's this piece going?" She asked about the flowers in Sara's hand.

"This is yours. I hope you won't take offense, Carolyn, but your office could use a little color."

"No offense taken. You don't find institutional white cheerful?"

Sara handed her the colorful bouquet with a grin. "These will help."

When they decided on the best spot on her desk for the flowers, Carolyn and Sara sat. "You said you remembered something?"

The two women sat in undisturbed silence while Sara sought words to describe the unsettling images. "I don't know if it has anything to do with what happened, but it felt weird. Not like a dream, but real. Kimberly and I were outside her house playing statues. You know, that game where one person turns their back and the other players try to sneak up, but if you turn around and see them moving they're out."

"Yes, we played that when I was a kid."

"It was only Kimberly and I playing, and I had my back to her, but when I turned around she was lying on the ground. I told her she could get up because I hadn't seen her move, but she stayed on the ground." Sara shivered despite the warm office. "I don't remember anything else, but when the image appeared I felt the darkness moving over me. I stayed focused and in control of my thoughts, but it frightened me."

"It may have frightened you, but two years ago it would have overwhelmed you and you didn't let that happen. You're a much stronger person now, Sara. Did you and Kimberly play that game often?"

"Not really. We did play it some, so I could have just been remembering that and made up the part about Kimberly not moving."

"Do you believe that?"

Her head moved slowly. "No. I remembered seeing Kimberly lying very still, but I don't know why."

As Carolyn asked specific questions, the decades old wall that blocked Sara's memory developed a crack. With experience and patience Dr. Kovecki, helped bring back ancient images. They appeared only briefly, and none stayed clear or long enough to explain the years of despair. Carolyn knew that Sara was on the verge of remembering everything, but not just then, and it was too dangerous to force her.

"Let's not go any further today. If the memories continue, let them in, but don't panic. Call me and we'll talk about them together. I don't want you to try and face this all at once, or alone." She hoped that when the wall tumbled and the past cleared in her mind, Sara could handle what was sure to be a terrifying memory. Carolyn considered the possibility, whether she was alone or with her, that Sara's memories could overwhelm her, but she hesitated to stop this close to recovery. "How are you?"

Sara held a tissue to her watery eyes. "I know I'm almost there and that terrifies me, but I can't stop. When the memories come, I'll handle them."

"You will." Carolyn said softly. "Come in tomorrow, and maybe every day until this is finally over."

Sara agreed, exhausted by the hour-long struggle to defeat her monsters. "I will. I'll tell mom about the session when I get home. She'll make sure I'm okay."

CHAPTER 27

Tracy intentionally arrived at Doctor Crawford's office before nine to beat the crowd, but as she stood at the front desk, his waiting room filled. "Hi, Lois. Henry's expecting me. How are you doing these days? It looks like half the Grove is here."

"I'm well, Tracy. I'll let him know you're here. Don't worry about the crowd. They're waiting for Doctor Lewis. She'll take over when Henry retires next year. He only sees a few of his older patients these days. Speaking of older patients, I'm glad you let your hair grow out. It looks good on you."

"I'm having a heck of a time getting used to it. I still scare myself."

"Most of us see it happen gradually, so it's not as much of a shock. If mine turned white overnight, I would have needed a few shots of Jack Daniels and a little time to adjust."

"You're a good person, Lois."

"Thank you." She lifted the phone and spoke briefly before returning it to the base. "Go on back. Henry's in his office waiting for you."

The door swung in as Tracy knocked, and a deep voice welcomed her. "Mrs. Kendall. I heard you'd joined the rest of the gray haired citizens in this town, but on you, it's lovely. Please have a seat."

"Thanks Henry. You're looking rather chipper yourself. Ready to retire?"

"I will be by next year. You and Dave are still keeping things hopping, I see. It wouldn't be much fun around here without the Gazette."

"I suppose that's true, although not everyone is a fan. As far as keeping things hopping, we started this investigation innocently enough." Dr. Crawford enjoyed food and drink far too much to bother with counting calories or cholesterol levels. His ample cheeks wore a perpetual smile, partially due to an inherited and unusual upward curve at the corners of his mouth. Those who knew him well thought the smile would be there even if his mouth were not a peculiar shape.

"I, for one, appreciate you're looking into it, Tracy. Louise suffered terribly after Jack's death and Kimberly's disappearance. How can I help?"

She reached in her purse and pulled out the pill bottle, still encased in latex. "We found these sedatives you prescribed at Louise's house, in her nightstand. One of her diaries said she stopped taking them."

"That was what she told me, and I was sure she did. She was quite pleased about it, but many things pleased her at that time. I take it the gloves are to preserve fingerprints?" When Tracy nodded, he pulled a pair of his own gloves from a desk drawer and opened the parcel. "Yes, it's the prescription I gave her." After a short struggle, he removed the cap and poured the contents on his desk, looking up suddenly. "Do you think someone killed Louise?"

"Am I that transparent?"

"I can't think of any other reason you'd be interested in the pills. Why do you suspect foul play?"

"We believe she found out who killed Jack and confronted him."

Even his natural smile could not hide the sadness as Henry considered the implications. "Whoever she confronted killed her. Another unimaginable tragedy."

"How many pills should there have been in the bottle, Henry?"

He turned it and read the label, and then counted the ones on the desk. "That's odd, the prescription is for thirty, and there are 26 pills here."

"Her diary said that she'd only recently started taking them."

"That's correct. She took medication for a while the first year or so after Jack's death, but stopped. In the last few weeks of trying to find out what happened, she had a few sleepless nights and I wrote her a new prescription. She'd only been on them a few days. When I dropped by to witness her sign her new will, she told me she'd decided to stop. If she overdosed, they came from another bottle and a different doctor. I was out of town the week Louise died and when I heard she overdosed, I assumed it was with these. Did you hear if they found another bottle?"

"No, I didn't. Can you find out if she filled a second prescription?"

"That'll be easy enough. I'll talk to the local pharmacies. What about the bottle, can you have the police check for fingerprints? You went through a great deal of trouble to preserve them." He indicated the gloves and orange plastic bottle.

"Scott can't even reopen a murder cases. We won't talk him into investigating a death by an overdose. If someone put a drug in your patient, you and I need to discover who and why. Henry, if you were out of town, who examined Louise?"

"Adam Collins."

Elaine watched from the kitchen as Sara, despite a trying session with her doctor, pruned the lilacs with delight. She told Elaine that she needed to focus on the things that made her happy and had gone straight out to work in the yard. She had a gift. The flowers and bushes looked even more beautiful than when Elaine did the gardening herself.

She gripped the wheels of the chair where she' would spend the rest of her days. Mysteries of the mind and the body were difficult to solve or even understand. Sara's darkness and her own crippling disease were alike in one way. Neither woman had any choice but to deal with things as best they could. She hoped their best would be good enough.

"Hi, Mom. Do you want to sit outside? It's a beautiful day."

"I'd like that."

Sara wheeled her down the long ramp and went back in for iced tea. When she sat, she took her mom's hand. "I'm going to see Carolyn again tomorrow. I suspect it won't be long before I know what happened. Are you ready for that?"

"I'm ready for you to have a life, Sara, whatever it takes. The most important question is, are you ready?"

"Yes, but I'm not sure dad wants me to remember. I'm worried about him. He doesn't look well and trying to stop me from working for Kate doesn't make sense. Why wouldn't he want me to be well?"

"He does want you well, child. I'm worried, too. I'll try talking to him again. Maybe together we can make him understand that you really are better. In the meantime, we need to make sure you stay that way."

❧

"Hello, Mr. Zabicki. Thank you for seeing me."

"That's not a problem, Ms Doyle. Please call me Peter. May I call you Janet?" She nodded. "What can I do for you?"

"I'm starting to understand the workings of a small town like Raccoon Grove, so I'm sure you've heard there's a possibility I'm Kimberly Vandenberg."

"Yes, I have heard."

"I want to look around the Vandenberg house to see if I can remember anything or if something could prove, at least to me, whether or not I'm Kimberly. I'd like to put this matter to rest as soon as possible and get on with my life, no matter what the outcome."

"I understand." Peter leaned back in his chair. "I take it you're not aware that the Vandenberg house burnt to the ground."

Janet stared blankly. "I don't understand. I was told that no one lived there."

"No one does. The police are relatively sure someone set the fire. They haven't discovered who or why."

"What about this person claiming to be a cousin or some relative from California? Would he have reason to try to burn it?" Janet asked.

"Joseph Vandenberg. I suppose anything's possible, but it wouldn't make sense for him to destroy what he wanted to inherit. Janet, Tracy Kendall told me you had memories of being here before. Are you able to understand them?"

"No. They are vague and disconnected. I recognized the Vandenberg house when Mrs. Kendall drove me around town. Did she tell you that?" He acknowledged she had. "I remembered visiting a lady with beautiful gardens. Me and another little girl with dark curly hair walked alongside a red haired woman." She stopped and shook her head. "I should have called before I came, but I didn't want to bother Mrs. Kendall."

"I'm sure Tracy wouldn't have minded. I'm sorry this is troubling to you. What about working with a hypnotist? They often help people recover lost memories."

"I might have to do that. Do you know if Kimberly had any friends that are still in town and might remember her?"

Peter thought about Sara and decided he'd check with Tracy before supplying her name. "Not right off the top of my head, but I'll think about it."

She stood and laid a piece of paper on his desk. "Please give me a call if you can think of anyone. Thank you for your time, Peter."

When Janet Doyle walked out of his office, Peter picked up the phone. "Tracy, guess who just paid me a visit."

⁂

Kate saw Jeff's number on the phone and answered. He didn't wait for her to say hello. "We have some news, but I don't know if it means anything."

"Should I grab a pen and paper?"

"You won't need it. A couple of days ago, Andy and I sent emails to everyone we are still in touch with from high school and asked if they remembered Herb Doyle being a janitor. We heard from a few people and some remembered Herb vaguely, but one guy, do you remember Jimmy Carmichael? He lived on Edgewood. Anyway, Jimmy talked to his brother and he remembered that Herb lived in a trailer outside of town with his girlfriend, Marge Serapin."

Kate's body reacted before her brain and she shot up in the chair. "Really? Marge Serapin. I'll have to pay her a visit. How is Jimmy?"

"He's fine, and said to say hi. So you know Marge Serapin?"

"Yes. You must remember her. She's been a waitress at the diner for years."

"I thought her name was Madge."

"No, it's Marge. Jeff, you two did great work."

Kate heard muffled noises before her daughter came on the line. "Hi, Mom, we're good at this spy stuff, aren't we? I almost hate to go back to my day job. Listen Janet was gone yesterday afternoon and came back with a guy who stayed the night. He looked in bad shape, sick or at least exhausted and his face was swollen."

"Can you describe him?"

She described a tall thin white male in his mid twenties who they thought had a bruised and swollen face. "Does that fit anyone around town?"

"I wonder if he could be that Joe Vandenberg guy. That would mean he and Janet Doyle are in this together. Does that make sense?"

"Can you email us a picture?"

"I don't know how, Andy, but Tracy could. Do you still have the same email address?" The two things Kate did on the computer were surf the flower sites and send emails, but only emails.

"It's the same."

"I'll see what we can do. Keep an eye on him, and her. I'll let Tracy know what you've found. You're both terrific. I'm not nagging, but remember, we don't know if these people are dangerous."

"It's okay if you nag."

"Thanks. How are you and Jeff doing?"

"We've been having fun. I know that's not the object of a stakeout, but it has been. When we finish the case, you and dad should come up and the four of us can go to dinner."

"That's a wonderful idea, Andrea, and I'll bet your father will agree."

"I asked mom and dad to join us for dinner."

"I heard. It could be fun. Andy, don't tell mom I said this, but when we were growing up I thought she was an airhead, the beautiful trophy wife."

"She thought so too, Jeff. She told me how frightening it was, but it took her a while to figure things out." Andrea made a face. "Listen to me, I'm forty and I haven't figured out a thing."

Jeff's eyes stayed on Janet's apartment, but his mind was on something else. "Do you think it's possible for us to have a family?"

"I do. Mom has changed, and I think I can. Even dad sounded different. If we make it work, I'll try to figure out how to do the same with my own kids. At this point, it will be a while before Mitch and I can work on anything. How do you feel about it, Jeff?" Andy's grip on the steering wheel loosened. Her younger sibling was now a middle-aged man, but when she looked to the passenger's seat, she saw her kid brother.

"I never thought much about it, but the older I get, the less faith I have in the word impossible."

CHAPTER 28

Except for the sheriff, who sat in a booth reading the paper, the diner was empty. Kate waved to Scott and took a seat at the vacant counter. "Hi, Marge. How are things?"

"Same old, same old, Kate. You're born, you work, and you die. Want a cup of coffee? This pot's fresh since the lunch crowd came through."

Since it was three in the afternoon, Kate chose not to take a chance. "Iced tea, please." Marge set a tall glass in front of her and pulled a straw from her pocket. "Marge, do you mind if I ask you a few questions?"

"No, go ahead. No one's here but the sheriff, the worst tipper in town." She spoke loud enough for Scott to hear, but he didn't look up.

"Do you remember Herb Doyle?"

For over a quarter of a century, Marge waited tables at Mike's diner. If that had been her intended career, she never said, and most people didn't ask. "I haven't seen Herb in years. Did he die and leave me money?"

Kate quickly ended any hopes of financial gain. "We don't know if he's dead or alive. I heard that you and he lived together for a while. Did you have any kids?"

"No. I didn't like them much. Still don't."

"What about Herb?"

Jean Sheldon

"He told me he had a daughter by his ex-wife. In fact, that was one of the reasons we split up. He said he wanted to try for custody. We lived together for about four years, but he wanted to move to Chicago 'cause he thought he'd have a better chance of getting his daughter. I told him to go without me. I'm not much for the big city, and like I said, I'm not much on kids. I have no idea what happened to him, or if he ended up with his daughter."

"Can you describe her? I mean, was she dark haired, or blond, or somewhere in between." Kate remembered the brown hair Janet Doyle shared with Kimberly.

"I saw a picture of her once. She looked to be two or three, but since I can't see a family resemblance in a set of identical twins, I couldn't tell you if she looked like him. She did have the same brown hair. If he had a picture of the mother, he never showed me and I don't remember if he said who she was, or even if she lived in Raccoon Grove. You know, it's funny your asking about Herb. I hadn't thought about him in years and then some kid came in here last week asking about him. Well, he wasn't asking about Herb. He was asking me if I had a boyfriend and I told him the last one was twenty years ago. I think he wanted a free cup of coffee."

"I hope you made him dish out the compliments before you gave it to him. Thanks, Marge. You've been a big help. Have a nice afternoon." She pulled a five from her wallet and put it on the counter as she stood.

"I've been a big help about what? Were you asking this stuff because of the Vandenberg case the Gazette's been writing about? How is Herb connected?"

Kate saw Scott peering over the top of his paper. "It is about the Vandenberg case, but we have too many pieces that don't fit together, or anywhere else. I'm not sure if Herb has anything to do with it."

"Are you working with Tracy?" Kate said she was. "I like that gal. She's spunky and doesn't take crap from people in this town. You tell her to keep up the good work and to get her butt in here to visit."

Kate left the diner and crossed the street to the Gazette. Dave wasn't there, but Tracy was in her office and looked up when she tapped on the doorframe. "Kate, I'm glad you're here. I found something interesting when I was shuffling through the scattered papers, a little gossip tidbit about Herb Doyle and his girlfriend."

"Marge Serapin. I just talked to her. She and Herb didn't have kids, but he showed her a picture of someone he said was his daughter from a previous marriage." Kate slipped into the chair in front of her desk. "Do you think that was Kimberly and he thought she was his?"

Obviously disappointed that her surprise was not a surprise, Tracy let the paper she held fall to the desk. "I must be slipping if the town gardener hears gossip before me."

"You're not slipping. Andy and Jeff called. They emailed their friends from high school. One of them remembered Herb and thought that he and Marge lived together. That reminds me, have you ever seen this supposed cousin, Joe Vandenberg?"

"No. Why?"

"Andy and Jeff said Janet had company, but he looked like he'd been in an accident. Remember the person in the woods? He wasn't in the greatest shape. Do you think that could have been Joe?"

"I guess we'd better find out what he looks like. If Joe Vandenberg visited Janet, then they're both fakes. If it wasn't

Joe and Janet turns out to be legitimate, he won't be happy about her appearance. Kate, if Janet is Kimberly, should we tell Sara?"

"If she is Kimberly, we'll have to tell her, but I don't think we need to say anything until we are certain."

"Oh, I forgot to tell you, Peter called. Janet paid him a visit." Tracy recounted the attorney's conversation and his visitor's vague memories. "She also said that she remembered a woman taking her and another little girl with curly dark hair to see the flower lady. She described your gardens."

"Really." That surprised Kate and sparked a foggy memory. "Shoot, that made me think of something, but I can't reel it in."

"Don't worry about it. I'll call Janet and ask if she remembers her cousin Joe Vandenberg."

"Andy asked me if we could email them a picture of Joe. I take it you don't have one?" Tracy shook her head. "If you can get him to talk to you, I can take a picture."

"Ah. Brilliant, Watson." Tracy picked up the phone. "Peter, can you have Joe Vandenberg come to your office? Oh, is he? Great. Kate and I want to take a picture of him without his knowledge. We'll wait outside. Don't worry, we'll figure out how to get him to pose." Peter described Joe, and Kate looked over her shoulder as Tracy wrote it down.

"That's close to the description the kids gave of Janet's visitor."

"Good. Did you drive here?" Kate nodded. "Let's take your van over and wait for him. Peter and he have an appointment in fifteen minutes to talk about the fire." Tracy stood and bit her lower lip.

"Is your ankle still hurting?"

"It isn't bad. It gets a little stiff after I've been sitting a while. I was afraid the pain would be worse and I'd have to walk around pretending it didn't hurt. Concealing my discomfort is not something I do well."

"Really?"

Five minutes after they parked in front of Peter's office, Joe approached. Tracy climbed out of the van and positioned her body to intercept him. He seemed preoccupied and might not have noticed her if she hadn't been in the middle of the sidewalk. She told him who she was and that the Gazette wanted to do a story about the heir to the Vandenberg estate. Joe said he wasn't up for an interview, but that as soon as he collected the money, he'd give her an exclusive. He never noticed Kate hanging out of the window with her camera. She took two pictures while they talked and when he went inside, Tracy returned. "How did you do?"

Kate viewed the images and handed Tracy the camera. "They should work. Would you send them to Andy in an email? I don't know how."

"I'll do it as soon as I go back to the office. I need to remember to give Janet Doyle a call and ask her about Joe. Do you want to visit for a while?"

"Not today. Don't forget to send the pictures."

❧

"Doctor Collins, this is Kimberly. You told me to call if I needed help, and I think I do. That columnist from the newspaper called me. She said she plans to expose me as a fake. I've been remembering more and more details of my life in Raccoon Grove and my friendship with Sara."

Adam gripped the phone and cursed under his breath as he listened to the frightened appeal. "Don't worry, Kimberly. I have an idea how to handle this. I'm going to send someone to talk to you. I want you to answer his questions as best you can. He'll be there in and hour and have a camera. Is that all right?"

"Yes, thank you. I'll do whatever you say."

⁂

Tracy heard Dave climb the stairs and arrived at his office just as he sat behind his desk. "Hi, Dave," she leaned on the doorframe. "Where've you been?"

"I had to pick up a part for one of the presses in Joliet. Did you miss me?"

"Of course, but I've been keeping myself busy so as not to wallow in self-pity. I called Janet Doyle earlier and asked her a few questions. I'm beginning to smell a rat, or at least some day old halibut. A week ago, she denied everything and now she has memories of her life here."

"I suppose as she looks into things, that's possible. What did she say?"

"She said the only explanation she could come up with for recognizing the Vandenberg house was that she must have seen it before. I asked if she ever lived in Raccoon Grove and she said she didn't remember everything, but she was beginning to think she had. Then I asked her if she knew that the estate was worth over two million dollars and she said she had no idea, but she had a feeling she might have lived in a very large home at some time. She was calm, considering, but I wasn't completely convinced. Do you think she's a scam artist after all?" Her head spun to the door. "That's my phone, I better grab it." She hurried to her office and immediately regretted answering.

"What is the matter with you? First, you try to destroy Sara and now you're trying to destroy Kimberly. Leave them alone. This has nothing to do with you."

She recognized the shouting voice. "Hi, Adam. I'm fine, thanks. How can I help you?"

"You think you're smart. I suggest you watch the Grove News on public access and see how smart you are." Adam slammed the receiver leaving Tracy stunned and able only to give him a belated and somewhat messy response with her tongue. She wiped her chin and returned to Dave's office. "That was Adam. He said I want to destroy Kimberly. She must have called him after we talked earlier. Flip on the TV, Dave. We're supposed to watch the public access news show at five and it's almost that now. Adam must not know the announcer reads the news from the Gazette."

It wasn't long before they saw what Adam arranged. To their surprise, a reporter spoke with Janet Doyle in her apartment. She now claimed to be Kimberly Vandenberg and her performance was so good that Tracy almost believed her. "I know Kate is our expert bullshit detector, but I'm picking up some pretty unpleasant aroma's myself. What is she after? If it's the two million dollar inheritance, this little human interest story could be pretty helpful."

"Boy, she was really convincing. Are you sure she's not Kimberly?"

"I can't be absolutely positive, but I don't think she is. Just in case, I'll try to gather a little more information to defend our position." Tracy shooed Dave from his computer.

"I don't suppose you could use your own computer."

"Mine is filled with nasty emails." She clicked away. Ten minutes later, she called him back and pointed at the monitor. "Look at this." While Dave examined her discovery, Tracy answered the phone. "Hi, Kate. Yes, we saw it too. Adam phoned to make sure. Apparently, she called him right after she and I talked. I imagine she told him I called her a fake, which I didn't. Then she told him she remembered who she was and the wonderful time she spent with Sara. If you want to win Adam over, say good things about Sara. I would be interested in getting a closer look at that locket she said she found in her dad's belongings. I wonder if Sara knows anything about it. Did she watch the Janet Doyle show?"

"We watched it together and all she said when Janet pointed to the locket around her neck was 'I wonder how she knew about that'. Tracy, Janet Doyle isn't the only person remembering things. Sara has too. She didn't want to talk about it but she is confident she'll know soon." Kate looked at Sara in the garden. "She didn't say anything else during the interview, not another word. She didn't look upset, in fact, if anything, she looked amused. When it ended, she shrugged and went back outside. Carolyn Kovecki called to see if Sara watched and how she reacted. She saw it too and thought Janet deserved an academy award for her performance."

"She doesn't believe Janet is Kimberly?"

"No, she doesn't. But after that show, we could be the only people who hold that opinion."

"We might be few, but we'll be right. I have a call coming in. I'll talk to you later."

"Hi, Tracy."

"Hello, Henry. Thanks for calling. Did you have any luck finding another prescription?"

"No, the only prescription Louise filled in the months before her death was the one you found. Those were the pills she told me she'd stopped taking. Tracy, I don't like where this is going. I've asked Scott to have Louise's body exhumed to see what killed her."

Tracy's pen tapped idly on the desk. "Henry, can we hold off on that for a few days? You know this town. Everyone will know what's happening before she's out of the ground, including the killer."

"I see. Of course. At this point, a few days won't hurt. Let me know what's going on, will you? I'll tell Scott about the delay."

"I will. Thanks, Henry. I suspect they'll be a number of secrets unearthed soon."

CHAPTER 29

Harold spent the morning breakfasting on beer and shots of tequila. When one of his mechanics came in to bring him back to the shop, Harold landed a fist on the side of his head and sent him staggering toward the door. Shortly, another figure arrived. "Hey, Hal. Why don't you come with me?"

"I ain't going nowhere with nobody. Take a hike." Harold didn't look at the person who spoke. When he felt a hand on his shoulder, he slammed his glass on the bar and stood ready to take a swing. The hand belonged to Scott, who in seconds had Harold's wrists in handcuffs.

"Let's go out to the car." Hal didn't struggle. In fact, the look on his face as he fell into the back seat of the squad was defeat. The sheriff was about to close the door when he saw a book by Harold's feet similar to the ones he'd seen Tracy and Kate reading. "Harold, after we take you to the station and make you comfy in lockup, I have to see a gardener."

Lockup in the Raccoon Grove Sheriff's Department was a small room with no windows, a table, and two chairs. It also served as the interrogation room, although Scott rarely used it for either. He removed the handcuffs, put Harold in the chair, and brought him a cup of coffee. "Drink this. I'll come back in a little while and drive you to the garage. Your car stays where it is until tomorrow." He left the door partially open knowing his prisoner wouldn't be going anywhere, and if he did, he wouldn't go far.

"Kate, are you back here?" She poked her head out of the greenhouse at the sound of Scott's voice. "I found something that might be of interest to you and Tracy."

She recognized Louise's diary and grabbed it from his hand. "Where did you get this?"

As he drove to Kate's, Scott had called Deputy Knowski and heard about the incident with Joe Vandenberg a few nights earlier. She'd forgotten all about throwing the diary in the back of the car. "This is the first I've seen it and I only found it because I had to take Harold in for a drunk and disorderly."

"He's not doing well?"

"He might be trying to replace Ben. He punched out one of his mechanics. Whatever's going on with him, I hope he works it out soon."

Kate waved the diary. "This means it was Joe who searched the house. Did he start the fire?"

"I suppose it's time I discussed a few things with Joe Vandenberg. If he started that fire and knew you and Tracy were inside, he'll be facing more serious charges than trespassing or arson. I'd better take Harold to the garage first. Could you and Tracy wrap this up? I don't like working this hard every day." He tipped his hat and closed the gate.

Kate sat in one of the deck chairs and opened the diary. It was dated April. The last one. *I visited Kimberly's room today. I still miss her so I can't breathe. I opened the lid to the jewelry box Sara gave her. She adored it. Sara should have it. She and Kimberly watched the little dancer for hours at a time while they giggled and talked. I took the locket out and remembered the day Jack and I gave it to her. She was excited and so proud that it had her name in it. Sometimes the memories bring too much pain.*

"The locket was still in the jewelry box. Louise only wrote this two months ago." Kate grabbed her cell phone and pushed Tracy's number. "Hi. Listen to this. Louise said in her last diary that the locket was still in the jewelry box in April."

"Wait a minute. What do you mean in the last diary? Do you have it?"

"Oh, geez, I'm sorry. Yes. Scott brought it by a little earlier. Linda found it on the road near the Vandenberg's house when she met Joe Vandenberg. Scott found it when he hauled Harold out of the bar a little earlier."

"Harold's still being a dope? Okay, don't read any more. I have to make a stop first and then I'll be over. Go play with your flowers."

Tracy left the paper and walked to Harold's garage. The remaining mechanic pointed her to the office, where she sat and waited for him to raise his head. He didn't. "Go away."

"Harold, you're being stupid. You didn't kill Jack and you know it."

He looked over his arms with bleary eyes. "This town sucks."

"Why, because people are concerned about you? You're losing your business. Since you didn't kill Jack, you won't be in jail for the rest of your life and you'll need the garage to make a living. So will your mechanics if you don't beat the daylights out of them."

"Why are you doing this, Tracy?"

It took her a minute to answer. "I could tell you it's because I care, but the real reason is I feel responsible. You were doing fine until I started the investigation."

"If it makes you feel better, I absolve you of any and all responsibility. You can leave with a clear conscience. So do that, will you?" He dropped his head.

"Damn you. You're as stubborn as a mule. Go ahead and kill yourself." She stood. "But, do me a favor and wait a few days."

"For what?"

"Because by then we'll have solved the case and found the killer, you jackass." She stormed out of his office and stopped to enlighten the mechanic who'd overheard the conversation. "I talked some sense into him."

Back at the paper, Tracy found Dave in her office. "What are you doing?"

"Answering your phone and taking messages. Do you want me to read them, or do you want to read them yourself. I'd say it's about a fifty-fifty tie."

"Fifty percent of the good folks of Raccoon Grove want to boil me in oil, and the other fifty percent want to run me out of town on a rail?"

"Give our community a little credit. Fifty percent of the folks who watched the news don't believe Janet Doyle is Kimberly, although they think she's a talented actor. The other fifty percent aren't sure. The only person positive Janet is Kimberly, is Adam Collins, but we knew that."

Tracy pulled the messages from Dave's hand and flipped through them. "These aren't all about the show. Some have information from and about people who've moved out of town."

"Right. You have a full day ahead of you."

"First I have to go to Kate's. Scott brought her the final diary, the most important one. I wonder why he didn't bring it to me."

"You don't have pretty flowers, and Kate hasn't been known to bite people's heads off."

"I'm taking your car."

❧

Scott pushed a chair in front of his desk next to the one occupied by Joe Vandenberg and offered it to Peter. "Thanks for coming. I didn't invite you here to act as Joe's attorney, but I thought it might be a good idea to have someone present while I ask him a few questions." At Peter's nod, the sheriff turned to his other guest. "Joe, did you set fire to the Vandenberg house?"

Joe's long body, draped across the chair, almost dislodged at the sheriff's words. "What are you talking about? Why would I burn my own house?"

"Maybe to burn the missing will." The sheriff directed a question at Peter. "If Louise's new will doesn't show up, are Joe's chances of inheriting the Vandenberg estate any better?"

"I suppose they might be, but it's rather meaningless now. From the looks of things, Kimberly Vandenberg has come home, and she's the heir. Did you see her on television, Scott? What a remarkable story."

Joe's eyes darted back and forth between the two men. "So, what happens now?"

"If she is Ms Vandenberg, then she will have to prove it," Peter told him. "After seeing her last night, I don't suppose she'll have a problem convincing the court. When she does that, you'll be out of the picture, Mr. Vandenberg. That is unless Kimberly wants to share her inheritance." Joe didn't find Peter's comment nearly as amusing as did the attorney and the sheriff.

Scott controlled his smile. "The inheritance isn't the reason I asked you here, Joe. Why were you in the house?"

"I told you, I wasn't."

"You dropped something the night Deputy Knowski saw you that says you were in the house."

When Scott told him about the diary Joe's brain was unable to come up with a believable lie. He decided on the truth, or at least his version of the truth. "Oh, all right. I wanted to see if I could find something to prove I'm related to the family. Since my dad's stuff burned, I figured it was my only chance."

"You look like you've been in an accident, Joe."

"That's right, an accident," Joe mumbled. "I tripped over a tree stump when I went for a walk in the woods. I'm not used to stuff like that."

"Are you staying in town?"

"Are you telling me to stay in town?"

"Nope. I'll call you if I need to see you again. For now, we all need to wait and see what happens with Kimberly Vandenberg. You can go."

Scott and Peter watched him depart. "What do you think, Peter? Is Janet Doyle really Kimberly Vandenberg?"

"Tracy and Kate think she's a fake. As convincing as she was in the interview, I'm betting they're right, which means there are two fakes in town."

❦

Doctor Adam Collins left his busy office to go home and tell Sara that he was sure Kimberly was alive and she'd be safe. "She's at Kate's, Adam," Elaine told him. He turned to leave, but she called him. "Adam, I saw the woman on the news last night. The one who says she's Kimberly. You know she's not. Kimberly died twenty years ago."

"No, she's not dead, Elaine. That woman knows everything about Kimberly's life. She must be her."

"Let's go sit out in the yard for a few minutes." Elaine turned her chair to the door and rolled toward the ramp, but Adam took the handles and wheeled her to the yard. "It's beautiful, isn't it? Sara's done a wonderful job, and she enjoys the work." Elaine looked at her husband who sat at her side. "Adam, she's worked hard to regain her life. You can't take that from her." He didn't answer. "Our marriage ended the day Jack died. I didn't know why. Eventually I grew used to living without you here emotionally. I never fought a decision you made about Sara even though I didn't agree with some of your choices. Now I have to insist you leave her alone and let her work with Kate. She's her own person and wants her own life. I won't let you hurt her."

Adam flew to his feet. "Hurt her. I want to keep Sara safe. That's all I've ever wanted to do. Why won't people leave me alone to take care of her?"

Elaine took his hand. "You've spent the last twenty years trying to keep Sara safe. It's time for you to take care of yourself. You need to let other people help you, including Sara. This person is not Kimberly, and if you try to make her Kimberly, it could prove very harmful to Sara." Adam fell back in the lawn chair and looked his daughter's work. Elaine reached over and held him as his head dropped into his hands. "Sara spent the morning with her doctor. She remembered what happened twenty years ago. She'll be safe now, Adam. Everything will be okay, and Sara will be safe."

⁂

Kate was practically sitting on her hands when Tracy arrived. "It took all my strength to wait for you. What took so long?"

"I stopped to see Harold. He looks bad. I asked him to hold off on killing himself until we solve this. I hope he does. Someone must know how he ended up parked by the creek. Let's see what Louise figured out."

The women sat next to each other in the gazebo with the diary open on the table. Their eyes widened and closed as they read different passages. Kate ran for a box of tissue, which they both used. When they finished and closed the book, they slid back in their chairs. For the last few pages, they'd perched on the edge. "Louise did a good job." Tracy tapped on the diary. "I can't believe what happened, and I'll bet she couldn't either."

"She was right about Ben knowing everything, and it wasn't difficult to help him loosen his tongue with a fifth of quality scotch."

"Now that we know, it all makes sense, doesn't it?"

"You're right, Tracy, but what do we do with this information? Scott told you he won't reopen the investigation."

"He'll have to reopen it when we get a confession. There are, as I thought in the beginning, two separate but connected issues. The first thing we need to do is talk to Kimberly and her cousin, Joe Vandenberg. Then, we need to talk to Jack Vandenberg's killer."

"Do you have an idea how we'll accomplish that?"

"Yes, I do. Kate. Tomorrow we're going to have a garden party."

"Any garden in particular?"

CHAPTER 30

The next morning, Kate spent a few hours preparing the yard for their gathering. Tracy was in charge of making sure everyone showed up, an enormous task for anyone but the town gossip columnist. Kate was in charge of the setting. Comfortable with her efforts, she returned to the house and found the phone ringing.

"Hi, Kate, it's Carolyn. Have you spoken to Sara today?"

"No, but let me check my voice mail." There was a message from Sara. She wanted Kate to know she wouldn't be over until the garden party, but everything was okay. "What's going on, Carolyn?" Sara's doctor explained that Sara had remembered the events that changed her life. She couldn't tell her what they were, but Sara really was okay. "Tracy and I read Louise Vandenberg's final diary. It told what happened." Kate explained the contents of the book. "Were Sara's memories accurate?"

"Yes, they were. Once she unraveled a few images, everything revealed itself. I wonder why Louise didn't tell anyone what she found."

"She might not have had a chance to tell anyone except Jack's killer. We believe he killed her."

"This has been a two-decade nightmare. It must have been horrifying for Louise to uncover the truth."

"I'm sure you're right, but she said it brought her peace. We also found Louise's new will. She left Sara the Vandenberg estate."

"That makes sense. What happens now?"

"Everyone involved will be at the gathering this evening."

"Sara is anxious for it to happen and frightened at the same time. I'm sure she'll be strong enough."

⁂

Tracy spent most of the morning in her office. She had been ready to beg, buy, and cajole people into attending, but it wasn't necessary. Everyone she called was anxious to be there. When all the names on her list had a check, she went to Dave's office and found him at his desk looking smug. "Open your mouth and let me see the canary."

"I just had an interesting conversation with Rebecca Doyle. Would you like to know who Rebecca Doyle is?" Tracy sat in the leather chair and waited for her husband's news. "She's Herb Doyle's daughter, the Herb Doyle who lived here in Raccoon Grove and worked as a janitor at the high school. He won custody of her right after he moved to Chicago."

"You don't say. The same Herb Doyle that died two years ago?"

"Yes, ma'am."

"Dave, what does this mean?"

Tempted to bask in the glory of his sleuthing skills, he saw his lovely wife preparing to jump across the desk and hurried his explanation. "Armando said that Herb's wife didn't fight for custody. She still lives in Chicago and she and Rebecca have a good relationship, as did Rebecca and Herb. It's funny when you think that we made the poor guy into this vicious killer and kidnapper, and he had nothing to do with anything. Rebecca said she hardly ever heard her dad mention Raccoon Grove."

"Janet really is one hell of an actress." Tracy pursed her lips and a smile crept across her face. "This party of ours should be quite interesting. We should get there before the others. I hope Kate understands the various players and possible risks."

That was the first question she asked when she and Dave arrived. "Are you sure you want to use your yard for this? I have no idea what might happen."

"I'm sure. Everyone wants this over. Besides, Sara and I are good at fixing flowers if someone finds reason to vent. Tracy, as much as I love my gardens, people's lives may depend on what happens today." Kate wrapped an arm around Sara, who arrived with Carolyn.

Soon, everyone in any way involved in Jack Vandenberg's murder and those involved in the settlement of the estate stood or sat in Kate's yard. A few curious locals attended because they didn't want to wait for the following days Gazette. The time had come to find out what happened in Raccoon Grove twenty years earlier and how it affected those involved.

Tracy called for everyone's attention. "Why don't we begin? Before we discuss the Vandenberg mystery, I have a question for our local mechanic. Harold, do know Stanley Brodsky?"

Harold looked sober, but for a minute, he also looked confused. Then he smiled. "Stosh, yeah, I know him. I haven't seen him in years. Why?"

"He lived here in town until about fifteen years ago, and has since moved to California, but he still has family here. They contacted him about the articles we ran, and he called me to explain his whereabouts the night of Jack's murder. He was sure his story would help." Harold raised a pair of weary shoulders. "It's not an easy thing for me to do, but I'll come right to the point. The night of Jack's death, Stosh was in his truck driving on Timber Lane by the creek when he hit a deer. The deer died, but Stosh didn't think it was a good idea to leave it in the road in case one of his buddies came by on their bike. It was a big buck, and he couldn't move it alone so he waved down a car. The driver of the car turned out to be a friend, who although stoned, helped him pull the deer off the road. Stosh couldn't hang around because he had a hot date with the woman he eventually married. He jumped in his truck, took off, and didn't notice his friend climb back into his car and go to sleep. He was covered with blood from the deer."

Harold stared for a second before the light bulb went off and he threw his arms around her. "Tracy, I'm sorry I've been a jerk. How can I thank you?"

She looked around for Dave. "See what happens when you tell me to let my hair grow out. The men are all over me." She hugged Harold. "I'm sorry you carried that for as long as you did, but I'm glad it's over. Harold, Stosh told me to make sure I gave you his number in California if you want it." He was speechless as he took the paper.

While Tracy and Harold concluded their business, Kate moved over and stood by George. Tracy spun in their direction. "George, we know you smashed Kate's flowers." She put up a hand as he opened his mouth. "We matched your boot to the prints in the garden. What we don't know is why."

George didn't argue. "I owed someone money. He asked me to try and scare you two to end the investigation."

"Did you set the Vandenberg house on fire for the same reason?"

"I didn't know you were inside. I didn't see a car and it was supposed to be empty."

"What about the anonymous letters we received about stopping the investigation. You wrote them I take it." Without lifting his head, he admitted that he'd paid a couple of the kids that worked at the sandwich shop to send them. "Who did you owe the money to, George?

"Doc Collins treated me for something and I couldn't afford to pay. He asked me to scare you to stop investigating because he was worried about Sara. I didn't know why he wanted the Vandenberg place burned, but I did it."

"Did you shoot at my car?"

"No. I didn't have anything to do with that."

Tracy startled George and everyone else in the yard when she spun and clapped her hands. "Let's go on to the Vandenberg case. Sara, I want you to meet Kimberly Vandenberg." Tracy pointed across the lawn to where Janet Doyle stood. "Do you remember her?"

Sara stood in front of Kimberly and studied her, saying nothing. Kimberly spoke first. "Hi, Sara. It's been a long time, hasn't it?"

The yard was quiet enough to hear a petal drop and when Sara spoke, it was through clenched teeth. "What you're doing is cruel and dangerous. There's been so much pain for so many people." She took a deep breath to reclaim her composure. "Was this all about the Vandenberg estate? Did you pretend to be Kimberly for the money?"

"I had no idea what my family's assets were. I had no idea who my family was. I didn't come looking for this. They came to me." She pointed at Kate and Tracy.

Sara crossed the yard and returned to Carolyn's side. "That's not Kimberly. She's a phony."

"How can you be sure? You haven't seen her in twenty years," Joe shouted.

Sara shook her head. "I know she's a fake. I shot Kimberly. I shot her and she died twenty years ago."

CHAPTER 31

No petals fell, but jaws dropped. Mouths opened, people gasped, a few even found a chair to support their stunned bodies. Joe was the first to speak. "What do you mean you shot her? You were five friggin' years old. How could you have shot her?"

"Are you okay?" Carolyn's hand rested on Sara's shoulder and squeezed gently.

"Yes." Sara spoke to Joe. "I found a gun in the glove compartment of my dad's car and put it in my pocket. When I saw Kimberly, I brought it out to show her and it fired. I tried to make her wake up, but she didn't move."

Adam stood frozen in place. He sputtered until he could finally speak. "No, Sara, no. Honey, you don't know what you're saying. You're confused. Don't you remember? You were home watching television the night Kimberly disappeared. She is Kimberly. You're still confused." Adam looked desperate. "That man is right. It was a long time ago." He turned to Janet. "Remember when I asked you where your room was at home? You knew. Tell them what you told me."

"At the top of the stairs. I kept my ballerina jewelry box that Sara gave me on top of my dresser." Janet smiled, but it faded when she saw Sara scowl.

"You're not Kimberly," Sara told her. "That's easy enough to prove with a DNA sample."

Adam was excited again. "Yes, Kimberly. Give them a DNA sample and we can request one from your mother's body. That'll prove you're Kimberly. You're alive and you weren't killed that night." Adam shouted. He didn't notice the defeat on Janet's face. "Give them a DNA sample and everything will be fine. You'll be alive, and Sara will be safe." The rest of the gathering realized what a few people already knew. Something was very wrong with Adam Collins.

Sara staggered slightly and Carolyn put her arm around her waist. "I think it's time for you to go home."

Her eyes filled as she walked across the lawn to her father and held him. "Thank you, Daddy. I love you." She and Carolyn left.

As the gate clicked shut, Joe spoke. "Since you know she's a fake," he pointed at Janet, "the estate is mine."

Everyone ignored him as Kate approached Janet. "I have to admit, you gave a wonderful performance, but none of that matters. We found the new Will and it names Sara as beneficiary. By the way, my associates in Chicago," she pointed at Andy and Jeff, "reported that you two live together. We sent them a picture and they identified you at her building. You planned to collect that estate one way or another, didn't you. That's why Joe wasn't upset that people believed you to be Kimberly. Janet, it was something you said that convinced me you were a fake. You told Peter that a woman brought you and Sara to my gardens. I just started growing flowers back then so you couldn't have seen a yard full of flowers. Joe told you about the photo he saw at the house with Kimberly, Sara, and Louise. Since he trespassed in my greenhouse looking for the diaries, he saw the flowers and thought that's where they were. Then, you suddenly remembered."

Janet glared at Joe. "You told me she had her gardens then."

Tracy suddenly realized that Kate was having all the fun. "Let me talk." Kate bowed and waved her forward. "Right after your stellar television appearance, I did more looking and found a photo of an actress from Chicago named Janet Braun. I didn't recognize you at first, because you wore your natural blond hair and no brown contacts. You made a mistake telling us you were an actress, and an even bigger mistake using your first name. I only looked for Janet on a hunch." Tracy pointed at Dave. "My super sleuth husband here found Herb Doyle's real daughter and she didn't remember having any sisters." Tracy gave her a sneer and turned to Joe. "You're no more related to the Vandenbergs than me. You read Peter's request in the paper. It's a popular con. You bought the phony identification and passed yourself off as Joe Vandenberg. Tell me why you took the diaries out and left them in the yard."

"I was in a hurry."

Scott and Deputy Knowski walked in prompting Joe and Janet to look for an exit. There wasn't one. "He was in a hurry because Linda showed up while he was paying a late night, unauthorized visit."

Tracy wasn't finished. When Scott approached Joe and Janet, she pulled him back and continued. "Joe, you were the sniper who shot at my car." She wasn't asking. "Did you find the ring in Kimberly's bedroom and bring it to your roommate?"

"No. I found it the first time I came out. I picked up a couple of rocks by the front door hoping to find a key and uncovered the ring. I knew it belonged to a kid and when I saw the KV, I figured it was the Vandenberg girl."

"You were right. So you gave Janet the ring, and the locket. You fed her every piece of information she needed. If you weren't able to prove you were family, there was a chance you could convince everyone Janet was Kimberly. It was a good plan, and if it hadn't been for Louise's diaries, Raccoon Grove's collective efforts, and Sara's strength, you might have gotten away with it. Whose idea was it?"

Joe didn't have a problem talking about his plan. "Mine to go for the inheritance, but Janet thought we should try the impersonation thing. After I found the lawyers ad, I did some research and came across your online edition of the Gazette. I didn't know small town papers put stuff on the internet. I showed Janet the article, and she figured she'd be able to fool everyone. She's a good actress."

"Shut up, Joe," Janet said sharply. He ignored her.

"After that, I came to town and started poking around. When I talked with the lady at the diner, I found out about Herb Doyle. We did some more checking and found out he'd died a couple of years ago and Janet figured we could make up a believable story about him being a kidnapper."

"So you two wrote the letters to the paper about Kimberly being alive."

"Yeah, but I screwed up the phone number." He didn't bother to check the disgusted look on Janet's face. "After I heard about the number not working, I wrote again."

"Joe, the good news is you won't have thugs coming after you for a while. No, that's not true. There are quite a few thugs in prison." Tracy smiled.

"How did you know about anyone coming after me?"

"They were at the diner yesterday talking about the beating they gave Joe Miller, and how much worse it was going to be if you didn't pay up. It's a small town. Everyone knew in an hour.

Janet, you tried to use Adam to support your pretense. You heard his desperation for you to be Kimberly. You didn't know why and you didn't care, as long as he could help convince everyone."

"You two have to come to the station." This time Scott pulled Tracy back.

"We haven't broken any laws," Joe told him.

"Fraud is a crime, Mr. Miller, so is breaking and entering. Shooting at people is illegal and it isn't nice. We have a few other criminal activities to discuss." As Deputy Knowski took them to the car, Janet sent an Oscar winning sneer in the direction of Tracy and Kate. Neither woman thought she was acting.

Adam stood alone, his arms wrapped around his body. He said nothing after Sara left with Carolyn. When Janet and Joe went through the gate, he fell to his knees. Tracy knelt next to him. "Was Ben blackmailing you from the beginning?"

"Yes, ever since that night. Then when the paper reported that someone knew who killed Jack, I knew Ben must have said something. I couldn't keep paying him, but if I didn't, Sara would have been in danger."

"You killed him and set it up to look as if he ran into that tree?" He could only groan. "Did Louise tell you to turn yourself in?"

"I couldn't. There would be no one to keep Sara safe. I couldn't go to jail."

"You gave Louise an overdose and reported that she took it herself from the prescription Henry had given her." He didn't answer and Tracy continued. "Why did you have George burn the Vandenberg house?"

"I was afraid she'd remember things and I wouldn't be there to tell her the memories weren't true. What if she went to the house?" he looked pleadingly at Tracy. "What if she remembered?"

Tracy shook her head, not in judgment, but in sympathy. "She did remember, Adam. You knew that eventually she would. Did you shoot Jack Vandenberg the night Sara accidentally shot Kimberly?"

Adam's head dropped to his chest. "Kimberly was on the side porch waving to us, so I took Sara to her and went back to the car for my jacket. When I heard the shot, I saw the glove compartment open and realized Sara might have taken the gun. I found her crying because she couldn't make Kimberly wake up. I gave her a sedative and put her in the car. I couldn't think. I didn't know what to do. I decided I'd put Kim in the trunk and get out of there, but Jack came out the front door. He'd been in the wine cellar and hadn't heard anything. I told him the girls were playing in Kimberly's room, and talked him into having a drink before Louise came home and we went to the card game. As soon as we went in, he yelled for her and ran up the stairs. He was going to find out what happened. I needed to make sure Sara was safe. I knew he kept his gun in his office and took it out of his desk drawer. When he came back downstairs, I shot him. It was my fault. Everything was my fault."

Scott came forward and extended his hand to Adam. "We have an ambulance on the way, Doctor Collins."

Kate stopped Adam as the sheriff escorted him through the yard. "Sara will be okay, Adam. I promise."

"Please, keep her safe."

After the ambulance left, Kate and Tracy went inside for drinks. "It's still hard to believe." Kate pulled beverages from the fridge and passed them to Tracy's already full arms.

"It is. It's also amazing to think that Janet and Joe could have ended up with the estate."

"She's a good actress, Tracy, but what a way to waste her talents. I suppose for her it was a million dollar part and they don't come along often."

"We'd better get out there and answer questions. That crew still looks a little confused." They returned with the refreshments and Tracy answered the quizzical faces with more details of the events that night. "Sara described what Louise and Adam confirmed. She didn't know her dad killed Jack for sure, but she suspected what happened."

"Why did he say everything was his fault?" Harold asked.

"He didn't leave Sara home alone that night. On his way to take Sara to Jack's house he'd left her in the car while he stopped to see a patient. Sara found the gun in the glove compartment. What compounded his guilt was that he hadn't stopped by for a medical emergency. She was an attractive woman and he'd dropped by to arrange to meet her later in the evening. Elaine was out of town and Sara was going to stay with Kimberly for the night. Kate was the one who suggested we get a list of Adam's patients from around the time of Jack's death to find out who had been his emergency. Scott talked to her. She only lived here for a year before moving back to Chicago. She and Adam did make plans to meet after his card game, but Adam never showed. She figured he changed his mind."

Kate grabbed Tracy's arm. "I think I figured out what Ben's police report said. It didn't say 'dog collar', it said 'Doc Collins.'"

"Oh, brother."

Andrea had a question. "Tracy, what will they do to Sara?"

"Nothing. They'll rule it an accident. After we read Louise's diary, I asked Scott a hypothetical question about a young girl accidentally shooting her best friend. He understood who the hypothetical girls were and said the court would find it was an accident. "If Adam had thought with his head instead of his heart, he'd have known the best thing to do would have been to report it. Sara still would have needed help, but not for over twenty years. Kate, between you, Carolyn, and Elaine, I'm sure she'll be okay. I'm amazed at how well she's doing after remembering she shot Kimberly."

Kate fingered the rose petals. "Sara understands that it was an accident and that she was only a child. She's relieved to know what happened. It meant a great deal to her that she hadn't forgotten watching the movie that changed her life. It turns out that bothered her more than anyone suspected. She has a lot to deal with, but the sadness for her father is the immediate and most important concern. She and Carolyn talked about her role in the tragedy, and Carolyn believes Sara understands she had no control over the events, or her father's actions."

Mad Dog, who hadn't said a word, shook his long curls. "I knew there was another explanation for Sara's behavior. That poor kid."

"How did Louise find out?" Andrea and Jeff stood by their father, and Kate joined them to answer Jeff's question.

"She spent five years searching for the truth, and much of what she gathered pointed to Ben. She decided to invite him for drinks and see if he'd open up. Good scotch did the trick. Ben told her he'd parked by the creek and was nodding off when Adam drove past. He decided to finish his nap, but when a loud noise awakened him a few minutes later, he remembered seeing Adam and gave up on the nap. He figured Adam was on his way to Jack's and decided to stop by to see if they were going to the card game. When he stepped out of the squad car, he heard a shot. He saw Sara asleep on the back seat in Adam's car, and when he walked through the open front door he saw Adam standing over Jack's body."

"Did Adam admit to shooting Jack?"

"He did, Harold. He offered Ben five thousand dollars to keep his mouth shut. He might have felt he had a better chance of protecting Sara if the sheriff was on his side. He couldn't have guessed that Ben would blackmail him for twenty years."

"If Ben and Adam were at the house, why weren't they seen when Anna dropped Louise off?" Dirk asked.

"After Adam left, Ben parked down the road to watch for Louise. He waited until Anna drove away and went back to the house. As he expected, he found Louise standing over Jack's body, just as he'd found Adam a little earlier."

"If Adam knew what really happened, how could he believe Janet Doyle was Kimberly?" Judging by the faces around the yard, Harold wasn't the only one who wondered.

Kate answered. "Carolyn thought Adam wanted so desperately for that night to disappear he would have believed anything. Janet was convincing, especially with Joe giving her the details. The events of that night over twenty years ago had taken its toll on Adam, especially after Sara became more curious. That proved fortunate for Janet. If she'd tried it a few years earlier, he might not have been as susceptible."

"I have a question, mom." Jeff waved his hand. "Why did Louise leave the estate to Sara? I mean, even if it was an accident, she did kill her daughter."

"I suppose that's the literal truth, but Louise didn't see it that way. She realized why Sara spent so much time in hospitals and felt Sara's punishment was unjust, though not intentional. Kimberly was dead and Louise could do nothing for her. She feared that when Sara learned what her father did, and why, she might not be strong enough to face it. I'm glad she was wrong."

"You're right, Mom," Andy said. "When you think about it, two million dollars can't make up for twenty years of her life, or the rest of her father's."

Tracy took over. "Louise confronted Adam. He told her he didn't know what she was talking about and that Sara hadn't done anything wrong. We don't know what happened for sure, but we think he went to her home and killed her. Since Henry Crawford was out of town that week, Adam Collins pronounced her dead of an overdose of the sedatives he thought she still took. They're exhuming the body, and I'm sure we'll find Adam injected her with something. Since he did the examination for her death certificate, no one suspected anything was wrong. The one thing we haven't solved is where he put Kimberly's body."

"I think I know." Kate pointed to a rose bush. "I'll bet she's buried under the pink rose bush in Sara's backyard."

That evening, Tracy and Dave redid the Gazette. They worked through the night and it appeared as usual on Friday morning. Much of the issue featured events that led to the previous day's arrest of Doctor Adam Collins, Joseph 'Vandenberg' Miller, and Janet 'Doyle' Braun. They also ran an announcement for a long overdue funeral service for Kimberly Vandenberg.

The two exhausted journalists sat by their phones and waited to see if they would have to put their house on the market. They didn't. Raccoon Grove citizens breathed a collective sigh of relief at the solution and were pleased with the Gazette's job. "Dave, old boy, they still love us here in the Grove."

"That might be pushing it a bit, Tracy, but I'm glad we don't have to move."

"Me too."

Sara felt a mixture of sorrow and peace for her long dead friend, and was grateful for Kate's company and advice as they walked through the gardens and gathered a beautiful assortment of flowers for her grave.

"Are you two ready?" Tracy, pleased to have her car back, opened the trunk with a big grin as the flower laden gardeners approached.

The grin faded when Kate pointed to a pile of books. "Hey, Tracy, what are those?"

"Oh, shoot. I thought Edwina was senile. Those are library books. Kate, will you take them in for me? Kate, did you hear me?"

About the Author

 *After three decades as a Fine and Graphic Artist, a musician, songwriter, and poet, Jean Sheldon tried her hand at fiction. She fell in love and has since written six novels and sees no end in sight. "My life has been a series of creative endeavors. For me, that works best. It was with surprise and delight I found the weaving of stories the most satisfying."*

Books by Jean Sheldon

The Woman in the Wing

A historical mystery that takes place in a defense plant. This well-researched book offers a glimpse into the lives of women who served at home during World War II, and sheds some light on the seldom told stories of the women who ferried military planes from plants to air bases around the country.

Seven Cities of Greed

A hand carved leather journal purchased at a Chicago book auction promises an adventure in New Mexico for Jacqueline Tracy and her friends, a group of women of a certain age. Instead, they find themselves followed by a modern day conquistador who will stop at nothing to have the book and the secrets it holds.

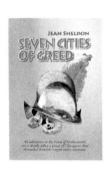

Mrs. Quigley's Kidnapping

When Mattie Draper opened her Chicago detective agency in 1968, she was one of only a handful of female Private Investigators nationwide. For the first three months, her cases offered no greater challenge than finding lost pets and wayward spouses—until someone kidnapped Diana Quigley. In a race to find the missing woman, Mattie tries to untangle the helpful information supplied by a growing lists of suspects. **Available as an eBook**

More information at:
www.jeansheldon.com

CPSIA information can be obtained at www.ICGtesting.com
Printed in the USA
270596BV00001B/1/P